LOVE ON GUARD

A Role-Reversal Romance

Nikki Kwiatkowski

To Chris,
I don't think I would have ever gotten this far if it wasn't for you. You coming home every day and looking forward to what I had written is what made me want to finish this book. If for no one else, for you.

To my parents, Angie and Raymond,
Thank you for supporting me in my choices in life, but most of all, thank you for encouraging my creativity at an early age.

With Loving Memory, To Kevin,
My only regret is that I didn't finish a book in your lifetime. You always knew I'd get around to it eventually. Thank you for always being my biggest fan. ♥

CONTENTS

Chapter 1 9
Chapter 2 18
Chapter 3 28
Chapter 4 42
Chapter 5 52
Chapter 6 61
Chapter 7 77
Chapter 8 94
Chapter 9 108
Chapter 10 115
Chapter 11 128
Chapter 12 133
Chapter 13 140
Chapter 14 150
Chapter 15 167
Chapter 16 178
Chapter 17 195
Chapter 18 202
Chapter 19 219
Chapter 20 229
Chapter 21 237
Chapter 22 255

Chapter 23 268
Chapter 24 277
Chapter 25 287
Chapter 26 301
Chapter 27 312
Chapter 28 322
Chapter 29 339
Chapter 30 354
Chapter 31 362

CHAPTER 1

The flames slowly simmered on the black Jaguar F-TYPE parked in the VIP parking space marked *E. Lowell*. The bomb had been a small one, only doing damage to a few vehicles parked outside the Lowell Enterprise building.

Local law enforcement were on the scene in what seemed like seconds. Soon after, the FBI was called in. With the country constantly on high alert concerning acts of terror, it was a given. It didn't hurt that one of the wealthiest hotel owners in the United States was on the phone with them the second he knew what happened. He had connections and insisted that simple police officers and detectives had no clue how to handle proceedings.

The avenue was constantly swarming with people; if the explosion would have been bigger, it could have easily killed dozens. Fortunately, only a handful were hurt, and only with minor injuries. One would have to stay overnight for a head injury, but that was the extent. What was certain, had Ethan Lowell been in his car, Owen Lowell would be on the phone making funeral arrangements rather than hassling the detectives and agents on the scene.

"I don't give a damn," Owen Lowell shouted at one of the peon agents who had absolutely no control over any part of the investigation. "Get the whole fucking FBI, CIA, Secret Service...get Interpol. I'm sure they can do a better job than whatever you think you're

9

doing!"

"Dad, calm down."

Ethan ran his fingers through his dark and spikey hair. It was still at a length where he could tousle it and spike it, though a haircut was in the foreseeable future; his father had said as much recently. He glared at his father with strained green eyes, attempting to calm him and pull him from the scene.

"Who the hell is in charge?! Do I need to call the Director again," he continued to bellow.

Any other person in the world would have already been confined, but this was a very powerful man, and as long as he stayed on the right side of the barriers that had been set up, they allowed him to rant away.

"That won't be necessary," a middle-aged man in a black suit announced. He tucked a pair of glasses into the pocket of his jacket as he approached.

"Oh really, and who are you?"

"Agent Delgado." He was firm and curt, even though he had spoken few words.

"Well, *Agent* Delgado."

Ethan immediately saw Delgado's jaw tense at the way his father's words came out. He wanted to distance himself from the old man who knew nothing of patience or decorum. Owen Lowell achieved what he had in life with persistence and shrewdness, and he never hesitated to point that out.

"I take it you're in charge of this mess then?"

"Yes, sir."

"Can you explain," Owen continued to shout.

"Mr. Lowell, my agents have a job to do. No matter

how much you continue to berate us, we cannot move any faster nor come up with a solution. I would appreciate it if you could head back to your offices and I can come and attempt to respond to—"

"That's your answer," Owen interrupted.

"Short of having you escorted off the premises."

"I'd like to see you try!"

Agent Delgado took a step forward, closing the distance with Owen, still on the opposite side of the barrier. He raised his right brow so much that it may have well extended his hairline. He was challenging Owen. It was one of those silent communications daring him to push just a little further.

Delgado couldn't help but laugh inside, only showing the faintest of smirks on the outside. He'd give anything for the billionaire prick to keep at it. He'd love to see him escorted away, still spitting vile epithets at the agents. Old man Lowell didn't allow him that privilege.

Owen huffed and stomped away like a child, beckoning his son to follow. Ethan gave Agent Delgado a grimacing look and nodded over his shoulder toward his father. Delgado understood and rolled his eyes as if it didn't bother him. He knew how people with money and power were. They wanted everything on their terms when they clicked their fingers. Unfortunately, Mr. Owen Lowell was going to be sorely disappointed.

* * *

"Alright, so what have you and your men gathered," Owen began as soon as Agent Delgado shut the door to the office that was far too big for one man. He didn't even allow him to speak before continuing. "Who did this? Why? Have you caught them?" Questions continued to spew from his mouth.

"Mr. Lowell, things like this take time."

"Someone blew up my son's car! What do you expect?"

"I need to ask the two of you some questions first."

Owen Lowell made a noise of frustration that sounded more like that of a dying animal of some sort.

"I'd like to start with you, Mr. Ethan Lowell."

Ethan had been staring out the window of the top floor office suite. He was numb. He didn't know what to think or how to feel. Now he had to answer questions from this FBI agent, questions he didn't even know if he could answer.

"Yes, of course," he finally acknowledged. The words of Delgado seemed to take a moment to sink in, but he was eventually able to tear himself from his melancholy daze.

"Alright." Delgado took out a small notepad to make a few notes.

"Oh! You've got to be kidding me! Don't you have a computer or a recording device," Owen spat.

Delgado rolled his eyes to the comment. He only needed a few notes so that he knew where to start.

"As the both of you know, our first reaction, due to the busy location and the fact that a bomb was involved...*and the fact that this turd knows the damn Director of the FBI and is a narcissistic asshole,*" he began, leaving his thoughts out of it. "We thought this might be an act of terror."

"I'm guessing that the next words I'm going to hear will negate that," Ethan responded before the man could continue.

"We still need to do an analysis on the bomb as well as your car; however, you are correct. With the location, we expected something more than this. The sole intent of this explosion appeared to be targeted directly for your car only."

"Why," Ethan gasped.

"That's why I need to talk to you a little more."

Delgado was frustrated beyond words with having to do this. He easily knew someone wanted Ethan Lowell and Ethan Lowell alone dead. This really wasn't his problem, nor that of this many FBI agents, but money and connections talked.

"Do you know anyone who may have any problems or vendettas against you?" It was a simple question, the most basic.

"No."

"No scorned girlfriends?"

"No," Ethan scoffed as if it was preposterous. "Honestly, I haven't had a girlfriend in my life."

What a prick, like father like son.

"I apologize for the confusion. Lovers?"

Ethan smirked slightly, dropping his face from the gazes of his father, Delgado, and some other agent present that had yet to be introduced, if ever.

He wasn't embarrassed about his lifestyle, though he knew it reflected negatively on his father at times. He loved ladies and ladies loved him. There was no point in having the same thing day after day when at his age, of twenty-nine, the world had so much to offer. He couldn't imagine why any man would ever want to have sex with the same woman twice if there were many more willing and equally attractive.

Ethan did grimace for a second once he looked at his father. His parents were an exception. His dad and mother were married since their early twenties, for nearly thirty-five years. That was different though; his mother was different. There wasn't a single woman he had ever encountered that could have even been ten percent of the strong woman that she was.

"Mr. Lowell? Your lovers?"

"I think they all walk away pretty satisfied," he acknowledged in his own cocky way.

"Have any of them seemed distraught in any way?"

"No?"

"Are there any business deals in the works that may not please everyone?"

That question was actually directed to Owen Lowell. His luxury hotel complexes were in several countries outside of the United States. He was known to be a little ruthless when it came to land disputes and getting what he wanted.

"Absolutely not!"

"I apologize if I've offended either of you. Aside

from terrorists, which we've almost ruled out, we believe that someone does have an issue with Mr. Ethan Lowell."

"What are you saying? Does he need to be in some sort of witness protection–"

"No, no, no," Delgado insisted, all but laughing.

"Then what do we do," Owen Lowell shouted as he slammed his fist on the vintage teak desk.

"Mr. Lowell, I cannot tell you what to do, but I believe this is an isolated incident. We'll look into a lot, my superiors have said as much, but I'm fairly certain that this is ultimately against your son. It doesn't appear to be an act of terror," he repeated.

Ethan heard most of what was yet to come. He couldn't help but zone out. Why would anyone want him dead? The sun set over the city. He was supposed to be gone long ago. For once he didn't have plans; he simply wanted to go back to his penthouse and just relax.

"Mr. Lowell?"

The name was foreign; most of the time his father was called that. He forgot that was also his name.

"Yes," he replied, taken off-guard.

"What time do you typically leave the office here?"

He didn't know how to answer that. He rarely even worked. Generally, he visited his dad, collected a paycheck, and knew that eventually he'd inherit everything. He just wasn't ready for any of that quite yet.

"You mean...when he does work," Owen corrected with a raised brow. He had been trying to get his son involved more, much to his disappointment.

"Yeah, sure, whatever." Agent Delgado really didn't care about technicalities. He just needed information so that he could close this shit.

"When I come to work," Ethan began, "I usually leave around five."

"Interesting."

"What does that mean?" Suddenly, Ethan found himself getting slightly aggressive.

"The bomb was detonated at 5:12."

Fuck.

He knew it. Someone wanted him, and only him, dead.

Owen and his son collided in a hug, although it was simply eye contact.

"I want agents everywhere," Owen immediately demanded. "I have guards here, but I need them at my son's penthouse. I need them with–"

"I'm sorry Mr. Lowell. That is outside of what I can do for you."

Delgado knew that he was in for a lashing; however, there was absolutely nothing that the FBI could do at this point, short of his superiors insisting.

"Then how can I have my son protected?! Tell me what to do!"

As much as Delgado hated the old man, the desperate look in his eyes did something to him. Sure, his son was a playboy and he was certain this whole incident was because of that. Delgado had a daughter though, and even if she was only four, he would move heaven and earth for her. The look in Owen's eyes touched him. He just knew that he couldn't go above

16

and beyond for this right now, for a rich kid to have special agents.

"If you insist, I would recommend a CPO. There are lots of places–"

"What the hell is a CPO?!"

The old man obviously wasn't too happy with his suggestion that the FBI would not be guarding them like the elites they thought they were.

"That would be a Close Protection Officer."

"Fine! Get me one!"

"I'm sorry, you'll have to go through something for that. We don't do bodyguards for–"

"What," Ethan screamed. "No, I don't need a bodyguard!"

His father completely ignored him. Despite being an adult, Ethan knew that whatever his father insisted would be the final word.

"I recommend talking with Perkins, he's head of The Agency," Delgado sighed. "It's one of the best. They do a lot of high profile events and celebrities."

That caught Ethan's attention. He couldn't imagine what it would be like to walk into a club with a bodyguard. Women would be into that.

CHAPTER 2

Ryan Beckett.

That was the name of the agent that Owen Lowell had ultimately chosen from The Agency. After speaking with the head, David Perkins, and going through several files of agents who were available for long-term protection. He decided that Ryan had some of the best qualifications for the main guard.

Lowell had insisted to Perkins that until something more was figured out, he wanted someone with his son twenty-four hours a day. It took a great deal of explaining to Lowell that one single person generally didn't do that; there would have to be rotations. It was also established that if Ethan were to go to any high profile events that it would be in his best interest to have extra protection consisting of more than just one.

Today, only a day since the bomb, one miserable day of being confined in his father's mansion, Ethan would meet the main guy hired to protect him. He had to admit, while he tried to find the good in having a bodyguard, it was a little weird. He was 6'1", muscular, not to the point that he looked like some football player on steroids, but he was very much in shape. It was a little emasculating having another guy protect him. Sure, celebrities did it all the time, but that's because a lot of them didn't look like they could take a punch to the face.

"I'm surprised you showed up," Owen huffed. He moved some papers around his desk as he motioned to a chair off to the side, a few feet away from the two chairs in front of his desk.

Ethan only grunted at the comment. It wasn't like he had much of a choice. His father had practically forced him to come stay at his mansion until he had adequate protection. He loved his parents, but there was a reason a man pushing thirty did not still live with them.

He at least dressed for the occasion, attempting to look like a respected businessman in his black three piece suit; however, he neglected the tie. He rarely wore ties to work. Dates, if you'd call them that, were a different story. Ties had a greater purpose for him than just dangling around his neck.

It was now two minutes after the hour of nine. Owen Lowell shook his head. Fashionably late did not exist in his world.

"Doing quite a bit of swiping right over there?"

Ethan laughed at the comment. His dad hadn't spoken to him since he sat down and his phone was more entertaining than anything in the office. "Since when did you become versed on dating applications?"

Before his father could begin to once again admonish his lifestyle, the office phone rang. Owen put it on speaker. It was just Allison, his secretary, announcing that two people were present for a meeting. His only response was for her to hurry along and send them in.

As soon as Allison opened the door, she shot Ethan that look that she always did. His father pretended not to notice. Despite knowing that his son would sleep with anything with a pulse, he knew that Ethan had a strict policy against doing anything physical with women that worked for the company. It didn't stop the flirting though.

Ethan did find Allison attractive. She was slightly older, and married, with at least two little demons. He knew because occasionally her husband brought them by for lunch. He looked like he was boring in bed; that's all Ethan got from him. Allison, however, with her edgy short hair and four inch heels, looked like she could be into kinky sex. If she didn't work for the company, Ethan knew that she would gladly discard her vows for one night with him. He quickly tossed the idea away as soon as she disappeared and two people in black suits strolled in the room.

The man looked to be around fifty. His brown eyes were aged; wrinkles sprawled from the corners. He still had a lot of hair, though it was speckled with more grey than the color it once was.

The woman that followed behind him was interesting to Ethan. She wore the same suit and jacket as the older man, but it had a much more feminine touch of alteration. Despite the suit, Ethan could easily tell that she was incredibly lean and thin. She was fairly tall; had she been a little taller, she could easily have the body of a model, not a Victoria's Secret model, but one of those that appear on the runway. She seemed to be lacking in certain areas that were necessary for a lingerie model. Ethan couldn't help it; whenever there was a new female around he had to check them out a little.

He had to admit, he hated her hair. She had offset bangs that swept more to her left than her right. The rest was so tightly pulled into a ponytail that not a strand looked out of place. If she were to let her hair down, it would probably fall somewhere below her shoulders. Boring. It wasn't feisty like Allison's, nor was it long and wavy like many of his conquests.

Ethan couldn't tell much from her face as most of it was hidden behind the darkest aviators he could imagine. Her skin was light and smooth; she obviously didn't bother with lipstick. That was all he gathered. Overall, he'd never give her a second glance.

His attention quickly drew to his father shaking hands with the man, David Perkins, head of The Agency. Every time his father had mentioned the name of the company, Ethan couldn't help but almost vomit a little. It was pathetic; one of the dumbest names that required no thought whatsoever.

The two men began rambling about procedure before Perkins could sit down. Ethan turned his attention to the woman. She hadn't been introduced yet, but sat in the seat next to Perkins. For a second,

Ethan thought that she might be Perkins' wife, that maybe they ran the business together. He quickly shook the idea. They were at least a quarter century apart in age, though nowadays, that mattered very little.

"Most of our agents aren't specialized in long-term, but I've pulled a couple of them from upcoming events so that nights can be rotated out."

"So, when will this all start?" Owen Lowell asked, completely ignoring the fact that his son was even in the room.

"We're prepared for today. You seemed to think that your son's safety is on high alert."

"Absolutely." He wouldn't admit it, but he didn't want his son staying another night in the mansion. It was large, but when they crossed paths, generally there was an unfortunate conversation. "I'm sorry. David Perkins, this is my son, Ethan Lowell."

All three men rose. Ethan took a step forward, while Perkins took several to meet his handshake.

"So," Owen Lowell clapped his hands enthusiastically. "You assured me that Ryan Beckett is one of the best, definitely extremely skilled...When can we meet him?"

For a moment the room stood in silence.

The woman that had remained seated now rose. If Ethan thought that she had no physically redeeming qualities that would elicit a second glance, he was dead wrong as soon as she took the aviators from her face and tucked them in her jacket. *Blue* became an understatement. If he had once been captivated by

Egremnoi, the Maldives, Cala Macarelleta, or any of those intense waters, it was nothing like looking into her eyes. All those places lacked in beauty to the set of eyes revealed beneath those dark glasses. He had to think for a moment that maybe that's why she wore them, to keep people from staring. With those eyes, her pale face and rose tinted cheeks made her look like a porcelain doll.

He forced himself to look away and rejoin the silence.

"I'm sorry if there was any confusion," Perkins began, only to be cut off.

"I'm Ryan Beckett," the woman announced as she held her hand out to Owen Lowell. The slight smirk on her face made it obvious that this wasn't the first time her name had led to a whole storm of awkward.

Ethan suddenly felt lightheaded and sick, very sick, so sick that the trashcan a few feet away at his father's desk looked inviting.

"What?!" He didn't realize that he was able to get a word out, but three sets of eyes, one he dared not look at, gave him full attention. He took in a deep breath and composed himself, trying to hide the shock and disgust. He was always good with burying emotions.

"I can't have a *girl* bodyguard," he spat. The word sounded like poison dripping from his lips.

For once, Owen Lowell was at a loss for words.

"I assure the both of you, Ryan is very skilled and impeccable with assessing the most dangerous situations," Perkins began.

"She looks twelve!"

Twenty-seven.

It wasn't the first time Ryan felt insulted by a man over her looks and profession. Whenever she told people what she did, there was a general shock, occasionally laughter, followed by ridiculous questions. She soon grew a thick skin.

"I don't see what my age or looks have to do with my ability." Her words were sharp and cold.

"Dad, seriously?" Ethan turned toward his father. If it were up to him, he'd dismiss the two other people in the room. If this was the best that The Agency had, he didn't want or need it. "This has to be a joke."

Owen sighed and grabbed a folder off his desk. Upon opening it, there on the front page, he realized his mistake.

Sex: f.

The Agency was in no way deceptive. It was a fact that he ignored. He had been so impressed by the contents of Ryan Beckett's folder that he only assumed it must come from a man. Now that he thought about it, perhaps the name could be unisex, but in his sixty years, he had never met a woman with that name.

"So, everything in here," Owen said as he held up the folder. "This is you?"

"You cannot be entertaining this idea!"

Owen ignored his son and focused on the woman in front of him. "You've accomplished all this in," he paused and opened the folder again. It had a birthdate, but he was too taken aback to determine her actual age. "Less than thirty years?"

"I had an abnormal childhood," Ryan laughed.

Owen raised his brow for her to continue. He had to admit that she was quite intriguing.

"My parents were both military. To say that we moved around would be an understatement. I got into a fight when I was in about the third grade. I'll just say that it didn't go so well. Rather than scold me, they put me in different classes. At first it was to learn to defend myself, you know, being a *girl* and all." She allowed her eyes to momentarily dart to the spoilt brat for a quick glare. "After a while, it taught me discipline, and strength, and as I got older I wanted to perfect my techniques."

Ethan scoffed as he grabbed the folder from his father. He hadn't looked at it until now. He recognized some of the words. Aikido. Krav Maga. Kickboxing.

"What the hell is Systema?" He muttered the words to himself, but she had obviously heard.

"It's Russian. Primarily hand-to-hand combat, knife fighting."

"Well, I don't care," Ethan said as he tossed the file back on his father's desk. He had to admit, a sick part of him thought it was a little hot. He could imagine her in some tight yoga pants, maybe a sports bra, training with a man twice her size, disarming him. *Oh, god. No.* "I'm not having a girl following me around. Congrats on your Chuck Norris résumé, but no. Sorry."

"Not that I want to be stuck with someone as

obnoxious and spoilt as you, but aside from the fact that I don't have a dick, what is your problem?" There it was. All the venom she had in her spewed from her lips. She had no reason to care; Perkins would have her on another job tomorrow.

Perkins, who had remained silent, rubbed his temple and shook his head. He'd be the biggest liar in the world if he didn't admit that the girl gave him headaches, even on good days.

Ethan was more than shocked. He knew she probably had a little fire in her, but he didn't expect that. He went with it though.

"Okay, fine. If someone is shooting at me, how are you going to cover me, how are you going to protect me? I'm like twice your size."

"You're telling me that what you're looking for is a big, muscular, hulking man to lay on top of you?"

Perkins had to stifle a laugh at that comment.

Owen glanced back and forth between Ethan and Ryan trying to do a deeper evaluation of the heated banter.

"Let me make one thing clear. I don't know what you've seen in the movies, but eventually, your human shield will be killed and then so will you. With me, you'd never be in that situation to begin with." Ryan quickly stopped herself. She realized that her confidence seemed more like persuasion.

"Are there papers we need to sign? How does this work," Owen asked, ignoring Ryan and Ethan and focusing his attention to David Perkins.

"Now that that's over," Perkins began. Oftentimes

he had similar meetings when it came to Ryan, but this was in the top five for the worst.

"Dad, no. I'm not a child–"

"You're right Ethan. You're not a child. You're my child!"

"I'm not having a female bodyguard!"

"Fine. No bodyguard at all then. Until whoever behind the bomb is caught, you'll remain confined to the mansion." Owen was a shrewd businessman. He knew how to get his way. He knew what triggered a person. Within minutes he could sense someone's weakness. His son's weakness was easy; he valued his freedom far too much.

Owen had no intention whatsoever of having his son staying with him, but he was better at playing games than his son was. The rage in Ethan's eyes and the clenching of his jaws told Owen everything. He had won.

Ethan continued his descent further into childhood by stomping from the room, no doubt cussing to himself, and slamming his father's door. By the time the office stopped shaking, there was another slam.

"His office is next door. Maybe he'll use his frustration and actually bury himself in his work," Owen announced casually.

CHAPTER 3

The rest of the morning was best described as awkward. Ryan had gone through Ethan's office, making mental notes of contents and locations. Ethan thought it was ridiculous. The building had security guards and they were on the 14th floor. He actually felt safest at work and his penthouse, but he couldn't confine himself to those two places.

Ryan spent most of the morning outside of his office. He expected that. She served no purpose simply watching him work. However, now she sat on the couch near his door; it was by far the seat farthest from his desk. Ethan pretended to work, but he couldn't help but be curious of the file she was skimming through. He didn't know how she could read anything with those glasses.

"Is the sun too bright for you? Should I turn it down," he asked sarcastically.

It got him what he wanted when she took off her glasses and folded them into an interior pocket in her jacket. She had unbuttoned it when she sat down and he noticed the black straps that fell over the shoulders of her white shirt. With the movement now, he saw the concealed gun on her left side.

"How many do you have?" He motioned to the

same spot on his left.

"On me now, or total?"

"Both." A rush of heat went through him. He didn't know why he felt like she belonged in some *Tomb Raider* and *Die Hard* mashup.

"Three and seventeen."

She motioned to her right side, but he couldn't see it. She then lifted her right pant leg and he got a glimpse of the one strapped above her ankle.

"What's the deal with the glasses," he asked, quickly changing the subject.

A small smile came across her face and she shook her head at the question.

"Habit."

Ethan noticed early on that she preferred short and concise responses. It was another thing about her that annoyed him. He let out a sigh of frustration that a deaf person could have picked up on.

"I don't like people to know where I'm looking. When I'm on a job, especially out in the public, I'm constantly scanning and looking for any movement that seems off."

"We're not in the public."

"Would you prefer that I not wear them when no one is around?" Her voice was mocking. She bat her eyelashes, not in an attractive way. It was the way one of his teachers used to do when he knew he was in trouble and she knew as well, but waited for him to incriminate himself.

The staring contest ended abruptly with the buzz-ing of a phone.

"I have to take this."

Ryan walked to a far off corner, near a window overlooking the city. Though her voice was low, Ethan picked up on every word.

"I'm working," were her first words.

"Hey, sweetheart!" The man's voice bellowed through the room. Ryan quickly hit a button on the side, turning the volume down.

"What do you want?"

"Damn, you're in a mood."

"I'll explain that one later," she sighed.

"Perkins got you with another bratty princess," the man laughed.

"Something like that." She couldn't help but smirk. One of her more recent jobs was as a bodyguard for a fifteen year old European princess touring the states. It was a miserable three days and the princess didn't understand that bodyguard and personal assistant were not interchangeable terms.

"I'll make this short. I'm just calling because you didn't tell your favorite brother good luck this morning." Jeremy was her only brother.

"Shit! I'm so sorry. Your race." She ran her hand over her neck and popped it to one side. She had been stressing over this job that she had completely forgotten. She never forgot to wish her brother good luck. While her job was more dangerous, she always felt on edge when it was race day for Jeremy.

"It's no big deal," he laughed. "It's not like it's Daytona."

"No, because I'll be in the stands for that one. I am

sorry Jer, good luck. You know I'll be checking the updates until it's over. Be safe."

"Love ya!"

"I love you too." With that, the conversation concluded.

Jeremy was a remarkable driver. Ryan never once doubted his skills. Accidents happened though, and she knew that she'd never be able to handle that phone call.

"Girlfriend?"

The comment jerked her from her thoughts and she swiftly turned around, glaring at the green eyes carefully watching her.

"Excuse me?"

"Was that your girlfriend? Partner? Whatever you call it."

"Is that your way of asking me if I'm a lesbian?" She was fuming at the suggestion, but didn't let it show through her words or body language as she made her way back to the sofa.

"You are, aren't you?" The smirk and narrowed eyes were too readable. He was messing with her.

"You should probably consider me as such."

She wasn't into girls. He knew that. Her words were an underlying comment telling him that he didn't stand a chance.

"Who is he?" He didn't want to pry, but there was always that hint of curiosity that got the best of him.

Ryan glared back at him. She didn't know if she was more upset that he thought her call was his business, or that he knew without a doubt there was

31

a man on the other end and he still proceeded with the lesbian comment.

"My brother. Not that my phone calls are any of your business," she spat.

"You could have taken it outside," he responded.

It took him a moment to put the pieces together. Beckett wasn't a name he encountered often, but it still seemed like a bit of a stretch. He went with it anyway.

"Wait, is your brother Jeremy Beckett?" He leaned forward over his desk, eagerly awaiting her response. His eyes lit up like a kid on Christmas when they knew that the wriggling box was going to contain a puppy.

"Are you going to fangirl," she huffed. She hated telling people about her brother. She wasn't embarrassed by him at all, but generally guys only wanted to talk to her about NASCAR and more than one girl had asked her if she had any shirtless pictures of Jeremy. The girls always made her vomit a little.

"Holy crap, that's awesome." It was the first time she had seen what his genuine smile looked like. His eyes softened and she found that the sight of that sent a shiver down her spine. She quickly dismissed it. "I can't believe your brother is Jeremy freakin' Beckett."

"His middle name is actually Paul."

Ethan rolled his eyes and went back to his computer. She would take something awesome and bring it down a hundred degrees.

From the corner of his eye, he saw his phone light

up with a text.

Zach: I'm headed up. Your rent-a-cops down here are dicks.

Shit. He and Zach did lunch often, that was, when he bothered coming to work. Ethan had mentioned to Zach that his father was upping security and that he'd probably have a bodyguard for a while. He knew once Zach walked in, he'd never hear the end of this messed up situation.

Before he could mention anything to Ryan, there was a rhythmic knock on the door. The text had obviously been delayed in the elevator.

Ryan's eyes darted from the door to Ethan with a questioning look.

"It's..." His words failed him. He rushed toward the door, but rather than pushing Zach from entering, so he could explain everything in the hall, Zach managed to casually slip past him.

"Honey, I'm home," he sang out. He was just about to plop on the couch like normal when he took a step back in shock. "Well, hello there." His brow raised midway through in an attempt to be seductive.

Ryan stood. She kept a flat and unemotional look as she eyed the man up and down. She didn't know who the stranger was. She thought to almost pat him down, but that should have been the job of security on the ground floor.

"Like what you see," he laughed as he swayed his hips a little. He was completely opposite in looks compared to Ethan. Blonde hair, dark eyes, but still just as fit.

"She's not checking you out," Ethan groaned. "She's probably wondering if you have any weapons."

"Don't even get me started. Dude! The fat hairy guy down there makes me feel like I need to go to therapy now. I mean, get some metal detectors or something," Zach squealed.

"Not all weapons are metal," Ryan coldly cut in.

"Wait, who is she?" Zach turned to Ethan again, searching for an explanation.

"First of all, if you give me any shit–"

Zach faked a laugh at the suggestion. "Seriously, why does it feel like Antarctica in here right now? Everything is so serious."

"She's my bodyguard." He blurted it out so fast and dismissing that it took the words a moment to travel to Zach's brain for comprehension.

"Wait...What?!"

He turned back to the woman and it was his turn to scan her. She didn't look like a bodyguard. He had actually seen female bodyguards before; most of them still looked like dudes.

The outburst took Ryan by surprise, not so much Ethan, he expected it from Zach. The laughter roared through the room. Never could something have been that funny to anyone. Zach gripped at his sides from the pain, but was still unable to compose himself. Ethan walked to his desk, ignoring his sometimes jerk of a best friend, and grabbed his phone and wallet. When he returned, the laughter had subsided and Zach was wiping away tears.

"Oh...god...too...much," he managed with the fading giggles.

"You know what," Ethan thought aloud. "Do you want to order something to be brought in?"

"Why? We always go to Moretti's."

Ethan motioned with his eyes to Ryan, which only caused a wide smile to form across Zach's face.

"Oh no, we're going to Moretti's."

Ethan quickly introduced Zach and Ryan in the elevator. Shortly after that, her glasses went back on and she faded into the background. Even when they hit the sidewalk for the three blocks to the restaurant, he knew she was present, but she had this creepy ability that made him forget that she was there, and he was able to fall into a normal conversation with Zach rambling on about stocks.

When they entered the restaurant, the hostess warmly greeted them as though they were best friends.

Ryan took this time to slip to the side and position herself against a wall in a perfect spot, away from the patrons, but overseeing everything.

"Wait," Zach stopped the hostess just after she grabbed two menus. "We need three."

All of them looked confused. Zach looked around for Ryan but noticed she was no longer with them. After glancing about for a moment he saw her along a wall. Her body was straight and professional and her wrists crossed just below her waist.

"No, we're not doing that." He looked to Ethan who

only shrugged like he didn't care what she did. "Sweetheart," Zach began, directing his words to the hostess now. "I'm ready to be seated." Then he turned his attention to Ethan. "Go get your *girl* and tell her she's joining us."

He knew his words jabbed at Ethan the moment his jaw clenched. Disappointment flashed on the woman's face and she tightly gripped the menus and motioned for Zach to follow her. She and Ethan never did anything, which was surprising for Ethan, but that didn't stop the mutual flirtation every time the two men came for lunch.

Zach watched intently as Ethan made his way over to Ryan. He couldn't wait to give him crap about this.

"That isn't how this works," Ryan spat.

"Don't cause a scene. And for the love of god, take those damn things off in here."

Ryan jerked her glasses off, only for her icy glare to meet Ethan's. He realized he hadn't been standing this close to her in his father's office. He had never been this close to her. He was close enough to touch her; he could even smell her perfume. It was one of those fruity floral blends, Bath and Body Works, or something like that.

"Are you just going to stand here and stare at me," she hissed, breaking him from whatever trance she had managed to put him in.

"It depends. Stop being so defiant and have lunch."

"I don't think you understand what my job is." She sighed like she was about to admit defeat.

"Fine, you can tell me all about the rules later, but if you don't sit down and eat with us, I'm never going to hear the end of it."

He didn't understand and she couldn't explain it to him right now in the middle of an upscale restaurant.

Rule broken.

"This is completely unprofessional," Ryan huffed as she followed Ethan to the table.

She stopped as soon they reached the booth and shook her head at the idea. Zach simply sat there with his beverage, no doubt alcoholic, and smirked. Ethan waited for a moment allowing Ryan to decide on the seating arrangement. When she didn't, he began to sit on the side next to Zach.

Before he could so much as touch the leather cushion, Zach's feet were all over him kicking like a kid in the supermarket candy section.

"Dude! Hell no! That's weird."

"Yeah, and you're a dick." Ethan glared at his concocting friend.

Zach turned his attention toward Ryan, still standing, like she was making a life altering decision.

"Look, sweetheart," Zach began, noticing the way she clenched at the word. "If you try to sit beside me, I can promise you I won't kick; however, since he's the one you're protecting..." He let his words drift off as he motioned toward Ethan.

Ryan sat as close to the edge as possible. The whole situation was throwing her off.

Ethan wasn't sure Ryan could have made a right

decision. Lunch would have been unbearable if he had to continuously meet her gaze across the table, but next to him was no better.

"So, Ryan," Zach began, focusing his attention to her.

"Let me stop you," she said, colder than she intended. "We don't do this." She motioned with her hand across the table.

"Eat lunch?"

"I'm not hired to be a friend."

"You really play by the rules don't you?"

"I'm not playing anything. There are guidelines that I like to follow," she growled. Although frustrating, she liked Zach's playful attitude. He wasn't as uptight as Ethan.

"Let me guess, if I offer you a drink right now, you're going to turn me down."

"If it's anything other than tea or water."

"Soda?"

"Asshole," Ryan scoffed.

Zach laughed and almost choked on the amber liquid in his glass.

"You're awfully quiet, princess." Zach directed that comment toward Ethan.

"I'm just letting you have your fun," he snapped.

Zach's eyes narrowed, and began studying his friend. He sensed how uncomfortable he was. A blind man could see how much Ethan didn't want to be there.

"What can I get for you," a cute waitress asked, announcing her presence.

They ordered. The service was quick. Zach was too hungry to bother with more teasing. He needed to let up with it anyway. He really did have something important to talk with Ethan about, and he knew that Ethan would give him more shit than he had given Ethan about a female bodyguard.

"Hey," the waitress nervously announced in Ethan's direction. "Umm, my shift is about to end, so someone else is taking over..."

Ryan shared a confused glance with Zach. He rolled his eyes and shook his head. He was all too accustomed to this when he went anywhere with Ethan.

"Anyway, here," she said as she slid a small piece of paper across the table in Ethan's direction.

In return he gave her a lustful smile; however, it quickly faded once she left and he slid the paper to Zach.

"Whoa, what?"

"She's not my type." He was calm about it, like he'd never give her a second look.

Zach glared at him, but Ethan wouldn't make eye contact with him. He glanced to Ryan, who was finishing her steak. Her face held no expression.

"Since when do you have a type?"

"Just drop it," Ethan growled.

"Well, I guess now is as good a time as any to tell you that I won't be needing this," he began, shoving the paper back at his friend.

Ethan looked confused. His brows furrowed, awaiting what Zach was about to drop.

"I need to tell you something. It's really important." It was the first time that Ryan was seeing Zach actually be serious.

"What?" Ethan drew out the word with hesitation.

"So, you know I've been seeing Anna–"

"But other girls too?"

"No. Just Anna." The smile on his face said it all to Ryan, but Ethan was slower to pick up on it. If he already knew, he was playing dumb to the fact that his friend was completely in love with this Anna person.

"Oh god, you're like in a relationship," Ethan groaned. Ryan shot him a scowl, but he only shrugged it off like he had done nothing wrong.

Ryan rose to leave; it was clearly going to be a conversation that needed to be discussed in private.

"Actually, I need you to stay," Zach nervously laughed.

"I don't see how this has anything to do with me."

"It doesn't, but in a minute, I might be needing your protection."

"Wait, what?" Ethan was on the verge of hyperventilating. "What could be worse than you being in a relationship and having an actual *girlfriend*?"

For a moment Ryan forgot that he was the person she was hired to keep alive. She had to refrain from slapping him. He made the word sound so vile and disgusting.

"It's a little more than that."

He reached into his pocket and drew out a black box, setting it in the middle of the table. It didn't need to be opened.

"What the fuck, man?!"

The restaurant went quiet and nasty glares shot their way. The attention they drew made all three of them feel uncomfortable, but Ethan soon became too consumed with the idea that his friend was about to propose.

"You've only known her like a month," he insisted. He was going to do everything possible to talk some sense into Zach.

"It's been longer than that."

"And you're just going to give up the rest of your life for her?"

"I'm not looking at it like that," he laughed. "I can't imagine being with another woman, ever. That's how I know this is right."

"No, no. You've just had a dry spell. We'll go out tonight–"

"Actually, tonight is the night," Zach announced proudly.

It only elicited more groans and whiny sounds from Ethan, who was now banging his head on the back of the leather seat. Ryan had never seen a man act so ridiculous; she had to separate herself from the madness.

CHAPTER 4

"Hey, Ryan, do you mind if I have a second with grumps," Zach asked as soon as they passed through the revolving doors of the office building.

Ryan nodded, told Zach congratulations again, and made her way to the elevator to wait for Ethan.

"You're not coming up for a minute?"

"And risk Elmer Fudd over there fondling me again?" He motioned to the heavyset guard eyeing him. "No, thanks."

They both chuckled at the comment; the security guard did share a close resemblance with the *Looney Tunes* character.

"Anyway, I'm sorry I sprang this on you, but you're my best friend, and I wanted you to be one of the first to know," he admitted.

"I know. I'll find a way to forgive you."

Zach shook his head and laughed. "You're an ass."

"I try."

"You do know that I'm going to need you to be my best man, if she says yes."

Ethan groaned at the mentioning of the relationship and wedding stuff again. "You know she's going to say yes."

"If it helps, most of her friends that she'd pick as

bridesmaids are single."

Ethan slightly laughed at the comment, but Zach was quick to pick up a flicker of something more at his lack of enthusiasm.

"Unless you're not into that?"

"Why wouldn't I be into that," he gasped, shocked at the suggestion.

Zach tipped his head in the direction of Ryan.

"What is wrong with you? No, absolutely not! She's a belligerent ass."

"You sure," he speculated.

"Absolutely."

"If you say so. Just don't mess things up."

"What the hell is that supposed to mean?" Ethan's voice rose and Zach knew that he had riled him just a little over the tipping point.

He laughed it off and they said their goodbyes. Maybe he was wrong, but something in the way Ethan looked at her against the wall in the restaurant made him doubt his friend's words.

* * *

The penthouse door swung open and Ethan motioned for Ryan to go in first. He couldn't stop from smiling when a gasp escaped her lips upon entering. She didn't strike him as a person to be in awe over anything, but as she strolled through the living room, fingertips grazing over the grey couches, making her way to the floor-to-ceiling windows overlooking the setting sun over the city, he knew she was amazed.

"I guess you want a tour?"

"Hmm?" It took Ryan a minute to register what he said. The view from the living room truly was spectacular. "Oh, I've already looked through the layout."

The living room, kitchen, and dining room went with the whole open concept floorplan. She just couldn't imagine why a single man would need such a big place. The kitchen was as big as half of her apartment. It was also too clean; he probably didn't know how to use much more than the coffee machine.

"Really, so you know where everything is?" He raised a brow as if testing her.

"Spare bedroom, bathroom, office, and another smaller bedroom that I believe you use as a gym," she said pointing past the kitchen and dining room and down a wide hallway. She then turned her finger the exact opposite direction. "Your master and attached bath that way."

He didn't need to tell her that she was right, the glimmer in her eyes said everything.

"Do you want to actually see the rooms?"

She glanced down at her watch. She thought it was closer to the end of her shift, but she still had well over an hour before Levi would arrive.

"Yeah, sure."

The house was exceptionally clean for a bachelor, meaning that he either didn't spend a lot of time at home, or he had a maid. Ryan actually thought both.

The gym was overwhelming; she became a little jealous of the night shift. Once Levi or Jeff bonded with Ethan, he would no doubt let them use it.

"Then here's the guest bathroom." He said it in a way like it was no big deal, but realistically it was the size of her bedroom. The garden tub and shower combination was a white marble with grey lines of sparkle that matched a counter long enough that she could sleep on it. Ryan had to remind herself not to let her jaw drop in amazement with each room.

"Guest bedroom." Unlike the other two rooms he stepped inside momentarily and motioned for her to do the same.

"Who stays here?"

"No one."

"Ever?"

"Ever," he laughed.

"Why is that so funny?"

His gaze fell on her and the laughter died. She could have sworn in that moment that his eyes darted toward her lips, but she had to be imagining things. Despite that, she could still feel her cheeks warming, and didn't know why.

"When I moved in here a little over a year ago, I decided not to have many guests." He turned off the light and continued back toward the other end of the house, to his bedroom. She didn't press any further.

It was ridiculous. No one person ever needed to sleep in a room so large. He held out his hand and gestured for her to look around.

He definitely was a fan of dark colors. Ryan noticed the bed first but refrained from allowing him to know that. It had to have been a California King.

From what she had seen in the tabloids, she couldn't help but wonder how many women had slept there.

She instead went along the nearest wall to her right. Three large paintings stretched over three of the walls, the last wall had windows dividing it. The paintings were impersonal and all black and white landscapes.

She ran her fingers over the bookshelf. Dickens. Faulkner. Fitzgerald. Hemingway. Twain. She didn't expect to see so many books, let alone such heavy reading. If anything, she thought he might have a few *Maxim* on the nightstand. She glanced back toward the bed. There were nightstands on both sides with wall lamps above them, but nothing on top of them.

Ethan said nothing to her as she slowly made her way throughout the room. He found himself fixated on her every movement. It was strange seeing a woman in his room. He made it a point to never bring any home. He had one shortly after college that stalked him like crazy. He had to admit, that was one thing bad about just one night with a random woman. None of them ever showed crazy until later on.

It wasn't until Ryan raked her fingers along the smooth black material of his comforter that he became undone. Something inside him lost all touch with reality and all he could think about was storming over to her, ripping her hair from that awfully tight ponytail and throwing her to the bed. No sooner than he thought it, she looked up at him. For a moment he wondered if he had vocalized his thoughts.

"It's a nice room," she concluded. She pointed to the bookshelf. "You have a good collection."

She was dry, vague, and unemotional. It brought him back to the real world. He needed to get out and get laid. It had been two weeks since he'd even kissed a woman. He didn't even want to think about how long it had been since he had more. That was the only reason thoughts of her had started to cross his mind. He could kick himself for throwing away the phone number from earlier.

"Oh, I almost forgot," Ryan announced once they were back in the living room. "Can I see your phone?"

Ethan raised his brow and shot her a speculating look, and for a split second he thought the blush she put on her cheeks more than nine hours ago seemed to intensify. Without asking any questions, he handed it to her and watched as she opened her own phone and clicked away at his.

"There." She handed it back to him moments later.

He flipped it on but didn't see anything different. He hit the bottom right icon to see what was last accessed. The only thing that popped up was the phone book.

"You have all of our direct lines, in case anything unforeseen should come up," she sighed when he didn't say anything.

"All?"

"Yes. Perkins, but only use that for an emergency. Then there's Levi and Jeff. They'll rotate off nights and anytime that I'm not available."

"And yours?"

"Obviously," she scoffed.

"Honestly," he began, changing the subject. "I'm probably safest right here. I don't need to be watched at night."

"I somewhat agree with you; however, your father insisted and if that's how he wants to spend his money, so be it. Besides, from what I've heard, he's all over the FBI, wanting this shit solved yesterday." She blew her breath upward and tossed her head slightly. The hairspray that once held her bangs perfectly had started to wear. "Maybe after a week we can look into backing off a little if all goes well."

"I'm going to go shower. You good waiting on…"

"Levi. Yes. If I'm gone by the time you're done, I'll meet you tomorrow at the office. Levi will drop you off."

"Sounds good."

Ryan waited until a few minutes after the water started running. Ethan's room and bathroom were so far away that she had to strain for any sound. Once she was certain he was in the shower, she pulled out her phone and dialed Jeremy's number.

The conversation was light at first. She congratulated him on third. She had kept up with the race from start to finish, checking every few minutes. Halfway in, however, she assumed that he had secured a spot in the top five. She was surprised he wasn't out celebrating, but he explained that he had an early day tomorrow for traveling purposes.

"So, tell me about this new gig you got," he laughed. He found humor in everything. Even when their parents divorced and he was already eighteen, he went on and on about getting two Christmases.

"I don't even know where to start!"

Ethan dug through his dresser for just a simple t-shirt. It was full of blacks, greys, and whites. He settled on a grey. He slid his hand into his damp hair and ruffled it a little, giving it his signature messy and spikey look; although, he made a mental note to make an appointment with his stylist in the near future for a trim.

He was about to open his door to make his way into the common area when he heard a voice. It was Ryan. He couldn't believe she was still there. He listened in, wondering if she was informing Levi of directions, or protocol, or whatever the hell they talked about. He quickly realized, after hearing no other voice, she was on the phone.

"You don't get it. This is the worst one Perkins has put me on. I feel like somewhere along the way I fucked up and he's handing me shit detail on a silver platter."

"Come on, Ry. It can't be that bad. I looked the guy up; he seems cool."

Ryan groaned at the suggestion. "He's spoilt and entitled. The only thing he needs protection from is an STD."

"I have to tell you, that was a little harsh," her brother sighed on the other end.

"Seriously though, I feel like I'm just going to be a babysitter with this one."

"I actually prefer that."

"I prefer a job where I'm doing something more than following around a rich guy because his daddy is paranoid."

That was all it took. Ethan had heard enough.

He tore through his closet and found a casual black button-up. He rolled up the sleeves and tucked his undershirt into his jeans. He quickly grabbed a tube of hair gel and smoothed a bit through his hair. Normally he put a little more effort into his looks, but it was just a club. He could show up in *SpongeBob* pajama pants and still get invited to go home with some random chick.

He quietly opened his door. Thankfully, she was in another part of the living room that swept a little to the left where the front door wasn't visible. He cautiously and quickly grabbed his keys and wallet from the stand by the door and he was gone.

"Hey, Jer, I'm going to have to call you back later. I'm getting an incoming call from my relief."

"It's no problem, I have the first flight out in the morning."

Ryan laughed. "I thought all you rich celebrities have private planes."

"Oh, shut up. You know I'm not like that. Anyway, goodnight, sis. I love you."

"Love you too." Ryan concluded with a kissy noise that her brother hated because it sent a piercing sound through the phone. She quickly swapped the conversation before Levi's incoming call was sent to voicemail.

"Hey, are you on your way?"

There was a pause. It was only faint and she could picture him opening his mouth just about to say something, but she didn't allow it.

"Levi, what happened?"

"Ryan, I'm so sorry. I tried calling Jeff to relieve you, but–"

"What is it," she pressed on.

"Whoa, don't go zero to a hundred just yet. I'm with my wife at the hospital. The baby has another fever."

"Oh."

"Yeah. I mean, I'll be there tonight, it's just going to take a little longer than I thought." He continued to apologize to the point that Ryan had to stop him.

"It's fine. I promise. This job is a piece of cake anyway, just as long as you can tolerate his attitude."

"Is it as bad as the princess," he laughed.

"The verdict is still out on that one."

"Awesome. Well, I'll be there a little later tonight. Again, I'm really sorry."

"Stop," Ryan insisted. "Your child comes before anything, including my sleep and sanity."

"You're the best Ryan. See you soon."

Once she hung up the phone, an eerie silence crept through the room, one that put her on high alert.

CHAPTER 5

Ryan sank into the couch. The house was so quiet. She was tempted to put the television on just for noise. That's when she tilted her head and peered down the hall toward Ethan's room; she could see a glimmer of light from beneath the door. She couldn't hear the shower anymore. It was difficult to hear at first, but now she was certain it was off.

Another ten minutes passed and that annoying voice in the back of her head kept telling her something wasn't right. She had to get up, had to move around. Sitting in one place with little to do was nothing more than self-torture.

She moseyed about the kitchen. She became shocked upon opening the refrigerator. It was full. For some reason, all she imagined was beer and left-over pizza boxes. Instead there were vegetables, fresh meat that would need to be used in the coming days, all kinds of condiments, cheeses, and other dairy. It looked like the refrigerator of someone who actually cooked.

Suddenly a different shock came over her when she looked up over the counters. She was certain that Ethan dropped his things off by the door. She replayed the memory in her head. When they came in, he put his keys, wallet, and phone on the stand. No. He was about to put the phone, but he didn't. He didn't because he had it on him when they left the bedroom. The keys and the wallet definitely stayed.

She rushed to the closed bedroom door.

"Ethan!" She pounded on the door. The only response was silence.

She swung the door open. No one in the bedroom. For a moment she hesitated going into the bathroom, but he should have been done and dressed by now. She was right. Her stomach sank and a sick and dizzy feeling ran through the length of her body.

"That fucking asshole," she screamed, nearly kicking the door off its hinges.

She whipped out her phone. Her finger hung over the contact box for Ethan, but she knew it was a waste of time. It was only going to be declined or go to voicemail. Instead, she opened her apps.

She had him.

She zoomed in on the red dot on the map and tapped the rectangular building outline. *Jupiter Lounge.*

Ryan had been there with clients before. It was an upscale nightclub for celebrities. The entry fee wasn't horrible for those sorts, but never in her life would Ryan have spent $100 just to get in the doors.

* * *

"Here!" Ryan all but threw the money at the taxi driver as she tore from the car.

Thankfully there wasn't a line at the entry doors. That was expected at such an early time and on a weeknight. Had it been a Friday or Saturday after ten, people would be lined up for blocks.

"Thank goodness," she sighed as she reached the bouncer. Donny. She had met him several times before. They first met when she was holding back the hair of an actress who went all out for her 21st birthday.

"Good evening," he greeted her.

She could feel the ache in her neck intensify when she looked up to make eye contact. He was easily 6'6" and she couldn't even begin to guess his weight with all the muscle latched to him. He had a long ponytail, more than five piercings in each ear, and a left arm bleeding in tattoos. He was a guy no one messed with. He was also the leader of the people who laughed at her choice of job.

"Hey, Donny. I need in."

"You look like shit." He didn't mind being blunt about it.

"I'm exhausted and frustrated. Look, my client is in there, unprotected," she admitted.

"Wait? You lost your client," he began to chuckle.

"Donny!"

"Sorry, darling. Unless you got a popstar paying your way..."

"Seriously?"

Donny arched his eyebrows and held out his hand. Ryan knew the rules, acquaintances or not. She dug through her wallet and handed him five twenties, which he tucked in a hip pack.

"I need a stamp."

"Like hell, top floor access is more than what you've got."

"Donny, please." She didn't realize how whiney her words came out until he gave her a look of pity.

"One time only, and don't you dare go around telling people that I'm going soft or any shit like that," he insisted. He pulled out a black tube and dotted her left hand with an eccentric black letter *J*.

Surprisingly, the club had more people than Ryan expected at this time. She was grateful that she had upper level access. She didn't expect Ethan to be there, but it gave her an entire view of everything below.

In a sea of bleached blonde, there he was. His arms were around two different women grinding against him, one a blonde, one a bright redhead. Rage fumed inside Ryan. This is what was so important for him to put not only her job in danger, but potentially his life.

The half-naked bodies, covered in scraps of designer dresses, swayed along his sides. It was what he needed. He felt like himself.

The redhead excused herself to go to the restroom and the blonde, Jessica, took full advantage of her departure. Her movements further intensified with more pressure as she danced against him. His body couldn't help but give away how much he wanted her.

Like a ravenous animal, she pulled him down for better access. Her lips, tongue, and teeth grazed over his neck. He flinched a little when it became too much. Even in his near drunken state, he was sober enough to know what a hickey would mean when seeing his father.

Her lips came to his ears. "I'm a ten minute drive away." She then began sucking on his earlobe.

"Is that an invitation?" He gripped at her hips and pulled her into him. She was overcome with giggles.

"Yeah." Her voice turned husky and lustful. "Want to get out of here?"

Before he could answer, there was a booming voice next to him. "I had the same idea!"

Something gripped his forearm and he felt himself being pulled away. If he would have been more sober, he could have pulled back, made his feet stop, but by the time he was able to process what was going on, he was against a wall, far away from the myriad of dancers.

His heart stopped the moment the blazing blue eyes latched on to his.

"What the hell is wrong with you?" Her words were screeching, something between a seagull and nails on a chalkboard, but magnified. It sent chills down his spine.

He stepped away and brushed past her, but she yanked at his arm and spun him around, reversing their original spots.

"We're leaving. Now!"

"Like hell," he roared back.

"What is your problem? You flipped from calm and mellow at your place to batshit crazy. Why would you leave without telling me?" She glanced around the club and waved her arm from left to right. "This is what was so important that you'd risk your own safety?"

He took a step toward her. When he did she instinctively took a step back. Then another. She could feel the wall brush against her elbows.

"I don't need a fucking *babysitter* following me around," he spat at her. He was so close that she could smell the whiskey on his breath.

He had heard her conversation with Jeremy; she knew that now. Hatred poured from his eyes over her.

He raked a hand through his hair before bringing it to the side of her head. He pressed it against the wall, steadying himself.

His glassy gaze flickered over her face. His tongue grazed over his bottom lip. His teeth clenched at one side and his eyes met hers again.

"After one day, you hate me that much." His words were barely a whisper

Ryan wasn't sure if it was a question or a statement. A million thoughts were running through her mind at rapid speed that nothing was coherent.

When she didn't say anything, his hand fell and he pushed himself away. Over his shoulder, Ryan saw the blonde headed their way with a fancy pink drink in hand.

She put her arm around Ethan's waist and whispered something inaudible in his ear causing his eyes to glaze over with lust. Ryan knew that if she couldn't get him to leave, she'd have to just stay, to make sure nothing happened to him. Although now, his only enemy was himself.

They began to dance, not far from the edge of the floor. Ryan remained pressed against the wall. She took a moment to update Levi on the situation should she need his help later.

"Watch it," a voice shouted not far from her.

Pink liquid streamed from a man's white button-up down to a puddle on the floor.

"Relax," Jessica spat at him. She tossed her hair and walked away, tugging at Ethan.

The man was quick and jerked Ethan by the other arm, causing him to slip from Jessica's grasp.

"Your hooker just ruined a $200 shirt," he roared. He was fuming.

"Great," Ryan said to herself. "An angry drunk." She began making her way to the escalating situation. If she thought it was simply going to be a verbal pissing match, she was dead wrong, especially when she saw the balled-up fist.

The man didn't know what happened as he stumbled backwards grabbing at his stomach. His fist had been so close to the jaw of the prick before him when a boot off to the side collided into him. Blinking and catching his breath he saw a female in a black suit. He wasn't about to let a woman get away with that. Ignoring the man, he went after her.

Ethan watched as the heel of Ryan's hand pushed the man's nose upward. He grasped at it with one hand and screamed, but Ryan wasn't done. In a swift and effortless move, his right arm was twisted behind his back. Ryan continued to apply pressure until he was pleading, begging, crying for her to stop. Then she did, pushing him forward to stumble through the crowd.

She turned to Ethan. The woman he was with had scampered away as soon as the altercation began.

"We're leaving."

Ethan knew it wasn't a question. They were leaving.

"I can't believe you drove knowing you were going to get so drunk," Ryan scoffed as soon as they reached his car. She got on the ground and using her phone's flashlight, skimmed under the car.

"People aren't going to keep putting bombs on my car," Ethan sighed. He was a little drunk, but it didn't dawn on him that he couldn't drive.

Minutes later, after circling the car, Ryan stood expectantly before him.

"What?"

"Keys."

"Over my dead body are you driving my car!"

Ryan took a quick glance over him. *Left pocket.*

"Give me the keys." She held out her hand. Her demand was firm, but he still didn't budge.

She pushed him against the car and his eyes widened in shock. His breath hitched when he realized where her hand was. Only the thin lining of his pocket kept them separated. His pocket!

Shit.

He was so taken aback by the action that he didn't foresee the purpose of her uncharacteristic behavior.

His mind was still on the blonde. Ryan wasn't like that. In one day he knew that much.

There she stood, a glimmer in her eye with the knowledge that she had gotten what she wanted. His keys dangled from her forefinger.

CHAPTER 6

The car ride had been silent.

When they made it to Ethan's penthouse, Levi was waiting. Relief fell over Ryan. She knew that if Ethan would have said anything to her that night, she would have unleashed holy hell on him because of his ridiculously childish behavior.

The next day flashed by. Perkins had words with both Owen and Ethan about protocol. Needless to say in that day, the words exchanged between Ethan and Ryan were at the bare minimum.

Friday morning Ethan woke too early. Unable to go back to sleep, he groggily made his way into the kitchen for coffee. On the other side, he could hear the clanking of weights. As soon as he had shown Levi and Jeff the room, he made sure that they knew it was at their disposal.

He genuinely liked the both of them. Levi was a little older than he was, already married with a toddler. He couldn't remember the age, two or three. Jeff was older, nowhere near his dad's age, but one of his kids was about to graduate college. Jeff had that Yoda-like wisdom that he admired.

He placed his cup down and ruffled through his hair. He felt tired, but awake, like he hadn't slept well. The knocking at the door sent a wave of energy through him.

He looked through the hole to see Jeff. That didn't make any sense.

"I take it you've seen better days," Jeff told him upon entering. It was a comment that would have come across less insulting if he would have had a hint of laughter upon delivery, but Jeff wasn't the sort to laugh.

"I'm confused. Levi is here."

"Yeah. I'm his relief."

"I was just under the assumption that he'd take me to work and drop me off to Ryan."

Jeff gave him a searching glance. "She has a few things to take care of this morning."

"Like what?" He didn't mean to ask the question; it just slipped out. He realized how insulted it made him seem.

"Don't know. She keeps her personal life personal, but I'd imagine her brother is passing through. Not much takes her away from work." He had a voice that drawled like Eeyore. Ethan could tell that he never got excited or worked up.

* * *

It wasn't until near lunch that Ryan burst into his office. There was one thing about her that had changed, and Ethan loved it. The damn hair.

Her bangs were the same; she must have had time

to straighten them. The rest was a mess of wavy locks. It wasn't like the waves from the machines that he was used to seeing on women. It was like she hurried through a shower, didn't have time to dry her hair, and that's just how it turned out.

He had to wonder if Jeff was right about her seeing her brother. Everything about her looked like she had slept somewhere other than her place and the morning had been just as eventful as the night before.

Then he remembered the conversation she had with her brother that night. He remembered how much he hated her, despite the fact that she was making it difficult on this particular day.

"Stop apologizing. Levi told me how little you cared about working extra for him to be at the hospital. We help each other when we can," Jeff insisted.

"Thank you. You know how I hate deviating from plans."

"Sometimes you have to."

Once Jeff left, completely ignoring the fact that Ethan was in the room, Ryan grabbed a smaller bag from her duffel bag and exited the room.

Ethan was a little disappointed when she returned with a messy ponytail.

"It looked better down." The words were quick and he grimaced as soon as he had said them. He looked up to a hardened blue gaze. "I mean, it doesn't make you look so old," he added, just for extra. If those eyes could have shot daggers, he'd have about a third of a second to pray to his maker.

Ryan went back to the same file she had been

looking over ever since she started. The manila folder had begun to wear. Ethan was more than tempted to ask her what it was she was studying, but he didn't dare. Ever since the nightclub incident, she had gone more robotic. Levi and Jeff were normal, but she came across as completely inhuman, at least around him. He saw how giddy and apologetic she was around Jeff; she even smiled. As soon as she returned from the restroom, she was back to a Dalek, no emotions aside from hatred and anger.

"Are we ever going to get past whatever this is?" It had taken another hour with her in the room before Ethan finally broke. "I can be on a good basis with Levi and Jeff, but you?"

"Is it because I'm a *girl*?"

He didn't tell her, part of it was just that, but he didn't know how much of a bad thing it was anymore.

"Is this still rolled over from the nightclub?"

"Yes!"

"Okay, fine." He threw his arms up rising from his desk. "I heard you on the phone talking to your brother and I got frustrated and pissed."

"And that's what you do when you're frustrated and pissed," she spat. This had been boiling in her for days.

"I admit, it probably wasn't the smartest move." *What*?! He couldn't believe he said that. He had just opened a door for her.

To his surprise, she didn't walk through with the insults.

"I'm good at what I do, damn good, and you not

only put my job on the line, but if there are people out there who want you dead, you put your life on the line. If something would have happened to you, I'm the one who has to live with that, knowing that I failed."

Her hard stare had turned soft; he could see it in her eyes. She had never failed at her job. He knew that if anyone would protect him, oddly enough, it would be her.

"Look, this whole situation is a little emasculating as it is; your words didn't help."

"Get over yourself, Lowell. People bond by complaining," she scoffed.

She went back to reading and didn't look up again. He didn't want to overthink her words, but he now had to wonder, how much of what she said to her brother were her actual thoughts and feelings?

"Hey, man." Ethan casually answered the phone. He glanced up to see if Ryan noticed; if she had, she didn't care.

"I'll keep it quick. I know you're working," Zach laughed on the other end.

Ethan rolled his eyes at the comment. He had never been one to work so many days consecutively.

"This work thing isn't so bad," he chuckled, not realizing that all the while he had been staring at Ryan.

"Whoa. I must have the wrong number."

"Actually, as soon as I can travel about freely, I'm looking at some spaces in Canada."

Ryan jerked her head. She wondered if what he

was saying was true, that he was thinking about a hotel venture in Canada. He never seemed to be the one to put forth any effort. She just assumed he came in to please his father.

"That's really awesome. You'll have to tell me more one day."

"I know you didn't call to talk about work, and lunch is long gone. So?"

There was a brief pause on the other end. "Look, I told Anna that it's really last minute and all," Zach sighed. "She wanted me to see if you could grab dinner with us tonight."

Ethan groaned at the suggestion. "Is that how girls get once they're engaged?"

Zach's laughter flooded through the speaker to Ethan's ear.

"She's only met you once and she wants our circles to blend," he admitted.

"What time?"

"Seven at Le Cygne Vert."

Ethan groaned again. It wasn't the sort of place he had hoped for. He was hoping for something more relaxed, not an upscale romantic restaurant.

"Hold on a second." Rather than put his phone on mute, he only covered the speaker at the bottom.

"Who's going to be with me from seven to about nine tonight," he called out to Ryan. She didn't need to respond. The narrowed glare was all the answer he needed.

"Hey, Zach? I don't know if that's going to work."

"Don't be embarrassed. I explained it all to Anna."

Ethan could hear Zach holding back on the laughter. "She's all about women empowerment."

"I hate you."

"Alright, so we'll meet at Le Cygne Vert a little before seven for the reservation?"

"Wait," Ethan stopped him. "How did you know I'd agree?"

"Because I know you."

They hung up and Ethan went back to his computer.

"Try not to be a major jerk like before," Ryan finally spoke. She didn't take her eyes from the papers sprawled out all over the couch and coffee table.

"Excuse me?"

"You were an asshole to him the other day. Don't do that in front of his fiancée."

"How did–"

"The phone doesn't have to be on speaker for me to read between the lines. Sorry that I'm the one you're stuck with tonight."

"Until when?"

"The nights aren't that hard. I don't sleep that much," she quietly admitted.

"Until when?" He asked again, a hint of uneasiness growing.

"Look, tomorrow is Saturday–"

"Until when?" He was almost screaming, and Ryan knew that by avoiding a direct answer, she was getting under his skin.

"Six."

"Oh," he sighed. She'd be gone before he even

woke up.

"Tomorrow evening."

"What," he roared. "That's more than twenty-four hours from now!"

"Wow, you are good with numbers." Her voice dripped with sarcasm.

Through all his huffing and puffing, she was able to explain. Levi's anniversary was tonight and she knew he'd be out late and probably drinking. He and his wife had gone through all the trouble to take their daughter an hour away to her maternal grandparents for the night. Ryan knew that he wouldn't be good to go until the following evening. Jeff on the other hand had missed several of his youngest child's plays. There was one Saturday afternoon and he had one of the lead roles. Ryan had insisted that Jeff go.

Ethan calmed listening to her explain. He couldn't understand her. She was so formal, played by the rules, unemotional, mechanical, but underneath she had a heart. Listening to her describe the situation, seeing the softness in her eyes, it made him a little envious.

* * *

Ryan looked at her watch. She was in disbelief that Ethan insisted they go back to his penthouse to change from one suit to another. What made even less sense was the fact that she had been sitting on the couch waiting for more than half an hour.

She'd never admit it to him, hell, she barely

wanted to admit it to herself, but once he came from his bedroom, her heart skipped a beat. He looked incredible. The navy blue suit, with light blue shirt, hugged his body perfectly. His shoulders suddenly appeared broader and the slimming pants made him seem to tower well over the six foot whatever. He had also shaven, much to her dislike. She wasn't a fan of a slick and clean face, and his messy hair matched better with a little scruff. Despite finding him incredibly annoying, his looks were extremely attractive.

His green eyes shot up to her and she immediately looked away. He felt a hint of satisfaction. He knew he looked good, and he was certain that she noticed.

"Do I look okay," he pressed.

Ryan remembered what he had said about her hair earlier. "You looked better with the scruff, not so prep school."

She didn't expect him to laugh, but he did, and it was melting. There was no doubt in her mind that he could do way better than the girl he was with in the club the other night.

* * *

Zach darted toward them before they had gotten near the restaurant. He and Ethan embraced in a bro hug, and he became apologetic at once.

"What are you talking about?"

"Look, Anna means well...It's just...Sometimes she doesn't think things through."

Before Zach could continue to apologize or even

make a statement about what he was apologizing for, two babbling women sauntered up. Ryan took a few steps back toward the windows of the restaurant and felt her arm hit something soft. A passing stranger.

He glared at her with dark and beady eyes, then spat at the ground a few feet to his left. "Watch it," he growled.

He continued on his way, crossing the busy street, but he didn't particularly go anywhere. He sat on a bench opposite the restaurant and his feet tapped at the sidewalk. He looked homeless, despite the expensive shoes. Ryan guessed he was a strung out druggie waiting for his next fix. His legs stopped and his gaze was set on her. The wide eyes pierced her; his look was nothing short of a murderous rage.

"Ahem." Anna cleared her throat. Ryan had not been introduced, but judging from the way Zach's arm was around the woman, she could deduce.

Ryan's eyes darted back to the stranger on the bench. He was gone. In that brief instant he had disappeared. Ryan ignored the four sets of eyes watching her as she stepped closer to the edge of the sidewalk.

He had just vanished. Something in her became paranoid. She felt like she was being watched; she felt eyes on her, but she couldn't see them.

"You guys should go in." Her voice was a little unsteady and she realized right away that Ethan had picked up on it.

He motioned down the sidewalk a bit and excused himself.

"Is everything okay?"

Thank goodness she was wearing her glasses, otherwise he'd see the panic in her eyes. A voice in her head kept screaming that she was overreacting. She did have the tendency to do that, but her job left her no choice. One wrong look from anyone, one little thing that looked out of place, one unnatural movement, it set her on high alert.

"Everything is fine," she whispered, glancing over his shoulders to three questioning looks.

Wait, three?

She pulled her glasses down an inch so that her skeptical eyes met Ethan's. He became uneasy and had a guilty look.

"Why didn't you tell me this was a double date?" The words fell from her lips before she could stop them.

"Would it have mattered?" His voice seemed to drop a little deeper and a chill ran through Ryan.

"No." She then pushed her glasses back up.

Ethan shook his head, smoothed over his jacket and spun around to return back to the group. Ryan took one last glance around. The brush of the cool night air subsided her stricken anxiety, but it didn't settle completely.

Though they had reservations, the hostess explained that it would be a slight wait, no more than five minutes. The foyer was packed, and the five of them stood in a space barely suited for two.

"I'm sorry Ryan, I didn't get a chance to introduce you. This is my fiancée Anna." He squeezed the woman wrapped in his arms and she beamed.

She was beautiful in a simple way. She had long black layers that were straight as a board, chocolate brown eyes, and skin the color of milk. When she shook Ryan's hand and said a few words, Ryan immediately picked up on a small hint of a British accent.

"And this is her friend Haylee." Zach motioned to the girl Ryan didn't expect to be there.

With one look, she knew this woman was exactly Ethan's type, right down to the strapless red dress plastered on her tanned body. She had long blonde waves that were loosely tied to the side; a few strands fell delicately over her exposed cleavage. Her eyes were a glistening amber. The black liquid outlining them did its purpose in making them look twice their size.

Ryan dropped her hand heavily after the greeting. It was at that moment that an electricity she had never felt before jolted through her. At the tight closeness of the situation, the back of her hand had inadvertently brushed Ethan's.

He didn't acknowledge it, but she saw the veins in his neck move as his jaw clenched. He stepped away slightly, distancing himself farther from Ryan and closer to Haylee. Haylee smiled and continued to eye him up and down. She held her left elbow with her right hand and batted her eyes like a shy and innocent school girl. It was a look Ryan saw right through.

"So, Ryan," Anna began, drawing Ryan's attention away from Haylee. "You're a bodyguard?"

"Yeah."

"That's so cool! I've never even met a male body-guard." Her excitement garnered the eyes of both Haylee and Ethan. "Have you ever shot anyone," she continued.

"Yes."

"Have you ever killed anyone?" Her voice was almost that of a whisper, like she was telling a horror story around a campfire.

Ryan always hated that question.

"Yeah."

"Wow! I don't know how you could do that. I mean, I know soldiers do and all–"

"I'm prepared to do whatever is necessary for the people I'm protecting," Ryan quickly interrupted.

She liked Anna, much more than that of Haylee, but the conversation was beginning to take a heavy turn and she didn't find anything amazing about the people she had killed.

She breathed a sigh of relief once their table was called.

Ethan looked over his shoulder as they were taken to their table on the second floor of Le Cygne Vert. Ryan wasn't with them. She had hung back and was talking to the hostess at the podium. The hostess nodded and pointed at various spots.

He clenched his left hand as their distance increased. A tingling sensation continued to run through it. Even if it was only for a second, he couldn't erase the warmth of her skin against his.

They were seated along the railing overlooking the

73

restaurant's first floor. The massive chandeliers and warm yellow lights danced and sparkled around them as though they were eating in a room full of bursting stars.

"Wait, we need a fifth seat," Zach insisted to the waitress, who looked confused.

"No we don't." Ethan flicked his wrist a little to the wall from the stairs they had come up not long ago.

"Is she really going to do this again?"

"It's her thing. Let it go. Trust me, it's probably for the best," Ethan sighed.

"I'm a little confused, but I'm not even going to ask." Anna then placed a kiss on Zach's face.

Dinner could not have gone any worse. Every time Ethan began to talk to Zach, he became painfully aware of Ryan's presence in the distance behind his friend. To make matters even more fucked up, he found out that Haylee was a ballerina. Heat rushed through his body when he thought of everything that she was capable of.

Occasionally Ryan watched the happy couples, but for the most part she watched everything surrounding them. She had a perfect view through the two story windows onto the street. Her concealed eyes spent the next hour scanning over the natural flow of the patrons of the restaurant to the well-lit street. With each passing minute, she became much more at ease.

She jerked her head to the table when Anna and Haylee excused themselves. Ethan watched as Haylee swayed away to the restroom. He was no doubt checking out her ass. Ryan couldn't blame him. Even she could admit when a girl had the looks, and Haylee definitely had them. Her breathing nearly stopped when she looked from Haylee to Ethan, only to find his eyes latched to hers, at least what he thought to be beneath the glasses. He quickly darted his attention to Zach, and Ryan cursed herself for not being able to hear what was being said.

"I'm guessing that's a no," Zach said in a matter-of-fact way as he took a sip of red wine.

"What are you talking about?"

"Haylee."

"What about her?" Ethan knew why his friend was apologizing earlier. He wasn't stupid; Anna had set this up.

"It's fine, really. I get it."

"What are you talking about," Ethan laughed.

Zach jerked his head backwards with a nod toward Ryan. Ethan forced himself not to look in her direction.

"Will you stop it with that crap," he hissed in a hush tone.

From the distance, Ryan picked up on Ethan's frustration and she remembered something.

"Shit. She's coming over here," Ethan whispered.

Ryan had meant to ask him this earlier so that she had more time to make adequate planning. She knew it was going to be awkward and had tried to delay it for as long as possible. Ethan and Zach fell silent and stared at her once she approached.

"Yes?"

She convinced herself the best way to mention it was to just bluntly put it out there, just like pulling off a bandage.

"Are we...Sorry," she corrected herself. "Are you planning on either going home with her or bringing her back?"

Wine spewed from Zach's lips, just barely missing Ethan's arm. A roaring laughter commenced to the point that he actually had tears in his eyes.

"Oh, god...I'm sorry...It's just...Ouch!"

Ethan had kicked him under the table. His pursed lips and blazing eyes said it all. *Shut it.*

Ethan directed his attention back to Ryan. "Piss off, Beckett."

Ryan yanked her glasses away and leaned over the table toward him.

"Look, I don't want to know anything more about your sex life than what I see on the tabloids," she spat. "But I need to know this. I especially need to know if you're going back to her place and where it's located ahead of time."

"No." His teeth were gritted and he looked like he was ready to battle it out with her.

Ryan would have pressed on. She genuinely wasn't trying to get under his skin; she had dealt with worse situations with a particular popstar. Given his reputation, she was definitely surprised she hadn't encountered something similar yet. She left it alone and excused herself, partly because the women had returned and partly because the way he said that one word answered every other question she could ask.

CHAPTER 7

The knots in her stomach returned when she scanned through the front windows again.

The homeless druggie was back. He slowly walked along the outside glass, his eyes burning through as though he was searching for something or someone. His movements equaled that of a lion preying on a herd of gazelle.

Ryan pressed herself to the top of the stair railing and leaned down ever so slightly. He hadn't looked to the second floor. Maybe the person he was looking for was on the ground level. He was probably just waiting on a rich patron to sell cocaine to. Then, just like that, he disappeared from the glass encasing Le Cygne Vert. Ryan breathed a small sigh of relief and straightened herself back up.

Ethan was staring at her with a raised eyebrow and she got the message. *Stop being so weird.*

Dinner finally came to an end, although not soon enough for Ryan. She waited for the four people to depart down the stairs first, but once they were near the entry doors, she slipped ahead. Before she could touch the door enough to open it, a pull on her elbow sent her backward.

She tore off her glasses and glared at the culprit.

"What?"

"You'd tell me if something was wrong, right?" There was an unsure and nervous look in his eyes. Ryan knew her insecurities had somehow bled into him throughout the course of the evening.

"Everything is perfect," she reassured him, yanking back her elbow.

Ryan stepped out, Ethan close behind her, the other three after him.

It was a beautiful night and the cool air once again subsided the perspiration that formed all over Ryan's body. Families walked with children. Businessmen leaving the office late shouted on their cell phones. A street vendor had several couples looking at her flowers for sale. Everything was just fine. Nothing was out of the ordinary. She had gotten on edge for no reason other than her insane ability to overthink every detail.

Ryan stepped near the wall, and watched the conversation take place near the line of parked cars on the bustling street, all the while still watching her surroundings carefully.

"This was so much fun, we should do it more often," Anna exclaimed.

"Yeah, and umm...Congratulations again." It wasn't the best, but at least he had tried.

"So, I know these two have an early day tomorrow," Haylee began. The shift in Ethan's disposition meant he knew exactly where she was going and he was thinking how to answer. "How about a couple of drinks?"

Ryan tried her best not to look at Ethan to give any indication of what she was thinking, but she could feel his eyes on her. She was furious. She had asked him earlier about the plans and he gave her nothing. That's just what she needed tonight, a drunk Ethan. The girl was already a little tipsy from the two glasses of wine; Ryan couldn't imagine what she'd be like after a couple shots. An image of Haylee and Ethan drunkenly going at it in a cab ride to Haylee's place quickly flashed in her mind.

It was going to be a long night.

"Actually, Haylee," Ethan sighed. "I have a really early day tomorrow too."

Haylee shot Anna a look of confusion. They both seemed surprised. Haylee was eager for a one night stand and Anna had assured her that Ethan was the way to go. Neither expected for him to decline.

"No offense, man, but you do look a little tired," Zach spoke. He sensed the awkwardness, and Ethan had told him long before this particular moment that it wasn't happening. He could only speculate that he needed to intrude.

They continued to talk casually, slowly beginning to separate and close the evening.

Seconds was all it took for the next events to play out.

A flash of silver flickered in the darkness, caught by a beam from the streetlights. That's when the dark figure came into view, rushing toward Ethan. Ryan didn't allow herself time to process the situation, as soon as the metal caught her eye in the darkness she was at Ethan's side.

She shoved him quickly and carelessly to get him out of the stranger's path. He collapsed into a nearby parked car, but before he could finish the curse word on his lips, Ryan had come into contact with the man.

At first, the easiest thing to do was to get him back, away from everyone, but she knew that the kick he took from her only fueled his anger and his mission. One more second passed. It gave her enough time to see what the flash was. Relief might not have been the best word to use, but a knife over a gun was a lot easier to deal with in her opinion.

The blade was easily eight inches, but it could have been far worse.

She thought about drawing her gun, maybe she should have.

The echoes of screams and people calling in to 911 were bouncing throughout the night.

The black eyes burned into her as another second went by.

He charged at Ryan. Rather than stabbing directly into her torso, his right hand was slightly raised in preparation to swing, slicing into her. She stepped back at the last minute and pulled her upper body backwards. The back of her right hand collided with his just as he cut through dead air. Her goal was to twist the wrist, to put just enough pressure and pain so that his fingers would slip from the weapon, but it all happened too fast.

The slicing motion continued past the target it was

intended for, with the help of Ryan's guidance.

The black eyes turned wide and a gasp escaped the assailant's mouth. He looked down in horror to find that he had used his own weapon against him. He stumbled backward, blood forming puddles with each step.

If he thought about running, slipping away into the night, he decided against it. It was too late. His body sank into a parked car, slowly crashing onto the sidewalk.

Ryan didn't have long. He'd be dead before an ambulance would get there. She rushed to his side and yanked him up a few inches.

"Who sent you and why," she demanded.

He laughed, coughing near the end. Blood started to seep from his lips. "Fuck you."

"You can do one good thing before your pathetic life ends. Tell me!"

"I'm not the last," he coughed.

That was it.

"Damnit!" She dropped him down as his eyes closed.

She started to run her hand through her hair in frustration and saw the blood that stained it. She rubbed it on the man's coat, but her flesh was already covered. Her hand was dry, but pink hues tarnished it.

A crowd had gathered and whispers bounced in the night air. Ryan ignored them all, but forced herself to look up at the four faces staring back at her. She couldn't describe their looks. Yes she could.

Shock and horror.

Ethan's was the only one that hinted at something different. It was a look of disbelief mixed with something she couldn't place, but she knew that she had changed in his eyes, and not necessarily for the better.

The three others turned back to Ethan, their attention focused on him, but he had a difficult time taking his from Ryan.

Ryan quickly ripped out her phone. Everything had played out in under a minute, she still had a little time before EMS and detectives would be trampling all over and ushering her away.

"It's late," Perkins answered.

"I don't have long. I just thought you should know," Ryan began. "There's a body."

"What the hell, Beckett?" Ryan knew that he had fallen asleep in front of the television. His groggy voice when he answered quickly changed and she could hear the noise in the background suddenly silenced.

"We had an attacker."

"Where are you," he demanded.

"Right outside Le Cygne Vert."

"Stay there." It was a pointless statement. Ryan knew she had to. "Has anyone arrived yet?"

"No, but they will soon."

"Good, get whatever you can. Once homicide gets in there, we won't know a damn thing."

"My thoughts exactly."

"Oh, and Ryan." His voice became uncertain and

he hesitated before continuing. "If it's Parker–"

"Don't even finish that." She then hung up before he could.

She rifled through the back jean pockets of the deceased, which took a little effort from his dead weight. It was worth it when she found his wallet. All she needed was a driver's license, but she went ahead and snapped pictures of credit cards as well. She put everything back and shoved the wallet into one of his outer jacket pockets.

Thankfully she had at least gotten a name.

She went through the front of his jeans. Nothing.

Her attention was then on the inside of his jacket. She ripped it open, trying her best not to get more blood on her.

In an inside pocket she found it. She skimmed through the pack tightly wrapped in a rubber band. If she had to guess, it would be somewhere around five thousand. She took a picture and shoved it back.

He had a tattoo on his neck. *Snap.*

She tugged at the sleeves of the jacket, pulling them up. He wore only a t-shirt beneath it. There was a snake tattoo on his left forearm that wrapped around his wrist. *Snap.*

There were no drugs present on his body, but the aged track marks showed a once heavy user. Ryan wondered if the money would have been used to revert back to old habits. *Snap.*

The sirens in the distance sent Ryan fluttering backwards.

She ignored the looks of bystanders, but she

couldn't ignore those of Haylee, Anna, Zach, and especially Ethan. They all screamed the same look of sheer revulsion.

Killing someone didn't look good no matter how it was twisted. Going through a dead man's belongings, even worse.

After establishing death, the body wasn't moved until detectives were on the scene.

Ryan sat on a bench, her legs slightly spread, one elbow on each, hands clasped and hanging between them. Nearby she could hear Ethan's friends; they were thankful he was okay, yet no one dared to speak to her.

Ethan couldn't focus on anything the three of them were saying. He felt Zach's arm on his shoulder, and for some unknown reason, Haylee had wrapped herself around his waist. All he could see, all he could attach himself to, was Ryan. He wanted to rush to her and ask if she was alright, but he knew the answer. Physically yes; however, emotionally might be another story.

She had saved his life, really saved his life. It wasn't a petty bar fight that would have left him with a broken nose. If she wouldn't have been where she was at that exact moment, he'd be the one on the concrete with a knife wedged in him.

As soon as a black car pulled up, and a man in a suit got out, Ethan noticed Ryan's grim and solemn demeanor change completely, like someone lit a fire inside her.

"Ryan Beckett." He sang her name, annunciating

each syllable. "I'd like to say I'm surprised."

He confidently strode up to her. Ethan became uneasy at the idea that Ryan must know the homicide detective quite well. He had to wonder how many times they had crossed paths in similar situations before.

"Don't start with me Parker." She glanced about, unable to see the deceased man as the yellow tape went up and officers and detectives started pushing the scene back. Out of the corner of her eye, she saw someone talking to Ethan's group.

"I take it he didn't fall on it."

"I was working." She started to walk off in the direction of Ethan. The scene started to grow in volume and she couldn't hear what was happening.

"Oh, right, the bodyguard thing," he laughed, louder than needed.

"Go to hell!"

Silence fell slightly, and movements slowed. Some unwanted attention became directed toward them.

"I'm going to need you to calm down or I'll be forced to take you into custody." He said this as he moved his jacket to the side, making his gun visible.

"Yeah," she screamed. "Well, detective, if you could stop harassing me–"

"Whoa, whoa," he nervously chuckled. "I understand there's some animosity–"

"Yeah! Because I wouldn't fuck you!" Her face was colored with rage. Red flashed in her eyes. Her heart pounded out of her chest, fueled from fury.

If Ethan ever wanted an answer about crossing

paths, he got it there. He had never seen Ryan so intense and angered.

He took his attention from the officer in front of him and eyed the source of Ryan's strife. He wasn't too tall, definitely under six foot. He was slim, not in that he worked out and was slim with muscular ripples from neck down like Ethan; he was just skinny. If he were any skinnier, he'd be as thin as Ryan, and that was saying a lot. He had that short military style of hair, probably because it appeared to be thinning near his temples. Ethan had to admit, he wasn't horrible looking, but he wasn't much to look at period. He almost found it hard to believe that Ryan had dated him, but then again, Ryan could be off-putting. She probably had a hard time finding dates. He was actually a little surprised that she dated at all.

"Okay, I'm going to need her restrained." He motioned his hands back and forth.

Ryan looked around to who he was talking to, but none of his subordinates paid him any attention. Typical.

He cleared his throat before continuing. "We'll need you to come in for a statement tonight."

"There are cameras everywhere." She pointed to the two outside the restaurant as well as another across the street. Detective Parker couldn't see them in the darkness, but Ryan knew they were there. "That's my statement."

"You know that's not how this works."

"Why don't you start your damn investigation so I

know why Tony Cohen was paid roughly five grand to attempt to murder my client?" Her yelling had subsided, but her cold stare and the way she spat her words didn't mean that her anger had left.

"How do..."

Ryan raised a brow and cocked her head to the dead man feet away.

"Jesus! Ryan! You searched him?"

She shrugged; a small smirk made its way to her face, knowing that she knew more than the investigators at this point.

"You're not a detective, not even close. Just mind your–"

"That's enough," Perkins' voice rang out.

"What is wrong with you people," Detective Parker screamed. "This is my scene. You have no authority whatsoever here."

"My agent will be in your office first thing in the morning, but right now, she's going home."

"Look, you may have been here back when dinosaurs walked the–"

"Parker. Just stop. It makes you look childish and uneducated."

Ryan didn't know how Perkins was able to keep so calm around the jerk.

It was true, David Perkins had once been a detective for about a decade in his younger days. Then one day he decided he wanted a change. For the last fifteen years he had been working his way up in The Agency and doing quite well. He had never worked with Trevor Parker, but the detective didn't hesitate making comments as though Perkins had taken a step down as far as career choices went.

"Fine," he whispered ferociously. He tried to assert himself without his subordinates knowing that he was really cowering down. "Get her out of here, but I swear she better be in my office the very first thing in the morning. I don't care if she oversleeps and shows up in her pajamas, she–"

"Oh, I'm sure you'd like that," Ryan grunted, taking a step forward, only for Perkins to step between the two.

"Done," he insisted. "We'll let you get back to your investigation."

Perkins shooed Ryan down the street with the four others. She was still fired up from her encounter with Trevor. She wanted to get as far away from people as possible, especially the ridiculous double date that seemed to never end.

Once they were far enough away from the scene, Perkins stopped.

"Lowell, I'm going to take you home. I've called Levi. He'll stay the night, and then–"

"Wait, what about his anniversary," Ryan interrupted. Her eyes clenched at the idea of ruining such a special evening for him.

Perkins only laughed. "Funny thing. He and his wife were so happy to get a break from the kid that all they did was order pizza and watch Netflix. He was already asleep when I called."

"That's not fair..."

"He's happy to come in. Whenever you finish with

your meeting with Casanova tomorrow, you can relieve him. Jeff will give you time off later that evening after his kid's stuff, or I can get other people entirely."

"I don't need time off," Ryan insisted.

Perkins looked back at the scene.

"I want you to take a day or two off after all this." It wasn't a suggestion. Ryan knew Perkins wasn't putting her back to work, outside of a couple hours the next day to cover the gap between Levi and Jeff.

"All of you need to go home and rest. I'd expect some calls in the future," Perkins stated, nearly forgetting the strangers hovering around, scared out of their minds.

They quickly said their goodbyes to Ethan. It was an awkward ending to a night that had taken an unexpected turn.

"I didn't think I could get through, so I had to park a couple blocks down. Give me a minute." Perkins rushed off. He wanted Ethan out of the general public as soon as possible.

Ethan and Ryan were left in darkened silence.

He stared at her. Emotions ran through him like he had never experienced. Shock. Fear. Disbelief. Awe. Gratefulness. Warmth. The feeling he felt most, alive, standing next to her, was something he didn't expect.

Ryan could feel his eyes on her. She knew what was to come, a million questions. The one she hated the most, past Anna asking if she had ever killed anyone, was the one that almost always followed it. How many? *Eight. No, make that nine now.*

From the corner of her eye she saw him take a deep breath and part his lips.

"Are you okay?"

Those weren't at all the words she prepared herself for.

"What?"

"Are you okay," he repeated.

She had heard him correctly the first time. It wasn't a question anyone had ever asked her. A part of her didn't even know what he meant.

"I'm fine," she finally responded.

"You didn't get hurt, did you?" His eyes moved to her hands, lined with streaks of dried blood.

Ryan followed his gaze and tried wiping them on her black slacks, but it was a futile attempt.

"If I was hurt, better me than you, right?"

Ethan smiled and shook his head. "No," he sighed. "I know it's your job, but I don't want anyone hurt because of me."

Ryan didn't have words to respond. No one had ever said that to her either.

She didn't mean to stare, but she couldn't take her gaze away from him. His back was pressed into the wall of the brick building. The streetlight above flickered over his face. His dark hair was a little messier, perfect for fingers to get lost in. When he turned to face her, the light caught his eyes perfectly, and revealed the brightest sparkling emeralds that no jeweler could ever compete with.

He scanned over her face, and this time she was certain where he was looking when his eyes fell from hers. A second later he brought them back up to hers and took a small step forward. His eyes had turned glassy and they clenched like he was in pain.

He opened his mouth to speak and just as he did, the horn from the SUV blared through the intensity forming, shattering it all to pieces.

"Get in," Perkins called out from the window that was only halfway down.

He would have to have a mess of briefcases and bags in the front.

"Sorry about that," he told Ryan as soon as she opened the door. Folders fell onto the pavement and she quickly grabbed them before their contents could blow away. "I didn't unload when I got home and–"

"It's fine," she grumbled.

She sat in the backseat with Ethan. There was enough space between the two of them to easily fit another person comfortably. That was for the best. Ryan found herself unable to look at him. She could never bring herself to ask him, but she knew that from this day forward, she'd always wonder if in that moment, if nothing would have interrupted, what would have happened in the seconds that followed. She could almost feel his lips on hers, and the thought brought about a pounding in her head and a fluttering in her stomach. She let out an exasperated groan as she came to a realization.

She didn't just find Ethan Lowell attractive, she was *attracted* to him.

"Everything okay," Perkins asked, watching her from the rearview mirror. Concern grew in his face.

"Yeah. I just…It's nothing."

Ethan watched as she fought with the thoughts in her head. He would have given anything to know what she was thinking. His only hope was that she was thinking of him. That was quickly squashed with Perkins' next words.

"You going to be okay tomorrow? Want me to be there?"

"I'm a big girl. I can handle myself."

His laugh echoed throughout the vehicle. "That's what I'm afraid of. You do know Parker will be the one interviewing you."

"I'm aware of that." She crossed her arms and her whole body clenched up.

Ethan replayed the encounter she had earlier with Detective Parker. He didn't know what their history was, but a stab of jealousy hit him.

Minutes later Perkins pulled up to an apartment complex. It was nothing special. It wasn't horrible and dilapidated; it was actually in a nice area. The plainness and simplicity didn't do much for Ethan.

As if by instinct, Ethan reached for his seatbelt. Ryan's eyes darted to the movement and she gave him a narrowed look. He quickly pulled his hand away realizing what he was about to do.

Open her door.

Walk her up the stairs.

Kiss her goodnight, praying he'd be invited in.

He could have ripped his hair out at the thoughts racing through his mind. He could have any woman he wanted, whenever he wanted. He could be tearing

Heather's...Hannah's...*Fuck*! He wasn't able to even remember the incredibly seductive woman he met only hours ago. She had wanted him; he could be having mind-blowing sex right now. No, instead he was thinking of the almost kiss that had happened with the most frustrating woman he had ever met.

CHAPTER 8

Levi sipped on his coffee and chuckled to the thoughts forming in his head. "What I wouldn't give to be a fly on the wall in that room." He mumbled it to himself, but Ethan shot a questioning look his way. "Ryan's little talk with Parker."

"What's the deal with that," Ethan found himself asking.

"It's a long story."

"I've got a whole pot of coffee."

They both laughed in unison. The morning news played in the background, but Ethan kept it so low that neither could make out the stories. He liked it on solely for a little noise.

"Last night, when he got to the scene–"

"Beckett turned into a force to be reckoned with?"

Ethan shrugged. That statement was a given for her regardless, but her whole demeanor had changed when Parker arrived.

"I'm guessing they dated?"

Levi nearly choked on his coffee at the question. "No, no. Not really. Ryan doesn't date."

"Why?" He didn't mean to come across as overly curious, but realistically he was.

"Ever since she got married and–" Levi quickly

noted his mistake, but his wide eyes of shock spoke even more. Ethan knew that fact wasn't supposed to be mentioned.

To say that he was stunned would have been the biggest understatement.

"She's married?"

"Look, it's not something I can talk to you about. Forget I even went there. It's a big deal to Ryan. She doesn't talk to many people about it, and I never should have said that," Levi blabbered.

Ethan felt sick. He couldn't believe he almost kissed a married woman. Okay, he had been with married women before, but they weren't Ryan. He knew she was fiercely loyal; she was nothing like the others. In that moment last night though, he could have sworn that she would have let him. How had he misconstrued that? His fists clenched at the idea. He wasn't angry with her; he was angry with himself. Recently there had been nights that he touched himself to the idea, the image, of her.

Married. No word could have been more repulsive at that moment.

A cough broke through the silence.

"So, yeah, anyway. Trevor Parker," Levi began. He twisted his hands around the coffee cup. He hoped that Ethan would ignore the slipup. After all, it wasn't a big deal; he just felt like it wasn't something he needed to be telling.

"What about him?"

"He asked Ryan out several times in the last few years. He was oblivious to the fact that she wasn't interested. I don't know what got into her one day, but she just gave in. He wasn't her type, but I think she felt sorry for him."

Ethan found his mind wandering as to what Ryan's *type* was. What physical features and personality traits was she interested in?

"One date, that's it. She said he acted like he was the one doing her a favor."

"Was that a long time ago?" It had to be if she was married now. He couldn't get past that idea.

"About six months, I think."

Six months! She went on a date six months ago with one man and now she was already married to another. Every stereotype Ethan had thought of Ryan suddenly became skewed.

Shortly after Ethan and Levi returned from the grocery store and lunch, there was a pounding on the door. Levi didn't even bother to look out before opening it to an exhausted and worn Ryan.

As soon as Ethan saw her, heat ran through every part of his body, parts that shouldn't react to her the way they were.

Despite looking like she hadn't slept well, despite the faded brown eyeliner, despite knowing that she had spent her whole morning giving statements, she looked incredible. She wasn't in her typical garb, which she had already explained to Levi, a bit embarrassed by the fact. Instead, stuffed into her combat boots, she wore a pair of skinny jeans with a loose fitting white t-shirt haphazardly tucked into the front. Waves of shoulder length brown hair glistened with the living room lights. It looked incredibly sexy down, but Ethan knew that wouldn't last long once he saw the band around her right wrist.

He then shot his attention to her left hand. It was plain. No jewelry at all. She gave no indication of being married.

Levi explained to her that all she was doing was covering until Jeff arrived around seven that night.

In Ethan's eyes, it was for the best; he needed some space from her. The last two days had been nothing short of weird. All he had to do was tough out the next six hours.

"What's on the agenda this afternoon," Ryan asked casually. Only now did she drop her duffel bag by the door.

"Nothing."

"Nothing?"

"No."

"You're just going to stay inside? All Saturday?"

"Yeah." He kept his answers short.

She crossed her arms and glared at him. She almost made a comment about how he didn't need someone for when he was just lounging around at home, but the final words of Tony Cohen echoed in her head. *I'm not the last.*

"I'll be in my office," he told her, exiting from the room.

He scrolled through the news, not reading

anything, simply trying to keep busy, to focus on anything other than last night and his conversation with Levi.

When Ryan arrived, she was friendly and talkative with Levi. As soon as he left, she was a robot, void of emotion once again. She acted like nothing had happened the evening prior. Nothing did, but it could have.

He soon became aggravated in his office, and it was only a little after three. The best way to clear his head was to workout.

He opted out of a shirt, just shorts. If he hoped to get a reaction from her, it was minimal, but enough to satisfy. Her reddened cheeks and inability to look him in the eyes said a good amount.

The silence in the room was cut short by the unexpected growling inside Ryan's stomach.

"I'm guessing you didn't eat breakfast or lunch," Ethan laughed.

"I was a little busy," she grumbled back.

"We can order something when I get done working out." He wasn't sure why he suggested it. It just slipped out.

"You have refrigerator full of stuff," Ryan pointed out.

He shrugged, told her to help herself, and made his way to the gym.

It wasn't until she heard clanking from a machine that she was able to breathe again.

Underneath the fitted suits, Ryan could still tell that Ethan had a nice body, but she never expected what she had just seen. He was incredibly lean and muscular. Visible veins trailed down his arms. Beneath his prominent pectoral muscles were hard ripples that continued all the way to a well-defined Adonis belt. Looking at him, when he stood before her moments ago, it was a joke to think that he needed her protection.

Ryan had stopped herself from looking more. She had to put any sexual thoughts of him aside. This was her job, and she was going to stay professional.

There was nothing in the refrigerator that was ready to eat. The quickest thing would have been a salad. A salad wouldn't suffice. He needed to use the raw chicken. He'd have to throw it out after today. Ryan wondered if he planned to cook it tonight, but she grabbed it anyway, along with onion, garlic, celery, and carrots; after all, he did tell her to help herself.

His workout took well over an hour. Zoned out, headed toward his shower, he completely ignored what was happening in the kitchen. The workout and cold shower put him at ease and the tense turmoil subsided. It wasn't until he stepped out of his room, barefoot, in jeans and a t-shirt, that the smell hit him.

"What the hell are you doing?"

"Fixing me something to eat."

Though it smelled amazing, the kitchen was a complete mess. When he approached he saw that the largest pot he owned was on the stove, a liquid bubbling inside. Completely ignoring him, Ryan took a cutting board full of shredded chicken and dropped it in.

"Are you seriously making chicken noodle soup," he laughed, after evaluating the rest of the tornado that hit his kitchen.

The comment was returned with a cold glare from eyes that could bring him to his knees.

"Your chicken was about to expire anyway."

"When I told you to help yourself, I didn't mean this."

"You have nothing that's ready to eat," she sighed. "Salad?"

The look she gave him made him remember the lunch with Zach and the fact that she had ordered a steak. Though she didn't look it, a salad wouldn't have been enough for her.

"What made you do this?"

"It's comfort food."

"Are you sharing?"

She scoffed. "After the morning I had, you're lucky there's anything left in your refrigerator."

"I meant to ask," he began. Noticing the freshly washed carrots, he opened a drawer for a peeler. "How did it go with–"

"Don't," she interrupted. She rapidly ran a knife through a pile of herbs.

He had to wonder if her cooking had less to do with her being hungry and more to do with occupying her mind.

"I don't want to talk about that ridiculous excuse for a detective." The growl in her voice made him drop the topic.

"So, in between all your fighting and training, or whatever, where did you learn to cook?" It was a lighter question, and it gave him the chance to get to know something personal.

"My grandmother. I spent a lot of time with her, what with my parents' jobs."

"Military, right?"

She went on to explain to him that her mother worked with explosives in the Marines and her father was a Navy SEAL. They had moved around a lot and tried to keep the family together, but sometimes work called them away. Her grandmother insisted that Ryan needed to learn more lady-like skills, cooking being one of them.

"I guess that's a better story than mine," Ethan admitted. Ryan arched a brow and cocked her head, momentarily stopping what she was doing. "I was eleven or twelve. My parents had a really hot maid that did a lot of the cooking and–"

"I get it." She coldly cut him off.

She was hard to read.

Once Ethan finished peeling the carrots, he reached for the knife on the counter that Ryan had used for the herbs. Unfortunately, he wasn't first. His fingers ended up wrapped around her hand that gripped the knife.

The electricity from the touch flooded through the both of them.

"I've got it," Ryan whispered, breaking the connection and yanking the knife away.

Ethan stepped out of the kitchen. He couldn't be that close to her right now. He still had two hours before her shift was over. If she was within reach, in those two hours he'd have her breathless, sweating, begging. He felt an erection coming on. It had been some time since he had gotten laid, which only made his desire more intense.

Her voice snapped him back to reality. "We didn't get a chance to talk about last night."

"What about." He hoped she couldn't hear the painful lust in his words.

"Are you alright? A lot of people go into shock after something like…"

Her voice trailed off. She was asking about the altercation. Of course she was. That was a way bigger part of the evening.

"I guess it hasn't sunk in yet."

"I wish it could have gone differently," she softly admitted.

"What do you mean?"

"I didn't intend to kill him. That's why I didn't draw my gun. It just all happened so fast." She put the lid on the pot and turned the stove down before making her way to the living room.

"It was unexpected," he admitted. "It's not like I've never seen a dead person. I've been to funerals." The image of the man, the handle of the knife protruding from his chest, flashed through Ethan's mind.

"If you need to talk about it–"

His laughter stopped her dead in her tracks.

"Screw you, Lowell," she hissed.

She was close, too close.

He tried to stop it. He knew it was wrong. He knew she was married. He knew she'd hate him for it. Everything that he knew didn't matter in that moment. He had regretted the interruption last night, but now, now she was right there.

In one swift motion, before he could attempt to rationalize, he swung his left arm around her waist and pulled her in. All the frustration drained from his body once their lips collided. His right hand ran along her face and down the back of her neck, absorbing the heat radiating from her silken skin.

She gripped at his shirt and pulled him down; he hadn't realized that she had been standing on her tiptoes. Even more to his surprise, she was the one that tried deepening the kiss that he had been so hesitant and fearful of starting. Once their lips parted and tongues swirled together in a battle for dominance, he was certain she could feel his erection grinding into her.

Ryan wasn't able to process what was happening at first. The kiss was wanted but at the same time unpredicted. It was unlike any kiss she had ever had, although her list was pretty slim.

She pulled her body from his and swatted at his chest. "What the hell," she screamed at him.

"Shit," he breathlessly managed.

"You can't do that! My god, why would you do that?"

The gravity of the situation hit. She should have stopped it sooner. She was irritated at her body for betraying her mind. She was even more upset that the kiss was so impossibly amazing.

"I'm sorry," he started to stammer. "I mean...I wanted that...That was..."

"Lowell!" She was screaming at the top of her lungs.

"I know. I know. I knew you were married. I knew I shouldn't have, but I couldn't help it. I just–"

"What the fuck are you talking about?"

"What do you mean what am I talking about," he rambled.

"Levi told you that I was married?"

"Don't be mad at him. It just slipped out and he didn't say anything beyond that," he continued.

"I don't believe this," Ryan groaned. It wasn't something that she told many people. It definitely wasn't something she told any of the people she worked for.

"I don't get it." He ran his hands through his still damp hair. "Why wouldn't you tell me?"

She stepped back, raised a brow, and crossed her arms. She looked at him like his question was outrageous. "That I was married," she scoffed.

"Yeah."

"*Was* you freaking idiot. I *was* married. Past tense!"

He let out a loud sigh of relief, which did nothing for her increasing irritation with him.

"Oh! That makes this better?"

"It helps." He tried to hide his smirk, but he was too ecstatic by the fact that she was very much not married.

"Stop." She held up her hand the second he tried taking a step forward. "I don't know what the hell you were thinking, but that was the first and last time for anything like that to happen."

"Wait," he said, a thought hitting him. "Levi said you didn't date because you were married."

"You're completely ignoring what I'm saying. I don't date because I don't fucking date. Not that it's any of your business."

He knew she really wasn't mad about the kiss. She couldn't be. She had kissed him back. She had been the one to want more.

"Did he die?" His face clenched as soon as he realized that his thought had become vocal.

"What is wrong with you," she screamed.

"I'm sorry. I shouldn't have asked. It's just that you seem so loyal and I couldn't imagine anything but–"

"I was!"

He was shocked when he saw her blinking back tears. He shouldn't have pressed her. He should never have brought it up. The best thing to happen today was now being followed by the worst once he saw that he had obviously brought up something excruciating in her past.

"I'm sorry." He took a step forward only for her to back away more.

"It's fine." She was cold and dismissive. She had stopped the tears before they had a chance to fall, and Ethan was certain that she had put up an even thicker wall than before with him.

* * *

She consumed herself with her computer and phone, pretending that he didn't exist. From time to time he heard a ding; he knew she was texting someone, and he hated how it drove him crazy not knowing who. He had to assume it to be her brother or a fellow agent, maybe Jeff, who would be arriving soon.

She didn't eat, didn't say goodbye, nothing.

When Ethan finally did eat, he was blown away. Not only was it absolutely amazing and satisfyingly comforting, but other than the maid, he had never had food cooked by any woman he knew.

He must have opened his messages a hundred times before he was finally able to form a sentence.

Ethan: The soup was amazing.

It wasn't a lot, but he had to say something, anything, to start a conversation with her.

Ryan: Glad someone enjoyed it.

He wanted to say that she could have stayed. She didn't have to act the way that she did. He decided against it.

Ethan: I just want you to know that I really am

sorry.

Ryan: For what?

There were many things that Ryan thought Ethan should be sorry for, but he was only apologizing for one.

Ethan: For bringing up something from the past that is clearly painful.

Ryan: Is that it?

He wanted to be delicate in addressing anything else, but that wasn't a characteristic he possessed.

Ethan: Yes. I'm not apologizing for any other actions because I'm not sorry.

He expected a bitter and sassy response, but none came.

CHAPTER 9

Monday morning was awkward to say the least. Ryan tried relaxing Sunday, tried clearing her head. She was able to get Tony Cohen out of her mind, able to look at her hands and not picture his blood. Killing someone was never easy. The first time she had done so, it felt like the world was caving in, so much that she considered going to therapy just to have someone to talk to about it. Then there was a second, and a third. It didn't get easier, but it became bearable. Killing Tony Cohen was just part of the job.

What she wasn't able to clear from her mind was Ethan. Every time she thought of him, she pictured the damn kiss. It was etched in her brain by now.

Since Matt, she tried to go out a few times, but she never felt comfortable enough to date. She had fun with a few of the guys, but no romantic interest in any of them. Other than the dinner with Trevor, in the last five years she had given up and solely focused on her job, but now there was Ethan.

Ryan pounded away on her laptop, refraining from glancing in his direction. They made eye contact once that morning when she arrived, and that brief moment almost unraveled her. Her thoughts were clear, she knew right from wrong, but she couldn't control the butterflies in her stomach with the way his face seemed to light up when she walked in the room.

Ethan watched as she put some papers in her laptop and closed it, leaving the room. He assumed to the restroom. When her phone buzzed with a text alert, he wasn't above crossing the office for a glimpse. Ryan had to be the only person he knew that didn't keep a lock on her phone. Rather than clicking on the message and marking that it had been read, he pulled down on the screen; he'd at least be able to read the first two lines. To his surprise, it was short and to the point.

JD: Call me when you get a chance.

Who the hell was JD?
Ethan quickly sat the phone back on the couch. He couldn't remember if it was face up or face down, but hopefully Ryan wouldn't remember either.

He impatiently waited for her to check her phone once she returned. He expected some type of reaction to the text, but there was none, nothing for him to read into. It was then that he came to the conclusion that he was losing it with her. He never thought about a woman this much before.

Ryan had made it clear where they stood, and the fact that she hadn't said more than a handful of words since arriving, he knew he needed to get over whatever feelings he thought he might be having toward her. Obsessively thinking about her in a romantic way was only self-torture at its best.

* * *

Ryan stepped outside Ethan's office, and eagerly awaited an answer. "Hey. Do you have some news?"

"Good morning to you too," JD laughed.

"Sorry. I'm out in the hall. I didn't want Ethan hearing anything in case–"

"In case it's really bad," he interrupted.

"Is it?"

"Depends. You were right about the bomb. We ran through surveillance footage outside..." He drifted off, the name of the club Ryan had given him was slipping his mind.

"Jupiter Lounge?"

"Yes. That place. Prior to all of this, he seemed to frequent it often."

"Get to the point," Ryan pressed on. She could hear a heavy sigh on the other end.

"The bomb was placed on his car there."

"And? Did you see by who? It's been days, do you have something more than that?"

"Jesus, Ryan. Calm down," he scolded. "I've got good news and bad news."

She waited. JD took the two seconds of silence for him to continue.

"Bobby Norman."

"The name doesn't ring a bell. Not a name I've seen anywhere."

"You probably won't. Small time drug dealer, few

110

arrests, a little jail time here and there."

"Did you find him?"

There was a pause. The bad news.

"He overdosed two days after the bombing incident."

"Shit," she screamed. It was loud enough that Ethan could have heard.

"Yeah. He left a big chunk of cash behind too."

"Payment?"

"Speculation."

"What now?"

"We need to find some sort of connection between the two. I was hoping it would be something easy so that I could wrap this up. You know, something like being involved in the same gang, but no such luck," he concluded.

"*We?*"

"I figured you'd pick up on that. I know you Ryan. You might not be a detective, but I'm all but certain as to how you're occupying your time when you're not saving Don Juan from the occasional stabbing," he laughed. Then his voice turned serious. "Look, there's a meeting today with old man Lowell. You'll probably be there?"

"I'm good at pretending if you are."

"Great. I'll see you this afternoon."

* * *

Ryan thought nothing of it when shortly after lunch Allison tapped at the door to inform Ethan of a meeting with his father.

When they entered, Ryan tensed alongside Ethan. It looked like a war room. There was Owen with Perkins and Agent Delgado, who had already started going into detail about his findings. Levi and Jeff stood to the side, listening, but staying out of it. There were four other men that Ryan didn't know, all she assumed FBI.

Conversation stopped when they realized Ethan had entered.

"Hurry along," Owen insisted. "They need you to take a look at this." He motioned to scattered papers all over his desk. "Oh, and everyone, this is the other bodyguard, Ryan Beckett."

For the most part, no one seemed to care. She already knew everyone aside from the four men off to the side, and she really didn't need introductions.

"Ryan, this is Special Agent Delgado."

It wasn't until then that Ryan remembered herself. She held out her hand and shook his.

"Nice to meet you, Delgado."

He gave her a smirk and a quick wink that no one took notice to before continuing.

She finally saw the image of the man who placed the car bomb. It was a mugshot from six months prior, and Delgado insisted that was the way he looked up until his death.

"I'm sorry," Ethan sighed. "I've never seen either of those men, and the names are foreign to me."

"It's not surprising. It was a long shot," Delgado admitted. "They don't exactly run in the same circles as you."

Ryan had so many questions, but she knew she needed to stay out of it. Close Protection Officer. That was her job. Not detective. Not investigator.

"Something you'd like to add, Beckett?" Delgado took her completely off-guard. He had a creepy way of knowing when the gears in her head were in overdrive. He was giving her a way in.

"How did you say that Norman died?"

He eyed her suspiciously. He had told her first on the phone, and had said it again moments ago. "Drug overdose."

"Heroin?" She quickly realized that she should have asked from which drug.

"Yeah. How did you know?"

The room had gone quiet and all attention was focused on their conversation.

"There were track marks on Cohen. They were older, but he was a heavy user–"

"What makes you think heroin?"

"Pure speculation, but it would be a commonality now."

"That's a long shot to go on considering the amount of people who shoot up every day. Then going from heroin to murder is an even a bigger one," he insisted, all the while knowing that she was making more work for him.

"I don't have all the pieces together, but I feel like that's a connection."

"Intravenous drug usage has something to do with a car bomb and attempted murder," he playfully

113

questioned.

She stopped speaking and glared him down. He was fifteen years older and had experience she couldn't begin to fathom, and he knew that.

"Since when did you go to detective school," he laughed, breaking his staunch composure and going back to the young man she remembered in her youth.

Ryan wanted to hit him. Their playful banter needed to come to an end. She felt uneasy with their reactions to one another.

Delgado coughed, collected himself, and continued. "Your input will be noted, Beckett."

The meeting started to wrap up, but little did Ryan know that another was about to begin.

CHAPTER 10

Ryan wasn't comprehending the conversation that had just taken place. She had heard them correctly, though. This couldn't be happening.

"What's wrong with the way we've been doing things?"

"We need to be extra careful. Lately the rotations have been adjusted for various reasons," Perkins began.

"He has a full-time guard. All three of us."

"We've decided that one of you isn't enough when he's in public. During the day, Levi or Jeff will be with you, unless he stays home. From my understanding and research, other guards are in place in the lobby and access to the penthouse is difficult."

"So you're putting me in for twenty-four," Ryan spat.

Perkins rarely gave assignments like that. He was a fan of rotations, as it should be. That was how it worked.

"It's only temporary. People are working on this around the clock," he sighed, but he could feel the storm brewing in Ryan's eyes.

"How long is *temporary*?"

"I don't know."

Levi, Jeff, Owen, and Ethan said nothing. They all knew about this. This was why Perkins gave her off. He and the two Lowell men made this decision without any say on her part.

"If I refuse?"

"Ryan..." His voice was soft and pleading.

She knew that he knew she wouldn't refuse. She had never refused an assignment, but none of her assignments had been Ethan Lowell.

"Can I just ask one thing?"

He nodded. His eyes were sympathetic. He hated to do this to her.

"Why me?"

"Honestly, it comes down to your lifestyle. I hate saying it like that, but if I had to uproot one of you, I'd choose you. Levi and Jeff both have families and..."

"No," she interrupted. "I get it."

"They both agreed to accept though."

She turned to the two men behind her. Each gave her a comforting smile. If it wouldn't have been so weird, she would have thrown her arms around the both of them.

"It was Ethan's choice."

"What," she screamed.

The warmth she felt from her fellow colleagues faded. It was replaced with icy flames of boiling rage. Her eyes bore into Ethan, but for once he didn't look at her. He stood solemnly, eyes fixated on the floor.

Ryan excused herself.

She had lost it. She never lost it. She got angry.

Trevor Parker made her angry. Ethan Lowell was something entirely different.

Her screams of frustration from Ethan's office echoed throughout Owen's.

"She just needs some time to process," Perkins nervously laughed.

Ethan knew that wasn't the case.

* * *

Ryan slammed her computer shut. She had to address it. She couldn't sit another moment in the same room with Ethan and not say anything about the change that was taking place.

"He gave you the choice?" She tried to speak as normal as possible. Her throat already ached from earlier.

"Yes." He stopped what he was doing and looked up at her.

"Why?"

He stood from his desk and confidently made his way toward her. The stupid organ in her chest, which unfortunately she needed for life, started working overtime. If she could have ripped it out to make the sensation cease, she would have.

Ethan sat on a chair diagonal from her. His legs were spread and his forearms rested on his knees, his hands clasped and dangling down.

"If you think Saturday meant–"

"Forget Saturday," he insisted. He couldn't forget it, but if it helped to play how she wanted, then he would. "It was a mistake. It never happened."

She looked relieved and satisfied.

"So, why?"

"Because I feel safest with you."

All weekend, since he and his father had talked with Perkins about the idea, Ethan had pictured this conversation. Now that it was taking place, he forgot everything he wanted to say and simply blurted it out.

She didn't respond, but the dropped jaw and wide eyes said enough.

"As horrible as I feel saying this, I know you'll protect me at any cost, even if it ends up costing you the ultimate price, which I really don't want." He couldn't look at her as he said those last words. "Just to make things clear, Perkins would have chosen you, lifestyle or not. After weighing out the options..." His voice drifted off, unable to make it sound good in any way.

* * *

Levi pulled an Agency issued SUV up to Ryan's apartment building later that evening.

"I'll only be a minute."

"Wait," Ethan called out from the backseat. "I thought I'm supposed to have more than one guard when I'm out in the public.

Ryan pursed her lips and held in what she really wanted to say. She glanced to Levi who shrugged. *He's right.*

She wasn't stupid. He could have sat in the

vehicle. This was his not-so-discreet way of getting inside her apartment.

"Don't touch anything," she growled, taking the key from the lock.

She then left the men to linger in the living room while she went to her bedroom to throw together a suitcase.

Ethan couldn't help but notice that her apartment had a grey color scheme like his own. Her couches looked new, but they weren't, just unused. While his couches revolved around an 88", twenty thousand dollar television, he didn't know why hers pointed to nothing specifically. He couldn't believe she didn't have a television.

She truly had no concept of decorating. He figured when she found something that suited her she bought it and stuck it in an empty space. A lion statue sat in one corner, while a gargoyle hung from a small bookshelf. Warmth spread through him when he ran his fingers over the books. That was the first thing she had mentioned in his bedroom, his book collection. He understood now. Every single book he scanned through could have been on his shelf. They had something in common.

He was thankful that she left her bedroom door open. He wasn't about to go in and interrupt her, but from the hallway he could at least get a view of where she slept.

His eyes went straight to the bed. Her suitcase covered it now as she hastily threw clothes into it, paying little attention to what she was packing. He wanted to tell her that she'd save space if she bothered folding and organizing, but he decided against it. He actually found it adorable. On a nearby chair he saw a pile of suits draped on hangers.

He hated the suits.

He couldn't forget how she looked on Saturday in jeans and a t-shirt. That's how he wanted to see her.

Only when she was standing next to it did he realize just how small her bed was. It was only big enough for one person. He liked that. Even though he knew he may have messed up any chance with her, he didn't want to think of another guy in her bed.

He laughed to himself at the thought. Her bed was too small to invite someone into; whereas his was the exact opposite, but he had never taken a woman into it.

"What," she hissed, glancing back to him.

There it was with the attitude again. He had no choice but to return to the living room where Levi sat, twiddling his thumbs and waiting.

* * *

"Are you going to be alright," Levi asked as he sat Ryan's suitcase by the door in the guestroom.

"No, but I'll make do."

"He's not so bad. He's really cool to talk to." He shrugged not understanding the mutual hate the two exuded toward each other.

"I'll see you soon, okay?"

"Don't forget to set the door up."

Perkins had given her a kit for the entry door. If anyone from the outside touched it during the night, it would send a shattering and deafening alarm that would have Ryan up in an instant. It also acted as what could best be described as an electroshock weapon, but on a larger scale. No one would do well if they tried to break in. She didn't think it was necessary. Sleep wasn't her best friend lately; it was more like an acquaintance you nod and smile to as you pass each other on the street.

She had to admit, she didn't expect it, but she was a little relieved that Ethan kept to himself that first night. What he told her in his office about choosing her had left her stomach in knots. If he were to say the right thing now, she'd have an internal battle of right and wrong that she wasn't ready to deal with.

When Ethan woke the next morning, Ryan was in the kitchen reading the day-old newspaper. She was already in her suit, makeup minimally done, and hair straightened and in a tight and pristine ponytail, just the way he hated.

"Good morning," he groaned, still not fully awake.

"You look like shit," she told him through a mouthful of toast.

He felt like shit. It was miserable trying to get to sleep with the way his body reacted, knowing that she was only two closed doors away from him.

"Jeff will be here in about twenty minutes," she grumbled, still stuffing her face.

"I'm not going in today."

He thought he might have to give her the Heimlich

after that comment.

Ryan gulped down coffee to wash the dry toast she was choking on.

"You have to." Her voice was shaky, still recovering.

"Believe it or not, I don't really go in that much. Last week was just a fluke." The cereal clanked in his bowl and he reached in the refrigerator for milk.

"You're truly serious? What do you plan on doing all day?"

"I don't know. Workout. Read. Video games."

The cocky grin showed through even as he shoveled cereal in his mouth like a five year old.

"Unbelievable. What a wasted day," she breathed in irritation.

"Sorry," he sang out.

Ryan quickly shot off a text full of expletive language to both Levi and Jeff. Jeff was ecstatic; his wife had a dishwasher that he was in charge of repairing, but he told Ryan to let him know if they planned to leave the penthouse. Levi simply sent a string of various laughing emojis, which she fully expected from him.

* * *

"You're free to use it if you want," Ethan breathlessly offered after finishing his time in the gym. He was nearly limping through the living room.

His hair was dripping and the longer strands were plastered across his forehead. Sweat continued to roll

122

down the muscular creases of his back.

"Noted," Ryan choked out, returning to the sheet of numbers.

It was going to be a long day. This job needed to come to an end.

Later that day, Ryan took every bit of a thirty second bathroom break, only to come back to the living room to see Ethan going through her things.

"What the hell are you doing?"

"You left all this stuff out. I was curious." He shrugged tossing the stack of papers back on the coffee table.

"Just mind your own business," Ryan huffed.

She stormed over to her things and began gathering them to take to her room.

"What's with all the call logs?"

"It's nothing."

A slight buzz filled the silence, but before Ryan could grab the phone from the couch, it was brightly lit with a text from JD, which Ethan saw.

"Who's JD," he skeptically asked.

"You're being really nosey." She quickly tucked her phone into her back pocket.

He proceeded to laugh. It wasn't a happy laugh as though he found humor in the situation. It was more like him laughing at being forced to throw his hands up in defeat.

"I don't get why you have to be so secretive with everything."

"You don't understand. I'm not here to be your

buddy. Normally I'm seen and not heard, and some-times I'm neither. I'm working for you and your father. You don't need to know anything about my personal life."

"The other day, in the kitchen," he softly began. "You were able to carry a conversation without being abrasive and defensive. It's like you were an actual human."

He didn't expect her to respond, nor did he give her a chance. She continued to put up wall after wall and he couldn't bear to look at her much less share another word.

The sunlight slowly crept over the city, fading by the minute. She had one day almost down; she didn't want to think of the countless more to come. She changed from the black suit and put on a pair of loose jeans and a t-shirt.

Her skull ached from the tight ponytail. The band fell on the dresser and she massaged the sore spot.

Glancing up into the mirror, she began a private conversation with herself.

Ethan had blurred the lines. At first she hated him for how he acted toward her that first day. She still hated him, but the times that he tried to be nice, tried to talk to her, those made her feel something else; yet, her responses were to snap at him, to push away any type of friendship.

She groaned and slammed her head against the mirror. She'd go crazy if she were left to her own thoughts. The rumbling of her stomach was a welcoming distraction.

"I heard you destroying the shit out of my kitchen," Ethan said, finally coming from his bedroom.

"Your dinner plans obviously didn't include leaving here."

"You don't have to cook for me." He slowly made his way into the kitchen like he was walking on eggshells.

"I need to eat too."

He stepped around her and grabbed a few of the spoons and bowls she had stacked near the sink and began placing them in the dishwasher.

"You don't have to do that. I've got it."

He aggressively threw a spatula and spoon into the sink. A shutter ran through Ryan from the sharp clanking. He was upset.

"I understand all your rules and shit, but this is ridiculous. I get it that you like to be not seen and not heard when we're in public. That makes sense, but do you know how freaking weird it is to be in an office with you all day and you don't say anything?"

"I do," she quietly admitted. Her brother had pointed out much worse over the years. What Ethan said was nothing.

"I don't get it," he stressed.

"This is how I'm used to being." She took a few utensils and placed them in the dishwasher. It was hard to look at him.

He ran a hand through his perfectly tousled hair

125

before bringing both arms up and firmly crossing them across his hardened chest. He pressed his back into the pantry door, as if he needed it to remain standing.

"I'm just not good with people," Ryan sighed again. She turned and went back to a pan on the stove.

"Understatement of the century." It was something he didn't mean to say aloud, but he did. He often did that with his thoughts.

Ryan shot up an eyebrow and shook her head. Any additional comment on her part wasn't needed.

"How are you with your friends?"

"I don't have any friends."

Ethan stepped away from the pantry and got two wine glasses from a high cabinet. Ryan heard them clank on the counter. Before jumping to conclusions, she waited.

He pulled a new bottle of red wine from the bottom of the refrigerator. A part of Ryan was a little surprised. She thought rich people were picky about how they drank wine, and she also thought red wine wasn't supposed to be cold.

"None for me, thanks though," she interrupted once he pulled the cork.

"Are you pregnant," he huffed.

"No. I'm working."

"Seriously?" He laughed and shook his head at her pathetic excuse, before pouring two glasses.

He walked over to her, keeping the distance wide so that he had to stretch his arm to its entirety to hand her the glass. She mumbled her thanks and went back to stirring the spaghetti sauce she had obviously made from scratch.

"Can you take a minute," he asked, motioning toward the living room.

CHAPTER 11

Ethan sat first. He chose a couch where Ryan could easily have joined him, but instead she went directly to an accent chair, like the thought of sitting next to him had never crossed her mind.

"Why don't you date?"

"Wow. I'm glad you're not being blunt." She smiled slightly, hoping to keep the conversation light. The serious look on Ethan's face said differently. "Is that why you gave me this," she said, holding up her wine glass. "You think if I get tipsy I'll talk to you?"

He turned his whole body attentively in her direction. "No, I gave you that because you look like you need to relax."

"What do you want Lowell," Ryan groaned.

He didn't hesitate on the question for a second. "I want to know why you are the way you are."

The way his eyes sank into her gave her a more warming sensation than the wine descending down her throat.

Maybe she could try. Maybe it wouldn't be so bad.

"That's a vague question."

"Do you really want me to get specific?" Ryan didn't answer him, but in the little time he knew her, he had learned to read her eyes perfectly, at least when she didn't wear those pitch-black glasses. "What happened with the marriage thing?"

Ryan grumbled and threw back another sip of wine. She knew that was going to be mentioned again. She was naïve to think he'd ease into it.

"We got a divorce," she began. "Actually an annulment." It felt weird saying it. She had talked about it before, but never to a client.

"How long ago?"

"About a decade."

Ethan looked confused. It had been established, it was even in her files, she was twenty-seven.

"After my parents divorced, my brother and I rebelled a bit," she told him, before he could ask. "I got married at eighteen, and they were pissed," she laughed, but the laughter quickly faded and Ethan saw the pain that came to her eyes.

"Did you love him?" He felt strange asking, but a part of him wanted to know everything there was to know about her.

"At the time you think so, because you're so damn stupid, and you don't know what that word means."

Guiltily, he felt relieved knowing that she hadn't loved him.

"About three months into it, I came home early." Her voice dropped and turned grave.

Ethan moved to the end of the couch so that he was closer to the chair she sat in, close enough to almost touch her. He knew what she was about to say before she even said it. The asshole was cheating on her.

"That wasn't the worst part that happened."

The way her fingers clenched and twirled the almost empty wine glass, Ethan realized just how difficult it was for her to talk about it. He decided to give her an out.

"That's fine. You don't have to–"

"I made it this far," she laughed, but it wasn't a happy one.

Ethan never expected what was left of the story.

"He yelled at me. He wasn't upset or remorseful, didn't beg for forgiveness. He was just angry for getting caught. He told me the cheating was my fault." She clenched her eyes shut to keep the tears from coming. She couldn't look at Ethan and tell him the last part. "Then he raped me. He said I owed him because I was his wife. When I cried, he beat me, to the point that my next memory was my brother standing over my hospital bed."

Her eyes were still closed when she polished off the last of her wine. The strangest feeling washed over her when she told the story this time. Relief.

She only opened them when she felt his hand on her knee. He didn't look shocked or disgusted, he looked genuinely hurt and saddened.

"Ryan, I–"

"Don't say anything. For the first time, it doesn't hurt so much." She thought for a minute; his touch was so soothing that the words continued to pour out. "Afterwards I was angry at myself."

"Why?"

"Remember how I said that I got involved with

different forms of martial arts in the third grade?"

"Yeah." He did remember. She had said it the first day when there was doubt about her skills.

"I was angry because I didn't fight back. I could have killed him and I didn't lift a finger."

"You were in a different position," Ethan sighed, gripping her knee more tightly.

"Well, after that. I threw myself into more intense training, more advanced ways of fighting, and I got really good with guns. Now, here I am," she concluded.

Her leg moved slightly, turning away from his touch. Her cheeks reddened. Ethan wasn't sure if it was from him or the wine.

When he rose to get more wine, she didn't stop him.

"I believe you asked why I didn't date," she began once he returned.

She felt like talking, telling him anything he asked. After telling him about Matt, it felt like a weight had been lifted from her. It had never felt like that before.

"I did try," she admitted, half a smile forming. "I had already started this job before I tried, so I didn't have much time. I can count the amount of men on one hand. For the most part, they were nice, and if I wanted someone to grab a drink with and complain about work, or go to a football game, that would have worked. I just never really liked any of them enough to pursue anything."

"What about Trevor Parker?"

"Oh, god! Why would you mention that?" Her

laughter was sincere. She was relaxed.

"You two seemed to have a nice little banter going," Ethan teased. "Probably built up sexual tension." The mentioning of that did nothing to help him. All his blood had drained to one organ.

"Parker is a rambling idiot. One dinner. I felt bad for him and I thought," she stopped. "Scratch that. I don't know what I was thinking."

Ethan quickly changed the subject to food. He had to focus on something else. Her honesty this evening only made things worse for him. A part of him wanted to throw her onto his bed, make her the first to have that experience, and listen to the screams of his name shattering off the walls. There was suddenly a different part, a part of him that wanted to protect her. He didn't want another man looking at her, much less touching her.

CHAPTER 12

The evening had been great after Ryan opened up. They ate an amazing dinner, had light conversation, and concluded as friends. He wanted to kiss her goodnight, but he couldn't, not after how she freaked out the first time. Desperately, he wanted her to come to him, but he knew she never would.

The next morning didn't help their situation at all.

Ethan stood in Ryan's doorway and they discussed the schedule for the day. As much as he didn't want to, he decided to go in to work. Ryan was already dressed appropriately in her suit and ready to go. She continued to scold him while she fixed her bed.

And that's when awkward hit the fan.

All she did was move the pillow back to pull the sheets up, but the clink on the hard floor directed his attention away from her and their conversation. She grabbed it quickly and threw it into the drawer of the nearby nightstand.

Ethan looked away before she turned toward him. He pretended that he didn't notice the small pink toy, but they both knew he had.

Now they sat in his office, not speaking, allowing work to consume them.

If Ryan was bothered by the situation, she hid it well. She continued typing on the keyboard and sifting through a messy pile of papers on the cushion next to her. Occasionally, it looked like she found something of value and she would twitch her mouth from side to side as she went into deeper thought.

Ethan, however, had a harder time focusing on anything other than what he saw hours ago. He let his imagination slip away.

If that was under her pillow in the morning, had that meant she used it the night before? Did he say or do something that turned her on to the point that she needed a release?

He pictured her writhing in the bed, moaning in pleasure, thinking of him, as vibrations shot through her until she was left breathless. Then he thought of her getting satisfaction from a fucking toy, when he was right there.

He watched as her eyes widened upon receiving a text. He was certain it was from whoever JD was.

JD: You're going to want to call.

She hit the call button before she could stand from her seat.

"Tell me something good," she excitedly spoke as soon as he answered.

"It's something alright, confusing as shit though."

Ryan sensed his frustration, and paced outside Ethan's office waiting for him to continue.

"After a little more digging, there's another connection between the two."

"Do you know who hired them to do the dirty work," she asked eagerly.

"Ryan, we aren't even close to that."

"Then what do you have?"

"Both men made visits to Mexico within the last year."

"Are you serious," Ryan growled. "That's what I needed to call about?"

"To the same–"

"Do you know how many people vacation in Mexico," she cut in. She was hoping for bigger news and was a little irritated.

"Guerrero."

Silence fell between them until a chuckle came from JD's end.

"I thought that would intrigue you. I'm guessing you know what's–"

"Poppies."

He laughed at her response, but it was true.

The Sierra Madre Mountains of Guerrero state were nothing more than a haven for drug traffickers. Poppies flooded parts of the area, and opium and heroin came easy. It continued to roll into the United States. Mexico was one of the major suppliers of the damn drug.

"I'm honestly so fucking confused by this. I really thought it was going to be a crazy ex-girlfriend thing. Now I'm looking into cartels and heroin." There was a thud. Ryan could picture him slamming his fist on his desk. "I hate to ask," he sighed. "You've been around Ethan a while, do you think–"

"Absolutely not," Ryan cut him off. There was nothing about Ethan that gave her the faintest thought that he might be involved in any sort of drug activity.

"I figured as much."

Ryan was a little surprised when no sooner than she concluded her conversation, Ethan popped out from behind the closed office door.

"Were you trying to listen to my call," she gasped, shoving the phone in her jacket.

"Get over yourself," he scoffed. "I don't care about your conversations with JD."

It was an assumption on his part, but Ryan couldn't hide her shock that he was correct. She also couldn't ignore the hint of jealousy that had escaped with his words.

"My father asked us to come by his office," he continued.

Ethan turned and made his way a few more feet to Owen Lowell's door.

Ryan didn't have the time to deal with whatever Owen had called them for. Her mind was still racing from her conversation with JD.

"Perkins?" She nearly stumbled backwards upon seeing her boss in the office.

He didn't look happy. His face was tense and he looked like he hadn't gotten any sleep. He stood straight, arms crossed, and shook his head at Ryan's acknowledgement.

"Great, I'll get straight to the point, because I have a call in twenty minutes," Owen began as he glanced at his watch.

"What's going on?" Ethan appeared more confused than anyone.

"I knew you'd forget," Owen huffed. "We need to talk about the charity ball at the Riverton Mansion."

"No. No. No." Ethan flailed his hands around and headed toward the door. "I'm not going to that crap again."

"It's a yearly event. That means it happens every year!"

"Then you go!"

"Of course your mother and I will be there, as will you and whoever you happen to be seeing come tomorrow night."

The jab Owen took at Ethan's personal life caused him to tense up. Ryan saw it in Ethan's eyes. *Go to hell.*

"Ryan, I'm going to need you watching Ethan very closely. Several hundred people will be there and–"

"We always do that event. You'll have plenty of guards," she interrupted.

She was mildly annoyed. She had been watching Ethan closely, so she didn't understand why Perkins needed to point that out.

Ryan was also familiar with the charity event he was talking about. The wealthy always feared someone was out to get them. Whoever rented out the mansion to host the lavish party in the name of charity had made sure there was adequate help in case something went wrong. To keep the guests from becoming uncomfortable, Perkins had everyone play parts, generally they took the place of servers. Ryan always loved that job, she could move around and sneak the occasional hors d'oeuvre.

"Wait, I can't have a date and *that*." Ethan waved his finger up and down, gesturing toward Ryan. "Also, since when have there ever been guards at this thing?"

"Always," Perkins chimed in with laughter. "Just because they don't look like she and I do at this moment doesn't mean they aren't there." He turned toward Ryan and hesitated. "Which brings up something I need to discuss with you."

"Why do I have the feeling that without a doubt, I know I'm not going to like this?"

"It would look awkward for a server to be fixated upon one guest, right?"

"Yes..." She drew the word out. She definitely wasn't going to like what he was about to tell her. He had two ways of dealing with her, being blunt, or justifying what he needed her to do before he actually told her what is was. Generally she hated the latter, as those were the more painful tasks.

"It would make more sense if you were a guest."

Ryan cringed. "That means I have to wear a dress."

"It does," Perkins laughed.

"That looks even worse," Ethan shouted. "I can't have her around me and be with my date."

"Now that we're back on the topic, who is it," Owen

asked. Ethan immediately knew why his father suddenly cared so much.

"I'm not taking that congressman's daughter!"

"Why not? She just graduated from Harvard. She's above and beyond anything you'd bring," Owen laughed.

"I'm not bringing anyone, and if you continue to fight me on this, I won't even make an appearance. I don't care what your repercussions are," Ethan insisted.

The rage in his eyes for his father was something Ryan hadn't seen until now. Ethan was more or less controlled by his father, expected to one day take over the business. What Owen was trying to do made sense. He wanted his son with someone that had a classy and reserved upbringing.

"Actually," Perkins nervously began as he interrupted the family drama starting to unfold. "That would work out quite well."

"What do you mean," Owen growled.

"Ryan can go as Ethan's date."

"No," Ryan screamed.

"I use the word loosely. You're already with him all the time as it is; this really won't be much different."

Ryan couldn't make a big deal about it without raising questions. What Perkins was saying was true; however, there had to be strong boundaries now. She thought that she had made that abundantly clear, but since that kiss, she was sure that one day Ethan would forget about the boundaries. Even more terrifying, she knew that she would too.

CHAPTER 13

The next morning, Thursday, the day of the event, Ethan decided to sleep in. He was being a drama queen, insisting that he couldn't work and go to the charity ball all in the same day. Ryan knew he simply didn't want to spend an entire day and most of the night with his father.

Ryan was quite surprised that he actually did work a bit, at least that's what she assumed when he buried himself in his office for most of the day.

At some point that afternoon, Levi dropped off a handful of dresses for Ryan. They were all approved by The Agency, though she would have preferred them to be a little more simplistic. Levi only laughed as he tried to explain to her that this was an elegant event, and a plain black dress wouldn't cut it. She needed to look like she belonged.

Ethan was dressed first, a full thirty minutes before Levi would arrive with one of The Agency's protection vehicles. He stood in the doorway of the guest bathroom attempting to follow along with Ryan ranting about procedure as she straightened her hair. All he could focus on was the fact that her t-shirt was a little short and her sweatpants a bit too low. Every time she reached up to grab a swatch of hair on the top, and her shirt rose with her arms, he could see at least two inches of toned skin. Just above her pants, the band of simple black cotton panties caught his attention.

"Are we clear?"

"I'm sorry. I missed that last part," Ethan nervously laughed.

"You haven't been listening for shit!" She pretended to throw the brush. Instinctively, Ethan put his arms up, but she never released it from her grip. He knew she was bluffing only after she turned back to the mirror, her reflection full of irritation as her eyes met his through the mirror.

He coughed and made a poor attempt to change the conversation to something else; he still wasn't sure what she had been talking about. "You do know we leave in thirty minutes?"

"I might not have gone to Harvard, but I'm well aware as to how clocks work."

His eyes narrowed on hers in the mirror. She didn't want to know what he was thinking right now. Her comment hinted at the snooty education of the congressman's daughter Owen had mentioned the previous day.

"Just go away so I can get dressed and finish my makeup."

"Have you picked a dress," he asked curiously. He

had only seen glimpses of them when Levi stopped by earlier. There was a white, a red, and a navy. He was certain she'd pick the navy; it was the closest to black.

"No."

"How can you do that? I thought it took girls hours to get ready."

She slammed the iron down and ran her fingers through her hair, ruffling it a bit. She turned, arms crossed, leaning against the counter. Her shirt had only risen slightly, which she seemed to be unaware of.

"I have more important things to do than spend that much time fiddling with my hair."

It wasn't until then that she noticed all of him. She wasn't into fashion, but with some of the wealthy clients she worked for, she knew a few things. Ethan wasn't in a typical suit. The Brioni tuxedo clung to his body; tailored just for him, it fit like a glove. One thing she had learned about Ethan was that he liked his suits fitted, and he had the body for it. She was a little surprised to see the silky black bowtie around his neck. She was under the impression that he wasn't a fan of ties.

Even more surprising was what he didn't do.

She eyed the dark stubble around his jawline and lips. As soon as she had settled on his lips, an ache in the pit of her stomach wanted them to desperately be on hers again. When they tilted up in a smirk, Ryan had to force herself to look away. She knew Ethan wasn't stupid, but more than that, she knew

142

that she couldn't encourage even the slightest flirtation with him.

"You're not going to shave?" He had shaved for his double date.

"No," he smiled. "I kind of like a little something here." He rubbed over the little amount of scruff and Ryan could feel her breathing momentarily stop.

She had to wonder if his reason for leaving it had anything to do with what she said that night.

"I really need to get ready." Her words were quick and dismissive, and a moment later, she had disappeared into her bedroom.

She hated all the dresses. They were beautiful for someone, just not her. Dresses served no purpose in her life. They made it difficult to conceal weapons and, depending on the length and the fitting, even more difficult to run.

All the dresses were floor-length evening gowns. While that wasn't ideal for running, she'd be able to have both her ankle holster as well as her garter holster, given that the fabric was loose enough below the waist. The navy one would have been her first choice, solely based on color; however, she found the plunging neckline to be too much for her to do it any justice. The white one was better, aside from the fact that it was white, and had a slit in the back that she didn't care for. She really didn't want to wear the red; the color was too vibrant and screamed for attention; however, as it rest splattered across her bed, the design appeared perfect. The top part was a crewneck cut, covering her from neck down, with dainty cap sleeves. The waist looked like it was going to be rather snug, and Ryan was thankful that she opted out of a second burger earlier. Past the waist, it spread out like a typical ball gown. It was surprising to find that it only had two layers of material. Aside from the bright color, it was the perfect design. She'd definitely be reporting her thoughts back on it.

That was until she attempted to try it on.

"I knew it was too good to be true," she grumbled to herself.

The back of the dress stopped about halfway down and opened up into a triangle. She hadn't seen it from the front because it stopped just at the sides of the hips in the back.

Once she finally put it on and glanced over her shoulder in the floor length mirror, she became even more frustrated. Her cotton bikini cut underwear, which were the ultimate comfy panties, were visible by more than half an inch. She could roll the band down a bit, but if it unrolled itself through the course of the evening, that would look tacky. The only positive thing was that no matter how she bent or reached, the top part of the back was long enough so that she could at least wear a bra. She wouldn't have been able to do that with the navy.

She rummaged through her things; all her under-garments were similar. Practical. Occasionally, through promotions and sales from the lingerie store she preferred, she would gain a pair that she'd never intentionally buy for herself. When she found the low-rise piece of lacy fabric buried in her things, she became suddenly aware that she had packed it. She honestly didn't recall half the things she had thrown into her bags the other night at her apartment.

She was only able to breathe a sigh of relief once she turned in the mirror again and everything looked perfect. For a minute, she actually thought that she looked every bit like the elegant women she'd soon encounter. She quickly popped back into the bathroom to finish off her makeup, this time closing the door so that Ethan wouldn't distract her.

Ryan felt beyond uncomfortable when she entered the room to two sets of eyes staring at her like she was something from another planet. She tried her best to avoid Ethan's gaze. She was positive that the congressman's daughter would have been better suited for the event. She had never put so much effort into getting ready for something like this, and she wouldn't be able to handle the look of disappointment she was certain had come across his face. Actually, when she thought about the upcoming evening, she had never even been to something of this nature unless as part of a job.

That thought stuck with her and she had to remind herself that this was part of the job. She was here because of her job. It was nothing more than that and it would never be anything more than that.

Thankfully, Levi broke her from the turmoil splattering inside her head. "Damn, Beckett! You clean up nice when you want to."

Ethan tried his best not to show his irritation. He genuinely liked Levi as a person, but he could have punched him at that comment. She didn't look like she had *cleaned up nice*. She was gorgeous, mesmerizing, breathtaking. She was perfect.

He couldn't tell her any of that, not with Levi. Then again, he wasn't sure if she'd want to hear anything like that from him at all.

He was a little surprised that she picked the red dress; the color was bold. Sure, other women would be wearing similar colors, but Ryan would easily stand out from them. The design of the dress was elegantly simple and tasteful. She must have picked it because of the wide skirt. As tight as it was from the waist up, Ethan could clearly tell that she wasn't concealing anything there.

Her hair was different than he had ever seen. It wasn't in her natural waves, but straight; he neglected to pay attention to that when she was in the mirror earlier. By not being in the slicked back ponytail he was accustomed to seeing, it came across as lighter in color. His eyes drifted over her face, desperately wanting to make eye contact with her so that she could see how enraptured he was. Her face looked like that of a doll. Her skin was so pure and flawless, cheeks a rosy pink, and she had done more to her eyes with a subtle brown eyeshadow, containing a vague amount of sparkle, and a darker brown liner along the top and bottom of the lashes. Her lips, however, remained bare, untouched by any cosmetic product.

"Are we ready," she asked, dropping any further conversation about her looks.

"I am if you two are. The driver, Jeff, and Brett are waiting in the vehicle."

Ryan watched as Ethan played with his wallet for a moment. He looked concerned, like he was missing something. He excused himself briefly to retreat to his room.

"How are you holding up," Levi quietly asked.

"I'm wearing an evening dress. Was that even a serious question?"

He responded with a hearty laugh and nudged her shoulder. "Perkins did remind me to tell you to stay on your best behavior. No cursing or arguing."

"Yeah, I get it," she sighed.

It wasn't until they were leaving that Ryan took a step or two in front of Ethan and he noticed the back of her dress. Blood drained from his brain and he became incapable of a single coherent thought. Seeing her midriff when she was getting ready was one thing, a tease, just a glimpse, but she'd be wearing that dress all night. He didn't want to gawk, but he was certain that the fabric came so low that he could see her Venusian dimples beneath her ridiculously toned back. There was no way he could get through the night with her at his side.

"Ethan, this is Brett. I don't think you two have met," Levi announced after opening the door to the SUV.

It had obviously been modified to suit their pur-poses. A row of seats faced the front and another faced the rear. It looked like a compact limousine.

Levi ushered Ethan in to sit on the side with the

man he had just met. He looked younger than Ethan. He was well sculpted, clean shaven, tanned skin, and a black ponytail hung between his shoulder blades.

Levi attempted to help Ryan up the step into the vehicle. She wasn't very elegant with her attire.

"Fucking piece of shit," she muttered under her breath, although everyone ended up hearing it.

"Get it out of your system while you can," Jeff smiled. His voice, however, remained monotone and void of any humor.

"No. Other side." Levi motioned to Ethan and Brett. "There's no way that you and gramps are getting all that room while we try to squeeze three big men into that side."

Jeff glared. "Watch it, boy."

Ryan huffed and puffed and finally situated herself next to Ethan. It was a large SUV, but she felt increasingly claustrophobic. Ethan could definitely slide a few inches closer to Brett and still not end up touching him; yet here they were, her left side plastered to his right. She clasped her hands together in her lap to prevent any further accidental touching.

Shortly after the vehicle began moving, Brett leaned forward so that Ryan could see him past Ethan.

"Hey, Beckett. I just want you to know, you look awesome tonight."

"Thank you," she said meekly.

"No, like really. You look gorgeous."

Ethan tried not to show his irritation, but he was fuming.

"Dude!" Levi's expression was close to that of disgust. "It's Ryan. Stop flirting with her. That's weird."

Ryan turned toward the window, but from the corner of his eye, Ethan could see her blushing. He had barely met this Brett guy and he already hated him.

Ethan knew he had to change things tonight.

CHAPTER 14

Ryan wasn't in awe once they entered the mansion like some of the women gasping before her. She had seen it before. It looked the same every year. It was beautiful, but she had seen better.

No one lived in the mansion. It was part of an estate and often rented out to elites for events like this or for weddings. Ryan had never seen much of it beyond the kitchen and the main ballroom.

"Here." Ethan gestured toward his slightly bent elbow.

"I'm fine," Ryan quickly said.

It's not a real date. The words continued to echo in her head every time she almost, for even a second, started to think differently.

"Suit yourself."

Ethan walked around the dance floor through the tables, like he knew where he was going. His family sat in the same area every year since he could remember.

Of course his sister and her family had come. She was in her early thirties and married with kids. Ethan hated her husband; he was too much like their father, aside from the fact that he was British. Whenever they came from England to visit, which was usually three to four times a year, he and Owen always had a grand time being judgmental toward Ethan.

He didn't understand why Leighton stuck with him. She was so full of life and whimsical and Oliver was a stick in the mud. No, he knew why. Their father couldn't have picked a better match for her if he had a catalog.

"Sweetheart," Gwen gasped as soon as she saw Ethan through the crowd. She rushed to him and gave him a hug. Ethan was careful in his mother's embrace so that her gin and tonic didn't spill all over the both of them.

His sister was next. Her eyes lit up at the sight of her brother. Ethan assumed she must be miserable with only their parents and her wretched husband.

"Oh, and who are you," Gwen squealed. She pushed past Ethan and made her way toward Ryan. Though she had asked a question, before Ryan could open her mouth to say her own name, Gwen began ranting away. "Ethan! Is this your date," she giggled. Ryan wasn't sure if it was an insult, but began speculating. "She's absolutely adorable! I, for sure, thought you were bringing some stripper like last year," she babbled.

"Sorry," Leighton interrupted. "That's supposed to be a compliment." She rolled her eyes at her mother and gave her a nudge.

"She's not my date," Ethan corrected. Everyone grew quiet.

From the other side of the table, Owen chimed in.

"Dear, I told you about her. That's Ryan Beckett."

Gwen gasped and took a step back. Her smile had faded as she eyed Ryan up and down. "I didn't expect a bodyguard to be so–"

"Mother," Ethan growled. Though Ryan hid it well, Ethan could sense how uncomfortable Ryan had become.

"Pretty," she concluded. She glared at Ethan and took her seat at the round table across from her husband.

"How many has she had," Ethan sighed to his sister.

Leighton laughed at the suggestion. "Sadly, that's her first one, but she's been listening to dad and Oliver discuss politics both the ride here and up until you came in, so give her some time." She motioned to the table, but Ethan hesitated.

"One second."

His hand tightened on Ryan's wrist and her body couldn't help but follow him farther away from the table. His eyes were desperate and if his hair wouldn't have been so perfectly fixed, he'd be running his fingers through it like he always did when he was nervous or uncomfortable.

"I realize this night is already painful for you," he began. His eyes clenched as he looked into hers and she could feel the sincerity. "I'll make this quick. My mom is a sweetheart but can be over-the-top eccentric. My sister is the easiest person in my family to talk to, but she reads too much into things and can be a little skeptical. You two share something in that," he softly laughed. "Her husband is the biggest cunt on the planet, and I use that word because he's British and according to him that is the most vulgar word in the English language."

"Why are you telling me all this?"

His smile was infectious. "If, up until this point, wearing a dress has been the worst part of your evening, you might be in for a rude awakening."

Ethan was definitely right about his brother-in-law. Though she had been informed several times to be on good behavior, she knew that stemmed from her screaming in a busy street with Trevor Parker over a dead body. Oliver was a different story. While Ryan didn't know him like she knew Parker, she disliked him immediately for no reason other than him opening his mouth. She had no intention of playing nice with a pretentious brat who thought his accent gave him authority.

"Do they actually allow you to carry a gun?"

"It would be a bit pointless if they didn't." Her words were cold through her gritted teeth. Oliver Miller made wearing a dress seem like a trip to Disney World.

"Have you actually used it?"

Everyone at the table started to tense up from the direction the conversation was going; however, Oliver thought it to be quite humorous.

"Many times." Her words held no emotion.

The smirk on his face said it before he could. "How many people have you killed?"

He thoroughly pissed Ryan off. She wanted so

badly to call him that uncouth word, instead she answered his question. "Honestly, too many to keep count at this point." She shrugged. It was a lie; she knew the exact number, but Oliver didn't.

His eyes widened and he backed off. Beneath the tablecloth, Ryan felt a squeeze on her knee. Her eyes darted up toward Ethan; he gave her a side smile and a nod. His touch had not at all been a romantic gesture. He was showing her pleasure in the fact that she had gotten Oliver to finally shut up.

The satisfaction was short-lived.

Owen jumped from his seat with the biggest smile. Ryan didn't even know he was capable of such a thing. "Daniels!"

Ryan's stomach churned. Congressman Daniels.

"Owen Lowell," the man laughed. "It's a pleasure to see you here."

Everyone but Oliver stood to shake hands; something on his phone was suddenly more pressing.

Ryan easily recognized the young lady with Congressman Daniels. She had worked other events where Ella Daniels attended. It was immediately clear that this was the girl Ethan's father wanted for his son.

Ethan would be a fool to turn down the opportunity. She was extremely educated and well-spoken. She held herself with grace and dignity. Her looks were even more of the coup de grâce to end it. She was tall and slim, as slim as Ryan, though Ryan knew she could easily trump Ella in pushups. Her naturally blonde hair fell down to her waist, but she had half of it pinned back tonight. Worst of all, her

154

chocolate eyes looked at Ethan like he hung the moon.

"Ethan!"

Even her damn voice was perfection.

"Hey, Ella."

She had attempted to give him a hug but he instead opted for a handshake, much to her surprise.

Out of habit, Ryan took a couple steps back, which Ethan followed. She shot him a look. *What are you doing?* He completely ignored her reaction to his action.

"Oh," Ella sighed. The disappointment came through in that one tiny word. "Hello. You must be Ethan's–"

Ryan didn't know what made her do it, maybe she was still riled up from Oliver.

"Protection officer," she blurted out, cutting Ella off before she could say that one word that Ryan couldn't bear hearing. *Date.*

"Come again?"

"I'm his bodyguard for the evening."

Ella looked at Ethan and raised a brow. It was an insinuation that it must be a joke.

"She's actually quite good," Ethan mumbled. For some odd reason, he was annoyed with Ryan.

The fact pleased Ella, and she became even more flirtatious. Ryan was just about to excuse herself, which would have definitely been unacceptable as per Perkins' orders, when Brett came to her rescue.

He had lucked out with his assignment.

He effortlessly balanced the tray of champagne glasses around the tables, finally settling near Ryan.

"It looks like you could use one most of all," he whispered.

"You're my savior," she whispered back, accepting his offer. "Although, I shouldn't be drinking on the job."

"With all of us?" He motioned around with his free hand and Ryan noticed that there were more guards tonight than she had ever worked with at this particular event. He gave her a wink and drifted off.

Ethan tried to overhear the conversation, but Ella's high-pitched laughter was enough to drown out the violinists. He didn't like how close Brett got to Ryan's face as he whispered something in her ear. He also didn't like that he made her smile. It was stupid and selfish. She rarely smiled, but when she did, it was the most beautiful wonder of the world. He didn't want her giving that to another man. There were a lot of things he didn't want her giving to other men.

At that moment, he realized he was losing it. The line was becoming too blurred with her.

"Excuse me, I'll be right back." His voice had lost most of its sound.

"Ethan, will you please stop?"

They were away from the main crowd, near a set of glass doors leading out to a lit veranda. Ryan looked at him with a panicked expression, curious as to what was wrong.

"Ethan Lowell," a scream wailed from far away.

"You have got to be kidding me," he murmured to himself.

He'd never get a moment alone with Ryan. She was going to drive him crazy the entire night, and until they got back to his penthouse, exhausted from all the socializing, he'd never even be able to tell her how beautiful she looked.

Two women were quickly headed their way. The more Spanish looking one that had called out to Ethan threw herself all over him. Ryan was a little surprised when he returned the hug and allowed her to kiss him on the cheek.

She went on to pull the other girl closer in, introducing her as Samantha; she was much shyer than the girl who knew Ethan. Ethan had yet to introduce Ryan, which she quickly read into. Half of her felt like he was using her. He had wanted Ella to think he was taken, but with this woman, a woman he clearly had a past with, he acted like Ryan didn't exist.

"I haven't seen you in forever, but I see you've been keeping out of trouble in the tabloids." She winked at him as she giggled the comment.

"Yeah. I meant to get in touch with you. Are you holding up alright?"

The smile on her face had obviously been forced before. "I guess as good as I can be given the circumstances."

"How about your father?" Ethan had only met him a few times, but he still thought to ask.

"I wouldn't even know," she scoffed and flipped her

thick black curls. "He's out of the country on business."

Ryan stood, feet away from the three, completely ignored. Ethan didn't need her, so there was no point in hovering over him. Just as she began to walk away to give him space, a hand clasped around hers. Before she knew it, she was at Ethan's side. She had to look down to make sure that her imagination wasn't running wild. It wasn't. Between their two bodies, their hands hung, fingers intertwined. Her heartbeat quickened at the gesture.

It's not real.

She tried to pull away without making a scene, but Ethan had felt it before she could follow through and tightened his grip. He looked down at her with soft eyes and a devilish smirk that awakened a swarm of butterflies within her stomach.

"Well, well. Ethan Lowell. I can't believe you haven't introduced us yet." The woman's voice was comforting and melodic.

He nervously laughed and allowed their hands to separate. "Sophia, this is Ryan Beckett, and Ryan, this is my friend Sophia Delacruz and her friend Samantha."

Sophia's eyes darted into a playful glare at the way Ethan made the introductions.

Ryan wasn't dumb, but she didn't know why Ethan didn't say it like it was. Sophia was obviously an ex-girlfriend, or ex-fling, or whatever Ethan called his conquests. Ryan also noticed that he called her nothing, not friend, not bodyguard, nothing.

"The name," Sophia exclaimed. "I love it. Very unique for a girl. What do you think Samantha?"

"It's hot, very sexy."

Ryan was a little surprised by how nice the girls were, but something seemed off. She couldn't quite place it. She also wasn't sure how to read the relationship between Sophia and Ethan.

Shortly after the encounter, Ethan appeared a little more relaxed, especially in the company of his family, particularly his sister. Once dinner finished, the orchestra started back up again and people took to the floor dancing. Although by now, most of them had already consumed their fair share of drinks and Ryan had a hard time calling what they were doing dancing.

"So, where did Mr. Sunshine run off to," Ethan asked. He playfully nudged his sister, but she could barely give him a fake smile.

"He's probably off kissing dad's ass." She leaned forward teasingly. "Do you miss him? Should I go find him?"

"Hell no. I couldn't be more comfortable with the two of them gone," he admitted.

"With them gone, I'll get to the point."

Ethan folded his arms and braced himself for whatever caused the devious glimmer in his sister's eyes. "Why do I have a bad feeling?"

"Interesting that you mention feelings..."

"Leigh?"

"What's the deal with you and Ryan?" She arched her brow and waited for him to lie through his teeth.

"I don't know what you're–"

"Bullshit."

They stared each other down for a minute. She knew he'd crack if given enough time, but she also knew Ryan would be returning from the bathroom soon.

"Fine, don't tell me what I already know."

"I don't know what you think, but–"

"I watched how you reacted to Miss Daniels. She's perfect for you and you know it. Is it because dad is obsessed with getting the two of you together that you dismiss the idea?"

Ethan hung his head, unable to look at his serious, and now overly curious, sister. "No," he answered quietly.

"Why didn't you bring a date tonight," she pressed.

He shook his head and ran his hand along the back of his neck in frustration. "I have someone trying to kill me, I don't have time for–"

"It might not be as obvious to them," she began. Ethan knew that she meant their parents. "And you should keep it that way for now. You know dad." He did. His father would never approve of someone like Ryan, but the thought that he needed his father to approve made him feel utterly disgusted with himself. "I know you're into her, and in case you can't tell, she's into you as well."

Ethan didn't want to show it, but the comment had caught his attention, to the point that his sister burst out in laughter.

"Baby brother, please don't make me go on. I'm a

160

psychologist for a reason and I will bury you if this conversation continues." Her voice then fell to a near whisper. "Plus, she's coming back." Her eyes narrowed and she leaned forward once again, her voice dropping below a whisper. "If you don't want me to embarrass you, I suggest you ask her to dance."

His parents always thought he was the troublemaker and the conniving one, but that was only because he learned from the best.

Of course Ryan rejected him at first, detesting the idea of dancing. It only became worse that his sister found humor in it and told Ryan that she had never been witness to any woman rejecting Ethan.

It wasn't until Oliver returned with a glass of scotch, that he clearly didn't need, that Ryan gave in to the idea.

"I've never really done this," Ryan admitted once they were on the floor.

Ethan loved seeing her out of her comfort zone. It gave him a feeling of control.

"Here." He carefully took her left hand and placed it on his upper arm. He could barely feel it, like she was afraid to touch him. He then snaked that same arm around her. There was no way that he could avoid touching her skin.

She jumped slightly from the warmth of his hand on her bare back. He quickly positioned their free hands together before she could change her mind.

"I can assure you that the music won't be fast-paced. Plus, your dress covers your feet well enough that no one will see if you're messing up."

Ryan brought her eyes to meet his. This was all so wrong. Even though it was just a dance, their closeness felt too romantically intimate.

"So, Sophia? An ex?" She had wanted to ask for a while now, and she was hoping that talking about another woman would stop him from looking at her with the intensity that he was.

He laughed at the suggestion. It was a genuine laugh reflected in the creases of his eyes as they clenched up. "I introduced her as a friend, a friend I haven't seen in a while."

"You didn't introduce me as anything." She felt his arm tighten around her as soon as she had said it.

"I'm not sure what you are to me."

Her heart was racing again. It was becoming too hard to tell herself that tonight was nothing more than a job.

Her words were flat. "I'm your bodyguard."

Ethan ignored the comment. Ryan was quickly becoming something else and he was going to make sure that she knew that soon.

"You asked how she was doing and the light faded from her." Ryan continued on, trying to come up with anything that would keep her from reading into the comment he just made.

His eyes turned dark and stormy. "Her family just hasn't had the best days recently."

Ryan felt her heart twist. The look in his eyes made it seem like they were clearly more than just friends, even if it was in the past.

"Her little brother died a couple months ago. It was

a disease that was caught too late."

Ryan felt like throwing up for feeling jealous in any way. Sophia had been quite amicable to her, and Ryan couldn't imagine what it would be like to lose Jeremy.

Ethan continued, his tone serious and full of pain. "He was only twelve. I hadn't seen him in more than a year, but he was always so active. I guess it was one of those things hidden beneath the surface and it just hit all at once."

"I'm sorry I asked," Ryan said softly, seeing how saddened Ethan became.

"That's not even half of what she's been through," he admitted.

Ryan was afraid to ask, but Ethan saw the inquisitive look flash across her face.

"I guess her mom couldn't take it."

Her chest clenched at what was to come.

"A couple weeks ago, she jumped off a bridge."

Ryan tried not to go into her robotic nature, but for some reason wheels began to turn in her head.

She didn't own a television. She didn't have time for the nonsense that was played, and depending on the channel, the media could be strongly biased. The only thing she had ever used a television for in recent years was the news, now she just found it on the internet and sifted through all the bullshit. She did remember seeing that a prominent businessman's wife had committed suicide. It didn't concern her line of work and she hated reading depressing articles, unless they pertained to murder, but now the name registered.

Delacruz.

Ethan interrupted her thoughts. "You're doing that thing."

"What thing?" Taken off-guard, Ryan accidentally stepped on the edge of her dress and fought to keep her balance.

Ethan laughed. It was different. He wasn't amused, but it wasn't fake. It was an unlikely laugh, just for her. "Your eyes dart all over the place. Your breathing changes. I didn't notice that before, but now I can feel it. You're overthinking something. What?"

"Nothing," she quickly answered, knowing that wouldn't be enough. "I just remember reading the article," she added. "So, it's just Sophia and her dad," she asked moments later.

"I guess. He's not really around much. He has a parts business for everything from vacuums to semi-trucks. It's pretty huge." Ethan shrugged like it was no big deal.

"She said that he was out of the country. Where does he go for a parts business?"

His steps faltered a little. He wanted to talk to Ryan, really talk to her. He hated when she was in her intrusive detective mode.

"Probably Mexico."

Bells and alarms went off in Ryan's head. *Mexico.* People went to Mexico all the time. She had to keep telling herself that. Stop reading into things that weren't there. Besides, there was nothing that Sophia had given that would lead Ryan to believe that she thought anything less than good-natured thoughts for Ethan. As much as she didn't want to, she knew she'd have to talk to JD.

Ethan pulled her in closer, far closer than ballroom dancing required. Her thinking deteriorated to the thoughts she had been trying to avoid all evening.

She closed her eyes and felt a fiery ecstasy run through her bones as he traced small circles along her back with his thumb. *It wasn't a date. It was just her job.*

"God, you look so perfect tonight." His words were dry and rough, like he was lacking air.

She needed to clear the fog that had obviously fallen over the both of them, but it was becoming one of the hardest things she had ever done.

"I tried, I suppose."

"Stop." In just that one word, he was fierce and direct, irritated with her for continuing to pull away. "I need to talk to you."

Ryan began to panic and tried to distance their bodies, which only made Ethan pull her closer.

"The other night was great." He swallowed heavily, fully knowing that Ryan could tell how nervous he was. "Everything changed the next morning. I know it was a little awkward–"

"Oh, god," Ryan groaned. "Please, don't do this."

"Did you think of me?"

Their eyes were locked on each other. Ryan wasn't sure they were moving anymore. The people around them seemed to be moving, but it felt like her feet were stuck in concrete.

"We're not talking about it."

Those words were enough of an answer for him. He didn't want to break away from her, but he knew it would only be momentarily.

His hands held both of hers as he took a step back, adding distance between them. The air was much colder now that he had separated their bodies. He tightened his grip on her fingers, the hurt and sadness in his face bleeding through to her with his touch.

"I can't do this, Ryan." The words came out with a swift intensity that cut through her.

When he dropped her hands from his and turned to leave, she realized the hollowness that started to grow inside. The more the distance increased between them, the harder it was for Ryan to keep her world together.

She couldn't be around him right now, but rather than go back to his family's table, he went down a darkened and secluded hallway. No one was with him; he was all alone.

CHAPTER 15

"Ethan," Ryan hissed. She caught up with him just as he reached a spiral staircase blocked off with a velvety green rope. "What the hell are you doing?"

He didn't answer her. He easily stepped over the rope and continued up the stairs.

"You have got to be kidding me! You can't go up there."

Ethan ignored her and continued on, making Ryan furious. She was as pissed as when he snuck out to go to the club, except this time he was deliberately refusing to listen and reason with her standing right there.

The rope didn't have a clasp to hook and unhook; it was tightly knotted around the railing on either side. Ryan proceeded to grab the bottom of her dress and pull the fabric above her knees so that she could climb over the rope as well.

She stumbled up the stairs after Ethan who was well ahead of her. Once she reached the top, she watched as he disappeared behind one of the many doors in the vast and unlit hallway. With each step she took in the same direction, she became even more irate with his behavior. One minute he wanted to talk about her damn vibrator, and the next he left her standing alone on a crowded dance floor.

She hesitantly stepped through the threshold of the open room. Her world then flipped a hundred thousand times in a matter of seconds.

Ethan had her tightly pressed between him and the wall near the doorway. He used his free hand to slam the door and flip the lock.

Hungry lips tugged at hers, begging for entry. One hand at her neck and another at her bare back pulled her closer. Once the shock faded, Ryan wrapped both her arms around Ethan and gave in to the second most amazing kiss she had ever had in her life. The mingling of his taste with hers sent her insides on fire. Her body reacted in ways that screamed for more than what he was giving.

"Wait," she mumbled, gasping for air and pulling back.

Ethan knew exactly where they were going once again. His want and need for her grew by the day and he was at his breaking point. He thought she wanted the same, but here she was pulling away, again.

He distanced himself from her and crossed the guest bedroom. He tried to collect his thoughts through the pounding frustration.

Ryan kept herself pressed against the wall, her yearning for him turning to concern. "What was that," she managed to get out, still trying to find her breath.

"Seriously?!" His arms were crossed as he glared at her. The same hands that had been all over her were now locked away.

"I thought you said you couldn't–"

He threw his arms up in the air. "Yeah, Ryan. I couldn't do that down there. I couldn't be that close to you, touch you, feel your body against mine." He ran his fingers through his hair and nervously paced the dark room, where the only light trickled in from the outdoor festivities below. "I couldn't be with you in that crowd a moment longer knowing that the entire time tonight all I've thought about was having you naked in my arms."

Ryan froze at the comment. She knew she couldn't do that; she couldn't give him what he wanted. She knew that one night with him would mean losing a deeper part of herself that she wasn't ready for. She knew a lot of things, but her body felt differently.

"After you freaked out the first time I kissed you, I backed off. I figured that eventually you'd come to me. That night when we talked, I was so sure that you'd at least try for a second time, but you're so focused on this being a *job*. I'm so fucking sick of that word."

With each word he spoke, Ryan found it harder to stay plastered where she was.

He started to go off on another rant. "If that's all this will ever be–"

She slowly moved from the wall toward his direction. "You knew I'd follow you, didn't you?"

"Of course I did," he scoffed. It was what he had wanted. Her. Away from everyone else.

She was never the one to be forward, but the ache in her core and the racing of her pulse left her no choice. *Just one night.* Maybe she could do that.

Her steps came to a stop once she stood close enough to feel his breath. The scent of his cologne had never been so intoxicating to her. It only caused the arousal between her legs to flood through to the skimpy panties she suddenly wished to disappear.

She had never been good at foreplay. She couldn't tell Ethan right now, but Matt had been the only man she was ever really with, and even then, sex was just sex. With Ethan, she wanted to prolong what was happening, but she didn't realize until that moment how much she wanted his body with hers.

She pressed her right hand on his lower abdomen and softly began sliding it up his chest. Through the fabric she could still feel every ridge and every muscle. She had seen him shirtless before; she knew what the crisp white shirt was concealing.

"Do you want me to answer your question," she asked with a voice she no longer recognized.

Ethan licked his lips. "I know you thought of me. I can see it in your eyes right now." His words were raw and confident.

In two swift flicks, Ryan had Ethan's bowtie undone and hanging around his neck. With her thumb and forefinger, she undid the top two buttons of Ethan's shirt. It was only then that he finally broke and touched her.

He held her hand tightly in his firm grip, pressing it into his chest. She could feel the pounding within. When their eyes met, the lust and desire in his washed over her, making her weak enough to fall to the floor.

"Ryan." Her name from his lips sounded like it was the most painful thing for him to say. She had to wonder if he was stopping her, if he no longer wanted this.

"Do you want me to stop," she quickly asked.

His soft laughter was reflected in his intense green eyes. "The last thing I want is for any of this to stop."

Before anything more could be said, Ryan yanked at the lapels on his jacket and pulled him into her. She needed to taste him, breathe him in. She let out a soft sigh once his tongue found its way into her mouth, and she could feel his lips finding humor in the fact that a kiss had done so much.

His hand drifted lower down the soft skin of her back. He allowed his fingers to slip below the fabric. Without meaning to, he jerked back a little.

"What the hell?" The feeling of the lace was unexpected.

"The dress was too low to wear normal panties," Ryan admitted, a little embarrassed at Ethan's shock.

The look in his eyes turned animalistic and desperate. Her eyes trailed down his body. The bulge in his pants pulsed at the mentioning of her underwear. Her hand cupped it through the fabric, and a shaky breath escaped Ethan's gritted teeth. With every movement of her hand along the material outlining what she knew would be something massive in pleasure, Ethan shuddered. Ryan knew he wanted her to give in first, to take the next step.

Though she had wanted to take things slow, to savor every moment, she found her hands tearing at Ethan's belt, then button, then zipper. His pants slid down, revealing blue boxers.

He didn't allow Ryan to go any further; she had made it clear that this was going to happen. He needed to be in control now.

He slid her hair to one shoulder and kissed the side of her neck, beginning near the bottom of her earlobe and trailing downward. Her body pressed into his and her sweet moans vibrated through him. He snaked his right hand to the back of her neck and slowly worked on the zipper.

"The dress has two of them," she breathed.

He sucked on her skin slightly, not wanting to leave a visible mark, as he felt the top of her dress come undone. "I know," he whispered in her ear, while his hand trailed down her back, sending goose-bumps across her skin. He had seen enough of the dress all night. He needed it gone.

Once the lower zipper had gone to its limit, Ethan forced himself to part from her, to allow her to wiggle from the dress on her own. While he watched her strip before him, he kicked off his shoes and slid out of his pants. After pulling his jacket off, he helped her step from the pile of fabric gathered at her ankles.

He could have lost himself at the sight of her. She was nothing like any woman he had ever been with. Everything about her was so real, down to the simple nude bra and the low-rise lacy black panties. It definitely didn't match, which only made it clear that she put little care in such trivial things, or that she hadn't expected for anyone to see her in such a vulnerable state tonight.

Though her body was lean and toned, Ethan couldn't get over the fact at how small and feminine she was compared to him. His eyes settled on her breasts longer than he wanted, and she clammed up at the attention. He didn't care; he had to take the sight in.

"Are you okay," he asked with a voice as smooth as velvet. He pulled her hands away from her body and to the remaining buttons on his shirt, which she shakily began to undo.

"I just haven't done this in a while," she admitted. She was unable to look him in the eyes. Once she did, she knew her face would flush with embarrassment.

Ethan rubbed his hands gently over her hips, slowly creeping higher, until his thumbs fought to get under the base of her bra. "Don't be nervous. You're beautiful." The words were foreign to him. Normally he'd tell a woman how badly he wanted to fuck, that would do it for her, and he'd be satisfied in the end. He couldn't do that with Ryan. He wanted something different with her.

The shirt fell from his chest and Ryan sucked in a breath. He looked like something from a dream; his body belonged in a magazine. It was impossible to think straight with the carnal desires racing through her mind and body. *Breathe. Keep breathing.*

He picked up his discarded jacket and withdrew his wallet from inside; upon opening it, Ryan noticed the gold foil that flashed in the faint light. That wasn't in there when he thumbed through it back at the penthouse.

She shot him a playful glare. "*That's* what you were forgetting before we left?"

His laughter only heightened the need between her thighs. "Yeah."

"I would assume you always had one."

"Not lately," he growled, slightly closing the distance between them. Before she could ask, like he assumed she would, "If I don't have one, I'm not tempted."

"So, why tonight?"

"As soon as I saw you in that dress, I knew I was fighting a losing battle." He pulled her so that her whole chest crashed into his.

"And you just thought I'd–"

"Hoped," he interrupted, correcting what she was about to say before she said it.

He reached for the thin bands of her panties and just as he was about to pull them down, she backed away and mumbled to herself. She began undoing the thigh holster on her right leg, until a strong hand pulled hers away.

"Leave it," he groaned. "It's hot."

With that, their lips collided again, unleashing all the pent-up desire they both had found through the course of their relationship. In seconds, the last bits of clothing were flung across the room. Ethan didn't have the easiest time getting Ryan's panties over her holster, and he was certain he heard something tear.

She stood between his legs, their kisses only taking the smallest breaks to catch air, while he positioned himself on the bed. Ryan finally broke free from her addiction to his tongue once she heard the crinkling of the condom wrapper.

Ethan didn't take his eyes from hers as he slid it over his rock-hard arousal. Ryan's lips were parted and she took in heavy breaths. Ethan watched with pleasure as she gaped at what she had ultimately done to him. When he was satisfied, he reached out and pulled her into him.

Ryan half-expected Ethan to throw her on the bed and fight for dominance, which would eventually lead to a passionate session of missionary. She didn't know what he wanted when he pulled her onto his lap facing him. Her ankle holster scraped the edge of the bed as she sat with her knees bent.

Her body shuddered when he ran his hand upward from her knee. The farther his hand went the more desperate she became. "Please," she breathed.

His hand stopped and her clenched eyes flew open to meet the devious ones staring back at her. "Please, what?" He wanted her to beg.

A week ago, she never thought she'd be demanding this from Ethan Lowell, but tonight, all rational thoughts ceased to exist. "Touch me," she managed to whisper against his lips.

Ryan gasped when he did just that. His fingers easily slid along her folds, and his eyes flickered with euphoria at her desire for him.

"Shit, you're so–"

Before he could finish the comment, she smashed her lips into his, moaning at the touch of his fingers skimming along her clit. He gave up with his hand as soon as she pulled herself closer into him, her wetness soaking the condom.

He pulled her back. "I want you to look at me," he lustfully demanded.

Ryan prepared herself for what was to come. She didn't want any more teasing. She wanted him.

Ethan lifted her a couple inches up so that his tip could glide along her entrance before he plunged into her. To his surprise, her patience hadn't been as good as his.

She yelped in a pleasurable pain as she forced herself onto him.

Ethan couldn't refrain the guttural groan that escaped when he was finally inside her. He dared not move, allowing her body to adjust to his size.

There was a hint of discomfort in her eyes from the initial penetration and she bit down on her lip, but a moment later she nodded for him to continue.

He gripped at her waist, and pushed deeper inside. He knew he was hurting her at first, but with each thrust, her whimpers slowly faded into moans.

Ryan's nails dug into his shoulders, silently begging for him to increase the steady rhythm they had fallen into. When his name slipped out in one of her sighs of need, he thought he'd come undone. He was aware that he was leaving marks on her skin with the grip he had.

When she tightened around him and began gasping for air, he was certain that she was close. The grasp she had on him was so powerful that it was challenging for him to follow through with the thrusts.

"Oh, god...Ethan." Her words were barely audible as she softly breathed them into his ear.

He pulled her closer. He wanted to feel all of her. Her cries of gratification echoed through his own body, sending jolts deep within that were about to send him over the edge. She shuddered against him, her climax irresistibly volatile. Only once her orgasm began to subside did he give in. He quickened the pace, sliding his hands from her waist to her ass. A small squeal escaped when he clenched her cheeks.

"Oh, shit," he panted. He didn't expect her to react much to his release, but when her lips sank into his, with such ferocity and madness, he was done for.

Ryan bit down on Ethan's lip once the finality hit him. She couldn't ignore the sensual pulsing inside her as he filled the condom.

CHAPTER 16

After the ecstasy wore off, Ryan felt sick. That person in the room with Ethan hadn't been her. She didn't sleep around. If it had been any other man, there's no way she would have done that in such a short time of knowing him. Worst of all, she did that with someone she worked for, someone she was hired to protect.

She wasn't sure what it meant for Ethan, but in the end, it couldn't mean anything, for either of them.

The rest of the evening Ryan remained silent. She tried her best not to make eye contact with Ethan. The few times she had nearly killed her. Every moment of what happened in the bedroom stuck, and her body craved more.

Near the end of the event, when everyone began leaving, Leighton pulled Ethan to the side. She talked about his niece and nephew, how they'd be in the states for a couple weeks and they should all get together. He reluctantly agreed to visit his parents' mansion that Saturday for a family get-together. He only hesitated because of Oliver.

The ride back to Ethan's penthouse was awkward. He and Ryan had barely spoken since the encounter. On the drive, the contact had seemed unavoidable in the space, but Ryan so was plastered to the door that she may as well have separated them with the Atlantic.

Jeff, Levi, and Brett went on and on about how they expected something to happen at the ball. Ryan didn't. Whoever wanted Ethan dead wouldn't do it at an event like that. It was far too public; however, because nothing happened, everyone thought that it might be the end. Ryan knew differently. Tony Cohen's words continued to haunt her.

Brett quickly exited the vehicle and ran around the side to help Ryan out. She didn't need it. She could ball the dress up now, crinkle it, get it dirty. It didn't matter.

He offered his hand to her and not wanting to be rude, she took it.

"Thanks."

He pulled her away, a few feet from the vehicle. "Are you alright," he asked with a great deal of concern.

"Yeah. It's just been a long day."

Ethan had exited by that point and hovered nearby, waiting on Ryan to finish the pointless conversation that he could clearly overhear.

"Maybe you can take a breather soon and we can grab a coffee?"

"Until all this is figured out, I don't really get a break," Ryan sighed.

Ethan was surprised by her response. She didn't directly decline. Did that mean that she wanted to get coffee with Brett? Did she not understand that he was asking her for more than coffee? He was asking her for her time, as in a date.

"Damnit, Brett. Stop flirting and get the fuck in," Levi hollered through the open door.

Redness came across Brett's face and he quietly concluded his conversation with Ryan.

Words remained unspoken, even after the door closed behind them and Ryan bolted it with all the mechanisms. When she turned, Ethan was right there, inches from her. Had she taken a step forward she would have crashed into him.

He breathed an exasperated breath and messed with his hair like he was frustrated. "You just don't plan on saying anything? For how long?"

"I'm tired," Ryan began as she made her way around him.

He grabbed her wrist, possessively but still soft and gentle.

"Are we going to talk about what happened to-night?"

Ryan knew they needed to, but she cringed at the idea that the man that stood before her had seen her like that. She still had a hard time coming to terms that they had sex. It didn't feel real.

"It was a mistake."

He dropped her from his grasp, and his face turned to stone, emotionless. "Mistake?"

"We just got caught up in...I don't know. I don't do that. I don't sleep with guys I barely know."

He took a step back, crossing his arms and narrowing his gaze at her. He flicked an eyebrow up for her to continue.

"Ethan, this is my job." The word ripped through him. "There are so many things wrong with what happened tonight."

It pained him to say his next words, but she didn't realize how much agony she was causing him. "Relax, Ryan. It was just sex."

He would have done less damage if he would have punched her in the gut. It took a second for his words to truly sink in. She couldn't help but feel used. The tiny voice screamed in her head so fiercely that she knew she'd be going to bed with a headache.

Ethan Lowell. Playboy. What the hell were you thinking?

She was just another girl to him. She had been stupid enough to break down and give him what he wanted.

"I'm glad we're on the same page, because that can never happen again. I have to stay focused and keep everything–"

"If it was just meaningless sex, why would it happen again?"

"It won't. Believe it or not, I'm not like the women you're used to. I don't have a different guy in my bed every night." Her voice was sharp and near that of a scream.

"I'm actually surprised that you could get any guy in your bed." As soon as the words came out, he felt like the worst human on the planet.

Her eyes clenched with hurt and her chest rose, taking a deep breath in and holding it.

Then something occurred to him.

"Shit," he began, shaking his head. "When you said that it had been a while–"

"I know what I said," she spat.

"I thought you meant that you just hadn't had sex in *awhile*, like a month or something."

The look in her eyes said it all, and he didn't know how to feel. The last guy she had been intimate with, if you could call it that, was her ex-husband.

"Screw you, Lowell."

What could have been a perfect night concluded with the slamming of her bedroom door.

✻ ✻ ✻

Ryan pressed her back to the door and allowed tears to fall. Confliction ripped her apart and she wasn't sure what she wanted anymore.

She couldn't pursue a relationship while she was being paid to protect him, not to mention that she had seen the tabloids. Ethan Lowell didn't commit to one woman, and she was nothing compared to the women with him in those magazines.

She felt so embarrassed that he knew that he had been the first man since that horrible day with her ex. He already thought he was god's gift to women. She couldn't imagine what he must think now, probably that there wasn't a woman on the planet that he couldn't get to screw him.

* * *

Ethan couldn't sleep that night. Every time he closed his eyes and tried, all he could see was her. The only thing he wanted was for her to be with him, to feel her, hold her, fall asleep with her. No woman had ever made him feel and think the way he was doing so now.

He replayed the events of the evening over and over, and those last moments before her door slammed made him feel sick to his stomach.

* * *

Ethan was surprised at how well Ryan was able to lock herself away from reality. The next morning she went about like the night before never took place.

They went to work. He mostly pretended to work. Ryan on the other hand worked tirelessly with her computer and a manila folder that she had worn to bits now. Occasionally her phone would vibrate and she'd hurriedly respond. At first he thought it might be JD, but after the way Brett looked at her last night, he couldn't be too sure.

He didn't understand, and he couldn't bring it up, but if she had all these men in her life, men who were clearly interested in her, why didn't she pursue anything? Why had she not been intimate with a man in almost ten years? It had to be something other than just the past. The question he wanted to know more than anything, the question that had kept him awake half the night, why him?

"Zach and I have a lunch meeting later," he told her, breaking the silence.

"Okay." Ryan didn't even look up at him.

"Regardless of what he says," Ethan began, feeling uncomfortable. "I'd prefer if you not join us. If you could just hang back–"

"Understood." The clicking on her keyboard had stopped and she brought her eyes up to meet his. "The same will go for all future social gatherings. Protocol and all."

It drove Ethan crazy. Her face was filled with no emotion. Her words were dry. He tried so hard to find an underlying meaning, but she had closed herself off so severely from him.

Back to day one.

＊ ＊ ＊

Zach sipped on his scotch and glared Ethan down. "Remind me again why she's not eating with us?"

"That's not how her job works."

Job. God how he hated that word.

"Besides, I need to talk to you privately."

Zach polished off the rest of his drink quicker than he should have. "Have things been weird since the whole kiss thing?"

"Forget about the kiss." Ethan ran his hands through his messy dark hair, his signature move when he was uncomfortable or nervous. "Things are much more convoluted than just a kiss."

"Like what? Sex," Zach laughed. When Ethan didn't respond, Zach quickly read the expression on his face. "Are you fucking serious?!"

The restaurant fell silent just like before, only this time the glares of the waitresses were so irate that the two men knew they were close to being asked to leave.

Ryan's eyes shot over the rims of her dark glasses. The look said it all to Ethan. She absolutely knew what they were talking about, and no shit she wasn't happy.

"How the hell did this happen," Zach whispered, though it was more of a quiet scream.

Ethan felt his face growing warm thinking about what had happened the previous night. "It just happened."

"That's it? That's all you've got?"

"We're not a bunch of girls. I think I can leave the details out."

"Then what's the deal with you two," he asked. He used his finger to motion between Ethan and Ryan, who stood quietly against a far wall. Immediately Ethan slapped Zach's hand to the table.

"Don't do that."

"Oh, I'm pretty sure she knows what we're talking about," Zach laughed. "Be real with me, what's the problem?"

Ethan went on to tell Zach the whole story, what happened after one of the best romantic encounters of his life.

Zach ultimately cut in before Ethan was done. "You want my opinion?"

"I have a feeling you're going to tell me either way."

"You're right on that." He leaned into the table and spoke quietly. "Both of you are a little messed up. So what if she said it was a mistake? You didn't need to say what you said either."

They gradually dropped the subject of Ryan and went on to talk about other events that had happened in the days since they last spoke.

Ethan described the issue of security that he and Ryan had been informed about only moments before his meeting with Zach. Since the ball had gone off so well, priorities had shifted in the levels of security. Though Ryan wasn't amused that she was still the sole person responsible for Ethan's well-being, her eyes did brighten up when Perkins handed her the keys to what he described as the ST-5.

Ethan hadn't seen it, and while Ryan wasn't exactly big on conversation with him at the moment, she did inform him that it was one of their top of the line security transportation vehicles. There were different levels and apparently the best of the best was level five.

"So now you can go out with just her? No other guards?"

Ethan wasn't amused with the devilish look in Zach's eyes. "I guess, at least until something happens."

"What makes you think that it's not over, that

someone is still after you," Zach pressed on, changing the subject of Ryan.

"I don't know what to think anymore. A few weeks ago I could do whatever the hell I wanted whenever I wanted. Now I have another person with me at all times."

Zach snickered like a little schoolboy at the comment.

"You're such a pervert." Ethan tilted his head in Ryan's direction. "If you can't tell, she's made herself perfectly clear with all this."

A waitress arrived with a little black book and pen. Ethan noticed that it was a different one than the one delivering their food. As she sat the check down, and quietly mumbled, Ethan remembered her. It was the same woman that had given her number not too long ago. She couldn't make eye contact with him, probably from embarrassment at her forwardness before.

An idea hit Ethan.

"Hey, I remember you," he quickly began before she could walk any farther.

The woman turned, her cheeks flushing a pale pink.

He stood up, and met the woman. In his peripheral vision he could see a stoic Ryan flinch by his movement. There was no way he was going to acknowledge her.

"We've met before."

She said nothing. What do you say when you throw yourself at a hot guy and he never calls?

"This is actually a little humiliating," Ethan lied. "I was wondering if I could get your number...again?"

"What," the waitress stammered. She was shocked by his words.

"I must have lost it somewhere along the way and I–"

"Absolutely!"

He handed her his phone rather than have her write it down this time. He watched her try to suppress an overly eager smile. She wasn't bad looking. Actually, she was quite attractive. Under any other circumstances, he definitely would have given her a night of his time, but something was different now.

"You're a fucking dick," Zach hissed as soon as Ethan sat back down.

Ethan's jaw dropped in shock. Zach wasn't joking. He looked generally pissed.

"I know what you're doing, and I'm going to tell you right now, if you were lucky enough to take one step in the right direction with Ryan, you just took about twenty back."

"What are you talking about?"

Zach shook his head at the fact that Ethan was so blind at understanding women. "She's not the kind of girl where you hit on the ugly friend to make the girl you want jealous. Given, that usually leads to awesome angry sex. That's not Ryan though, and–"

"Oh, you know her so well now," Ethan interrupted.

"I'm not saying I do, but I think she's more than the girls you're used to."

"What is that supposed to mean?" Ethan asked the question, already knowing that his friend was right about one thing. He had never met someone like Ryan.

"She's serious. She knows what she's worth. She's not the type of woman that you meet at a club for just one night." He laughed as he continued on, shocked that he was giving female advice to the one guy who could get any woman out there. "Look at her line of work, man. She'd give her life protecting you. You need to show her that she's different, that she means something. Jealousy isn't the way to go. You're only going to push her away with that childish bullshit."

"You know, I don't like you since you've gotten in this relationship garbage," Ethan admitted, trying to lighten the intense impact Zach's words were having on him. "Besides, how do you know it wasn't just one night with her too?"

Zach laughed to the point that he almost choked. "I've been your friend for too long, and I have never seen you look at any woman the way you look at her. Even when you talk about her, your eyes–"

"Okay! Okay! I can't take all the girl talk."

If Zach and Leighton could tell how taken he was with Ryan, she had to know. She was so perceptive with everything. The worst realization came to him just then. Maybe she knew that he was falling for her and that's why she was pulling away; she didn't want him. Maybe it was all just a mistake to her.

It didn't help matters when as they were leaving, Sophia walked through the doors. She wrapped her arms around Ethan and squealed like a boy band had just come onto the stage.

"Wow! Ethan Lowell! Twice in twenty-four hours," she giggled.

Ethan watched as Ryan stepped away, closer to the doors. Sophia was the last person who should make Ryan jealous, but after his stunt with the waitress, this must be the icing on the cake for her.

"And Zach! I haven't seen you in forever either."

She was exceedingly excited. Both Ethan and Zach were aware that she had always been prone to self-medicate. Since her brother and mother, it could be assumed that she had started again.

"How are you doing," Ethan asked. It was the blandest and most generic thing he could say, but he had to say something.

"Really well actually. Daddy comes home soon, so I'm trying to use up all my freedom before then," she laughed.

Her father had always been very strict. He wouldn't have entertained half the things his daughter did. Despite the fact that she was an adult and had been for some time, she heavily relied on one thing. His money.

Ryan closely watched the interactions with the three. She hadn't told JD to look into Sophia yet; she didn't have enough to go on besides her overthinking. Sophia truly seemed nice enough, but the fact that her father was in Mexico didn't sit well with Ryan.

"We should all get together soon."

"Yeah, that would be great." Ethan tried not to be

rude, but he was certain that Sophia's ideas of getting together hadn't changed over the years; however, the wild party scene wasn't doing much for him recently.

"Yeah, Zach could bring Anna. I heard about the engagement. I'm dying to meet her. And Ethan," she began with a wink. "If you're still with that sexy girlfriend of yours when the time comes, you should bring her."

"I'm sure he'll screw something up," Zach laughed. He nudged Ethan and was surprised that Ethan hadn't corrected Sophia on a word he hated so much.

"Well, I better get going. I see my table is waiting for me. It was so good seeing you guys again."

Ryan tried to ignore the conversation between Ethan and Zach on the way back, but when the topic of Sophia was brought up, she couldn't help but listen in. She had hoped to find out something, anything, that would raise a flag, but there was none. All they talked about was how much she must be going through with the deaths in her family.

Upon returning to the office, Ryan made a beeline for her computer. She knew Sophia would be the type of person to be huge with social media activity.

Sophia Delacruz.

Twitter. Facebook. Instagram. YouTube.

She opened tabs for all of them. She wasn't surprised that Sophia made her profiles so publicly available.

Ryan had to admit after going as far back as a

year, she began to feel like a stalker. Sophia's Instagram page was ridiculous. She had never seen so many selfies in her life. Sometimes there were four posted within a day. Sophia's Facebook page was a little more toned down. There were lots of vacation albums and check-ins at various posh places. Ryan went through an album of friends and came across a face she recognized. It was a picture from a couple years ago, but it still made Ryan sick seeing the three girls hanging all over Ethan. She looked down at the caption. Everyone was tagged except for him. She typed his name in the search bar, but no profiles matched anything that could be for him.

Just when she was about to give up going through the posts, she found an album that triggered something in her.

Family Vacay in Mexico.

There were only twenty pictures, and no location was tagged. She could have been anywhere in Mexico. There were pictures of her mother and brother, but none of her dad. The mother was beautiful just like Sophia, though lighter in skin tone. The little boy was nothing short of adorable with his radiant smile and bright green eyes. Ryan continued scrolling.

There are people that believe in coincidences. Ryan wasn't one of those people.

The picture of a beautiful Sophia in a skimpy white sundress would grab anyone's attention, but that wasn't where Ryan was focused. It was the field of flowers beyond the gorgeous model.

Ryan slammed her computer shut and grabbed

her phone.

Rather than taking the chance of Ethan overhearing, she locked herself in the restroom across the hall.

"Hey. I'm sorry but I'm a little–"

"I need you to look into someone."

The panic in Ryan's voice forced JD to push the rest of his work aside. "What do you have?"

"Something that might be nothing."

"Ryan," he started, mildly annoyed. "Are you about to send me on a wild goose chase?"

"Last night, I met this woman. I think she's an ex-girlfriend or something. Anyway," Ryan began rambling, trying to catch JD up on everything as quickly as possible. "Her mom and brother both died in the span of a couple months, and her dad is in Mexico for business."

"I hate to tell you, but you're not making any sense."

Ryan tried to calm down, but the wheels turning in her head made conversation difficult. "I went through her social media accounts and I found a picture that makes all of this not feel right."

"I hope you're about to tell me that she was at a family picnic with Cohen or Norman?"

"Not exactly. It was a family vacation–"

"Look, Ryan," he interrupted, but she only ignored his disappointment.

"There was a field of poppies behind her!" There, she had gotten it out.

Silence ensued, but Ryan had expected that.

After a few more seconds, "I need a name."

"Sophia Delacruz."

CHAPTER 17

"What the hell is this?"

"It's one of our special transportation vehicles," Ryan answered, not understanding his shock. "It's just a revamped Chevrolet Tahoe."

"Revamped is putting it mildly. What's up with the tires?" He kicked at the front passenger tire; he had never seen anything like it. "They have holes in them?"

"Honeycomb. They're non-pneumatic, so they aren't supported by air pressure."

"Is this whole vehicle bulletproof," he asked, becoming intrigued with the black beast in front of him.

"About as close as it can be. The seats are Kevlar and the windows are bulletproof glass. It sounds nice and all, but shit can still happen. This just makes it more of an effort."

Ethan's face held an expression of childlike wonder. Ryan knew the vehicles they had were pretty awesome, but she had been around them for years.

Ethan opened the driver's door and Ryan had to fight back a laugh when he tried to get in, thinking that he would be driving.

"Thanks." She slipped between him and the open door, blocking him from completing the act. "That's very chivalrous of you."

He pressed himself against the outer part of the half opened door and leaned in toward her, pressing his right hand to the side of the cool metal, pinning her in a very tight space. Her eyes widened and he sensed that he was making her nervous.

"Let me drive." It wasn't a question, more of a demand, but one that Ryan would never go along with.

She forced a laugh; his closeness was causing her skin to heat up. "No way. This car is worth more than your little toy that got blown to bits."

"It's not worth more than my Veyron."

The smirk on his face was enough to cause Ryan to unravel. She reminded herself of his true nature. This was how he operated to get women to turn to a puddle of mush. She wouldn't do it again.

"Congratulations, Lowell. You own a Bugatti." She knew he hated being called by his last name. She remembered the first time she had done it and how he flinched. She tried to limit its use to only when she was irritated or extremely angry, but found that this time was more along the lines of playful banter. "Bragging doesn't look good on you. Also, in my experience, men that put that much money into their toys are just compensating for something that's missing in their life."

As soon as that smirk of his turned into a full on devilish grin, she knew he had a statement waiting to get out. He leaned in closer. She could smell his damn cologne. It had to have magical aphrodisiac powers to make any woman in her position want to pull him in the few inches left between them. She wasn't any woman, and as much as her body screamed at her for being such a fool to resist the pleasure she knew he could give, she did just that. Resisted.

"Tell me, *Beckett*," he teasingly hissed. "What exactly am I compensating for?"

She wasn't sure if this was a game to him at the moment, but anything that she answered with, he'd turn into something sexual.

He looked at her with such intensity. He'd have to be deaf if he couldn't hear the pounding in her chest. When his gaze flickered down to her lips and his chest rose from shaky and uneven breaths, she felt like it wasn't a game. He wanted to kiss her just as much as she wanted him to, and that was bad. The waters were already too muddy.

Ryan was stronger than temptation.

She broke through the heavy blanket of lust sweeping over them.

She swiftly rose and pulled herself into the driver's seat. "I don't have all day to argue. Get in." Before he could say anything, Ryan yanked the door from his grasp and slammed it shut.

Ethan stood in awe for a moment. He felt like someone had just dumped a bucket of icy water on him. He couldn't have totally misread that situation. Her eyes had given her away.

Ryan wasn't at all surprised when Delgado and two other agents requested a late visit with Owen Lowell. She had hoped he could have done it before she and Ethan had left for the evening, but when Ethan got the call later, Ryan didn't hesitate upon returning to the office.

Delgado sat Ethan and Owen down. He thumbed through a folder, but Ryan knew he was only doing that for effect. He was here to gauge a reaction on one particular name. He didn't call her prior; that was disconcerting. She had to wonder if he had anything yet, or if he needed to try to pull information from the two men.

"I won't take up too much of your time," Delgado began.

"Have you found who the main person behind the bombing and attempted stabbing is? Who paid those lowlifes," Owen quickly asked. He wasn't amused that it had been well over a week, nearly two, since the first attack on his son's life.

"We have some names we'd like to run by you and see if you can give us any personal information about your relationship to these people."

Again, that was a load of crap. Ryan was certain that there was only one name Delgado was after, but he was still going to make it look like he really had some information.

He did just that, mentioned several names, both male and female, and pretended to take notes.

Ryan watched the men's reactions to each name. Owen appeared annoyed that this was going to be a waste of time. Ethan genuinely tried to think on some of the names, especially the women. Ryan knew he probably didn't even know or remember the names of half the women he'd been with. She felt gross at the thought.

"Sophia Delacruz?"

Ryan was perplexed when both father and son froze at the mentioning of that particular name, and two different reactions appeared.

Ethan's sight shot straight into Ryan, daggers flying from eyes that were now full of rage. She could tell that he was thoroughly pissed at her. He knew she had suggested Sophia as a tip to the FBI.

It was hard to break contact with Ethan, but she found herself more interested in Owen. Upon the mentioning of Sophia's name, the blood drained from his face and his breathing patterns changed. Neither one had answered the question.

"Why would you mention that name," Ethan growled. His eyes still sank into Ryan.

"It's just another name on the list," Delgado replied. It was a name that they'd look into further, although so far he had little to go on. "Do either of you know her?"

Owen didn't reply, but shook his head. Ryan knew it was bullshit. There was something going on with Owen Lowell and Sophia Delacruz. Her first reaction was an affair, albeit that would have been messed up if both father and son had slept with the same woman. She had to wait, she wouldn't jump to conclusions this time.

"Yeah, she's an old friend," Ethan admitted. His voice was tense, growing angrier by the second.

"And how long ago did your *friendship* end?"

Ethan didn't like the way the question came out. "What exactly are you insinuating?"

"What I mentioned at the very beginning. Given your reputation, could Miss Delacruz be a scorned lover with motive?"

Ethan shot up from his chair like he had been hit by a bolt of lightning. "Are you fucking serious?"

His screams caused a chill to run through Ryan. She didn't know if she had ever seen him so irate. There was something else besides anger boiling over. Hurt. He was hurt.

"I don't know what delusional asshole suggested that!" It was Ryan, but he couldn't even look at her. "Look you want the truth. I told you, we were friends a long time ago, not so much now. That's not good enough, right?" He didn't give Delgado a chance to respond. "How about this agent? How about I give you another 'L' word? Lesbian."

"I'm sorry, I–"

"Sophia is lesbian. She has been ever since I've known her. So fuck no she's not a scorned lover and fuck this damn conversation."

Ethan stormed from the room, the door rattling behind him as it closed.

"You should probably follow," Owen huffed. "Knowing him he'll end up in a bar."

The vibrations of another slamming door dismissed that. Ryan thought about letting Ethan cool off, but she also knew that people could often be most honest when emotions ran high. Right now, Ethan's emotions were through the roof.

Ethan was pacing the room when Ryan walked in and softly closed the door behind her. He had taken his jacket off and rolled up the sleeves on his dress shirt. Something about him, despite the anger seeping through his skin, made him unbelievably attractive. She hated how that worked.

"What the hell, Ryan," he irritably sighed.

Ryan couldn't stand the way he was looking at her. She wished that he would bring back that furious fire to his eyes, rather than a look like she had betrayed him.

"The FBI is just looking into—"

"You suggested Sophia's name to someone didn't you? After everything she's been through." He shook his head, tearing his eyes from Ryan. "Just because you're jealous—"

"I am absolutely not jealous," Ryan scoffed, growing annoyed that he would think that's the case.

"I mean, god, if anyone should be jealous it should be me." He said the words before he thought them over.

"Look, Ethan," Ryan began, quickly changing the subject from where it could have gone. "There were a few red flags and—"

"Last time I checked, you're not a detective," he growled, shoving his finger at her.

CHAPTER 18

Ethan woke early Saturday morning. He knew he'd be at his parents' mansion a good portion of the day and by the time he would be able to finally get away, he wouldn't have enough energy for a workout.

He was chugging a glass of water when Ryan entered the kitchen to make coffee. He had already made it, knowing that was the first thing she did in the morning, even prior to going pee, which said a lot about her priorities.

"Thanks," she mumbled as she filled her mug.

He had to admit, she looked like hell, like she had tossed and turned all night, but seeing her with a knotted mess of hair, baggy pajama pants, and an oversized shirt, was just about the cutest she'd ever been. He wouldn't mind a few more mornings seeing her like that.

Once the warm liquid eased down Ryan's throat and she yawned away the sleep, she became very aware of the shirtless person standing in the kitchen.

Sweat dripped down Ethan's dark hair, rolling over his face, neck, and chest. She had to stop there. She couldn't get over his body; it was too perfect. What made matters worse was knowing that only a couple days ago she had all of that. She was losing it. This assignment needed to end. The sooner the better. She kept burying everything she thought and felt toward Ethan, but he had a way of drawing it back out.

"Are you alright," he smirked. He saw her admiring him, and that made him feel more fulfilled than any workout.

She immediately turned with her mug and started back to her room. "Yeah. Fine. Just a little groggy," she lied. He had awoken her, in more ways than one.

"Don't forget, I have to go to my parents," he reminded her.

All he heard before the closing of her door was a groan of frustration.

He didn't have high hopes for the day. Of course he was eager to see his mother and sister as well as her little ones, but his dad and Oliver were something else.

He wanted to make sure Ryan felt comfortable and more so, didn't freak the kids out, so before she could settle into her plans for the morning he knocked on her door.

"It's open," she called out from within.

She sat on the bed, legs crossed, already on her computer, the mug of coffee half empty. It killed him how perfect she looked, like she just belonged. A part of him knew it was temporary, but another part liked how it felt always having her around. He didn't want to think of an end.

"What do you want?" Her words weren't cold, just to the point.

"I have a weird request."

Her eyes tore from the computer at that point, unsure the direction of the conversation. With Ethan, there was no telling.

"My sister has two young kids, and…" He thought for a minute.

"Kids, got it. Kids love me."

He couldn't suppress the laugh.

"They do." Her voice was elevated and insistent. "Kids are easy. Adults, not so much."

"Well, what I was going to ask is if you could tone it down a little for them," he hesitated.

"What does that mean?"

He motioned to one of her suits she had draped across a chair.

"Oh, you mean dress like I'm not working?"

"Something like that."

"I'll still need to carry a gun," she pointed out.

That didn't bother Ethan. Most of the time he never even knew she had one on her. He just didn't want his niece and nephew asking about the broody woman in the *Men in Black* getup.

* * *

A small girl ran to the door as soon as it opened. "Uncle Ethan! Uncle Ethan!" She couldn't have been more than five, and as adorable as could be in a little pink dress with yellow flowers and her hair pulled back in a messy braid.

"Mia," Ethan yelled, grabbing the girl, and tossing

her into his chest.

She wrapped her arms tightly around his neck and buried her face into his shirt. Looking up with eyes of adoration she whispered how much she missed him.

Ryan turned to a puddle of mush at the connection between the two. Never in her wildest dreams could she ever picture Ethan being a family man, and maybe he wasn't, but the way that child looked at him and the way he looked at her said something immensely different.

Trailing behind the energetic Mia was an older boy. He had to be somewhere between eight and ten.

Ethan shifted Mia to his side, propping her up with just one arm while she clung to him like a little monkey.

"Hey, Danny. Wow, you've gotten big," Ethan greeted.

The kid held a skeptical look on his face and tucked his hands into his front pockets, acting as though he were years beyond his real age.

"Mom told me you were bringing a hot chick," he casually said, getting to the point.

"Damnit, Danny," a voice screamed from far away. "I did not fucking say that!"

"Watch your mouth," a man hissed, though everyone could hear him. Oliver.

"I'm just messing with you," Danny said, looking down and shuffling his foot around. "Mom didn't say that, but I did notice."

"Yeah, umm," Ethan fumbled for words. "Well, this

is…This is–"

"It's cool. I know. Dad already told me that you have a girl that beats up bullies for you," he said with a shrug.

Just like that, Ryan could feel the walls come crashing down for Ethan. Obviously he had been an idol in their minds, and while the little girl probably didn't understand, or hadn't been told, in the boy's eyes it looked like Superman had been stripped to nothing more than a powerless and normal human.

"Anyway," Ethan went on. "Mia, Danny, this is my friend, Ryan."

Mia giggled shyly and pressed her face into her uncle's chest. Danny eyed Ryan suspiciously. He was definitely his father's son.

"Ryan?"

"Yes."

"That's a boy's name," he laughed.

Okay, so Ryan got along with *most* kids.

"Actually," she began. *Choose your words wisely. He's just a kid.* "It can be unisex," she told him, albeit through gritted teeth.

Danny doubled over in laughter. "Does that mean you can be a boy and a girl?"

Her lips were pursed and her eyes widened as she flung her attention to Ethan. He raised an eyebrow and shook his head. The kid was turning into a brat, just like his dad, and he knew it.

Eventually adults came to the rescue in the forms of Gwen and Leighton.

"Ryan," Gwen squealed. "We're so glad you could

make it."

Ryan refrained from pointing out the obvious, that she didn't have a choice. She watched as Leighton pulled Ethan away. His sister looked nervous and concerned, but she couldn't make out the conversation.

"Shit, Ethan. I'm so sorry."

"What's going on?"

"Mom and I talked about all of us getting together while my family was in the states, but we tried to keep dad out of it," Leighton began.

Ethan didn't know why his sister was rambling, but he could smell lunch, obviously catered from an amazing restaurant, and his workout and slim breakfast was taking its toll.

"It's fine," he insisted. "I can deal with him, and that wonderful husband of yours." He didn't even try to hide the sarcasm. Leighton was aware at how much he detested Oliver; he'd never like him.

"No, it's not that. Dad–"

"Everyone is ready," a voice rang out from the dining area.

The four of them made their way farther into the mansion. Ryan wanted to stop and admire the architecture and paintings, but she felt like an invisible cattle prod pushed her on.

"Fuck," Ethan whispered as he rounded the corner before Ryan.

Congressman Daniels. And Ella.

"Ethan," Owen shouted, holding up a tumbler of bourbon, or scotch, whatever, Ryan couldn't tell.

A woman and man in black pants and white shirts were bringing out plates of food. Ryan speculated that it had been catered from a local restaurant, and rather than Owen Lowell actually making his own plate in front of such esteemed guests, he hired people to do it for him.

As everyone but Ethan gathered in their seats, Ryan noticed one thing. There was only one space left, next to Ella Daniels. She showed no emotion, she had grown accustomed to bottling everything in, but damn if it didn't hurt.

"Wait," Leighton spoke up. "We need to make a space for Ryan.

"No, that's quite alright," Ryan began before Owen could interrupt. She had told Ethan prior to this that she needed to follow protocol. Eating with them wouldn't be right; that's what she continued to tell herself.

"Sweetheart." Ryan saw Leighton cringe at the term of endearment. "That's not appropriate," Owen said as he shook his head and took another sip of the amber liquid.

"I'll share my seat," Mia piped up. She scooted over in her chair making barely enough room for a friend equal to her own size.

Ryan had to get out of there. She'd never belong in a world like this, but the way Owen Lowell pointed it out made her want to vomit.

"Thank you, I might take you up on that," Ryan lied, speaking only to the girl. If she could have told Owen to fuck off, she would have. "I just need to look around a bit."

"You're not eating with us," Danny exclaimed. Ryan was surprised. She thought the kid hated her.

"Sorry," was all she could manage as she slipped from the room.

"Son, we don't eat with people we hire to work for us," Oliver laughed.

"No offense, dad. This isn't *Downton Abbey*. She might have a boy-girl name, but she's cool. She can beat up guys Uncle Ethan can't." Danny stuck his tongue out after finishing.

Ethan wanted nothing more than to high-five his nephew, even though it was a little insulting to him.

Ryan fought back tears as she walked the premises. She didn't like all the glass doors and windows. Even as she made her way across the grounds of the massive backyard and pool, she could see the movement of the elites eating their lunch that they couldn't even bother to make for themselves. The entire dining room was encased in glass. Ridiculous.

She finally brought herself back to reality. The reality was, she felt something for Ethan. Since she arrived, she was also painfully aware as to where her place was.

Going back inside would be difficult, but she couldn't walk around outside forever, not to mention that they could see her from all the freaking glass.

She hovered in a nearby corner, her eyes firmly planted on the ground.

"That's wonderful," Owen exclaimed.

"Since I heard your daughter was home for a bit, I

was able to arrange for eight tickets to the symphony," Congressman Daniels told him proudly. His wife was rarely present at most things, but he did indeed have one.

Leighton wasn't having any of it. She had suffered under her father's wishes and she wasn't about to allow her little brother to as well. Just as she was about to speak up, Ethan found his voice and she couldn't have been prouder.

"Actually, that's this coming Tuesday, right?"

"It is," Daniels confirmed.

"I'm so sorry. I think I'll be out of town," Ethan lied.

"Doing what?" The tone in Owen's voice came through loud and clear. He wasn't happy with his son rejecting a possible date with a congressman's daughter.

"Working on an investment," Ethan concluded. He still hadn't let his father know how close he was to closing a property in Canada, and he wouldn't. He wanted something to be his own creation for the business, without his father's guidance; however, he was lying about the fact that he had to work or even leave the area that particular evening.

"That's a shame," Ella cooed. "I was really hoping you'd be able to attend."

Ryan had to force herself to look away as the pretty blonde rubbed her hands along Ethan's arm. Judging from his demeanor, it looked unwanted, but Ryan never knew with Ethan.

"We'll talk about it later," Owen said, staring

Ethan down. "I'm sure something can be arranged."

Ethan let it go at the time, but there was no way he was going to that symphony with Ella Daniels.

The meal went by the best it could. Ryan remained bored out of her mind, while Ethan and Leighton spoke very little. Owen, Oliver, and Daniels did most of the talking while Gwen made little people talk with Mia.

Relief washed over Ethan when Congressman Daniels and Ella announced that they'd be departing. He had planned on attempting to enjoy time with his family.

"Ethan," Leighton began as she shooed the kids through one of the glass doors to the pool and lawn. "Mom and I are going to sit outside while the kids play. Care to join us?"

"Of course."

"Sounds like a good idea," Owen chimed in.

Rather than just his mother and sister, everyone moved outside.

Ryan lingered by the pool, giving the family some space for personal talk. Leighton eyed her suspiciously, a devilish, yet playful glimmer in her eye. Though she and Ethan were very different, they were all too similar as well. Ryan cringed when Leighton took another sip of her wine and called out to her.

"Ryan, won't you join us?" Before her father could protest, "You've been on your feet all day. I'm sure you're entitled to a break at some point."

Reluctantly, Ryan made her way to the area filled with exquisite patio furniture. It was nothing like what she had growing up. Her family used the plastic folding chairs, the ones that were falling apart by the end of summer from the melting heat.

Leighton quickly moved over so that the only open spot was near Ethan and Ryan's heart stopped. She could read Leighton's look clear as day.

She knew.

Ethan tried not to stare as Ryan came closer toward them; he had succeeded most of the day in pretending she wasn't there, but now he was able to really look at her, and he wished they were anywhere but with his family.

She had dressed comfortable, as comfortable as it got for her. She had a light pair of skinny jeans, slightly torn at one knee, stuffed into black combat boots. He had seen that look before. Her oversized white t-shirt was tucked slightly into the front of her jeans, draping perfectly across her arms and chest. Her hair drove him crazy. She didn't straighten it, only pulled the waves partly back with a little clip so that some still hung wildly around her neck.

He broke his trance as soon as she sat down next to him. His father was going to need a better reason than work for him to decline a date with Ella, and he didn't want to give any indication that Ryan was that reason.

"Would you like a drink," Leighton asked.

Before Ryan could respond, Ethan grabbed a bottle of water from the bucket of ice near him and handed it to her.

"I'm sure she wants something more than water,"

Gwen coughed.

"Actually, I prefer not to drink while I'm working, but thank you."

"Your job is very demanding isn't it," Leighton continued.

Ryan liked Leighton, but she knew that she was being set up for something. "I suppose." She wasn't going to give more detail than needed.

"Do you have a significant other?"

Ryan picked a wrong time to take a sip of water. She composed herself quickly from the way it went down; however, Owen and Oliver had stopped their conversation and brought their attention over.

"I'm sorry, what?" Ryan pretended not to understand, still not sure where Leighton was going with this.

"Boyfriend?"

There was no need to elaborate or explain herself. That would only give Leighton more to go on. It was simple. One word. The truth. "No."

Ethan knew that was the answer, despite JD and Brett.

"Stop asking inappropriate questions," Oliver scolded Leighton.

"I don't mind," Ryan cut in. She didn't like the way Oliver talked to Leighton, or anyone really.

Owen pulled up a chair near them. "Speaking of significant others."

"Dear, now is not the time. Let it go," Gwen whispered.

Owen completely ignored her and carried on. His

eyes were serious and showed that he was displeased with his son.

"Why did you turn down the symphony with Ella?"

"I didn't turn just her down. I turned down going with all of you."

Ryan bit her bottom lip to keep from smiling. She couldn't believe that Ethan didn't mind riling his father up like that.

"So you'll go on a date with her, alone?"

"No," Ethan scoffed. It was like his father was asking him to take the ugly smelly girl to prom, and Ella was anything but.

"Why the hell not? She's perfect for you." Owen slammed his fist on one of the side tables and a glass of wine shook enough to tip over, but didn't.

Ethan's eyes fell to the ground and he shook his head. Nothing was ever enough for his father; it always had to be his way.

Leighton knew she was overstepping, but the wine had given her an unexpected confidence. "He's seeing someone, dad."

Silence.

Ethan's eyes grew twice their size when he allowed his sister's words to fully sink in.

What the hell?

The intensity was broken by the obnoxious laughter of Oliver. "That's hilarious," he shrieked. "Since when did Ethan ever have a girl for more than a night?"

Ethan could have punched him; he wanted to so badly. He was sick and tired of Oliver and his father constantly throwing his reputation in his face. Then he realized something. His sister had just done him the biggest favor in his life. Their eyes met, and she knew it too.

As casually as he could, "She's right."

"What," Gwen screeched, ecstatic with the statement. "That's wonderful! What's her name? How long have you been together? When can we meet–"

"Whatever," Oliver cut her off. "If you have a girlfriend, why didn't she come to the gala the other night?"

Ethan had to think quickly. That was a good question.

Owen's finger darted between Leighton and Ethan. "Did the two of you concoct this? All so you could get out of a symphony?"

"No. I really am seeing someone, and it's serious." Ethan couldn't believe he was actually saying those words, even if they were lies, they felt good. He felt relieved.

"Then why wasn't she with you the other night," Oliver pressed on.

"Not that it's anyone's business, but there were several reasons. One, the relationship is new and we didn't want it all over the tabloids–"

"Oh, so she's famous? God, Ethan, not another model," Owen derided.

Ethan ignored the comment. "Two, as long as all this is going on, I didn't want to drag her into it. Three, *Oliver*, I didn't want her to have to put up with your shit. Four, would you like me to go on?" It felt good finally getting just a little jab in with Oliver.

"Ethan," Gwen reprimanded, shaking her head.

Ryan could tell that Gwen and Leighton didn't do well with confrontation and arguing.

At first she thought the same thing that Owen did, that Leighton was helping her brother out of a sticky situation. Now she had to wonder. She had only known Ethan for around two weeks. She didn't know who he texted and it was none of her business. If he was dating a model, she could be out of the country on a shoot. What made the most sense of all was that he didn't want to drag another person into the madness surrounding him right now.

Shit. He has a girlfriend.

"If it's that new, and she's the usual type, I'm sure it will be over before it starts," Owen told Ethan. He flipped his wrist, dismissing the idea.

Ethan wasn't going to let him have the last word. "It's more than that."

"What's that supposed to mean?"

"It means I'm in love with her and I have no intention of things ending." Saying those words made him feel lightheaded. Even though the whole girlfriend thing was garbage, the words he just said couldn't have been more true, and he never thought they'd come from his own lips.

Aside from a gasp by Gwen, no one said anything. Eyes were wide and jaws hung. None of Ethan's family ever expected for him to say something like that.

Ryan's insides turned to knots. If she would have

eaten lunch with them, she'd be throwing it up right about now. All of this was new to her. Reading people was always easy. She thought she had Ethan pinned as well. A girlfriend was one thing, but how could he say what he just said, knowing that he had cheated on that very person he said those words about. Ryan hid her emotions well, but right now she would have given anything to punch Ethan Lowell straight into the pool.

Leighton composed herself from the blow her brother had just delivered faster than the rest of the family, and in what Ryan presumed was her typical style, she dove all in as well.

"Since we're sharing so much, I will not be outdone little brother," Leighton began, her lips pursed, fighting back a smile, though her words were no laughing matter. "We're getting a divorce."

Another gasp came from Gwen.

"Damnit, Leigh! We were going to wait," Oliver spat at her, angry that she just announced it like it was nothing.

"Finally," Ethan huffed.

"What the hell is going on with this family," Owen roared. "You're not going to continue dating some bimbo tart," he began, pointing at Ethan. "And you two are not getting divorced. Work through whatever phase is going on."

Too much anger was boiling up. Ryan watched a vein in Ethan's neck flicker as he clenched his fists. His father's description of this newfound girlfriend triggered something possessive in him. It was attractive as hell, but she had to put that thought away, forever.

The situation, the family, all of it was chaotic madness. All she wanted was out. Another job, another place. Anywhere but with Ethan Lowell and this messed up family.

Then the unexpected happened. The wine glass had just been sitting there. No one touched the table and it simply shattered, bits flying everywhere.

CHAPTER 19

Before anyone was able to process what had just happened, to their shock, Ryan's Glock was already drawn.

"Get inside, now!"

"Oh my god, the kids," Leighton screamed.

"I'll get them," Ryan quickly responded, noting that the kids were several yards away on the lawn. They had no idea what was happening, but Mia was already bursting into tears. "Everyone just get inside!"

Shooting at what she couldn't see was pointless, but Ryan fired off several warning shots at where she estimated the bullets had come from. She wasn't confident, knowing there were multiple shooters.

Danny was running toward her, dragging the wailing girl with him. As soon as she scooped Mia into her arms, she felt her being torn away.

"What the hell are you doing?! What part of get the fuck inside do you not understand?!"

"I've got them," Ethan insisted. "Just help us get out of here."

Another bullet tore past them.

"Try not to run in a straight line," Ryan quickly spat out. It wasn't the best advice she could give, but now wasn't the time for a PowerPoint presentation on what to do.

Seconds became too much passing time without knowing where the threat was. She stayed close behind Ethan, firing rounds into what was nothing more than darkness in the trees. The only thing saving them now was the fact that their shooters weren't bothering with aiming.

Then, once they were feet from the glass doors which would soon shatter, Ryan saw it. She had only turned for a moment and it was the faintest movement behind a tree, but it caught her attention.

They were safe. Ethan and the kids had made it inside.

Ryan ducked behind one of the pillars near the pool. It was just enough to conceal her, depending on where the other shooters were.

"Ryan!" Ethan was at the doors calling for her.

"Get away from the glass! Get inside!"

As soon as she had gotten the words out, one of the full length panels of glass shattered, spraying throughout the dining area.

"Ethan, I'm begging you." She needed him away. She needed to focus. More than anything, she needed him safe.

The look in her eyes said it all, and even though it was the last thing he wanted to do, he retreated inside to his family. He was unarmed and a target. If she wouldn't come with him, there was nothing he could do.

Bullets rained down, but intermittently. Either

they didn't have much ammo or they were using guns that required a lot of reloading. She couldn't recall how many shots she had fired. She couldn't have more than five left, and she only had one spare magazine, making it a total of twenty.

She could see one of the shooters stepping from behind a tree now. As much as she wanted one of them alive for questioning, she wasn't taking any chances. She was an excellent marksman, so three shots to the chest was overkill for her. When he collapsed she couldn't help but allow the tiniest sigh of relief to escape.

She flung herself towards the opening, knowing that as soon as she moved bullets would be all over her, and she was right. Two more panels of glass shattered. She could feel the shards landing in her hair.

The entire family was waiting near the front door, unsure what to do next.

"Do you have a cellar? Basement?" Ryan's words were fast and demanding.

"No," Owen answered.

"Fuck," she hissed. "The vehicle is too far. I can't take that chance."

"Just tell us what to do," Oliver insisted. He was annoyed, but that didn't mask his panic.

Thankfully the alarms had been triggered and in the distance Ryan heard Leighton on the phone with 911. She just didn't know how soon help would arrive. "I have to get back out there. There's more than one."

She briefly met Ethan's protesting expression, but she knew what she had to do.

"I need all of you upstairs, the farthest room from any point of entry and stay away from windows."

Though she still had two rounds left, she put in a new magazine. The last thing she needed was to reload in a shootout.

"You heard her," Gwen chimed in. "Kids, everyone, come," she yelled with a shaky voice on the verge of tears.

Ryan hated to kill time in tense situations. Every second counted. She watched as they ran up the stairs, disappearing to the left. Ethan was the only one who stayed.

He grabbed both her hands in his, the coolness of the gun in her right making him flinch.

"You need to go," Ryan growled.

"Law enforcement will be here soon, please don't go out there," he pleaded. He knew his words meant nothing to her. "You're going aren't you?"

"I have to."

His insides shattered. He didn't want her to leave him. It had nothing to do with her protecting him and everything to do with the simple fact that he wanted her with him, safe.

She pulled from him and swiftly made her way to the front door.

Ryan had no proof as to what she'd meet upon opening the door, but she went on a gut feeling that any danger was coming from the backyard. She didn't dare take her chances going out the back way with all the glass and openness.

She kept close to the walls of the mansion, but she knew she had to move fast. Whoever was out there would be making their way through the shattered back entry soon, and find the entire Lowell family upstairs, unprotected.

Ryan hid low on the ground, concealing herself with the massive red tip photinia that led into the backyard along the house. Already halfway between the heavily wooded trees beyond the lawn and the swimming pool, stalked a man in black. Ryan saw a gun in either hand. They were nothing serious, but he had the ability to fire more shots than she did.

Something seemed off. Just as she was about to fire, which would give her hiding spot away, she noticed him glance over his shoulder, and she stopped herself.

Someone was guarding him. That was the only explanation as to why he was so casually drifting about in the wide open. She scanned over the premises and her heart sank when she found another attacker and in his hands a much larger gun than expected. She didn't think it was an assault rifle, but she couldn't tell from where he was standing. In that moment she was thankful that they didn't have more powerful weapons.

If she were to shoot at the man on the lawn, she didn't know if she'd have enough time to get a clean hit on the one that was partially hidden. She needed him out first. It killed her to let the man on the lawn continue toward the house.

Ryan zeroed in on the assailant in the trees. All she had was a barrel and a glimpse of his arm. She needed him to come out of hiding; at this point all she'd be able to do would be to scrape some skin. She had to take a chance.

She'd have about two seconds after a wasted shot to take him down for good. Her heart pounded as her finger began to squeeze the trigger.

Just like that, the bark of the tree from where he was standing blasted behind him. When he turned, assuming the shot came from behind, he took one fateful step too many and Ryan got a good shot at half of his body. Not taking any gambles, she aimed for his neck.

He screamed in agony and dropped the gun, stumbling forward. Ryan wasn't sure how clean the shot was, so she made a final one, toward his head, and looked away as soon as the trigger pulled back. Then, there was silence.

Ryan knew there was no one else aside from the man that was already in the mansion, if there had been, she would have been fired at by now.

Hastily, she moved, but she was sure to keep herself guarded in the process. It wasn't until she reached the broken glass of the remains of the dining room and entrance to the backyard that she became extra cautious, hiding behind one of the pillars near the pool and now peering inside.

The gunman had been just as careful, not yet reaching the staircase. Now that she saw him, she could see that he looked nervous and unsure. Something told her not to go for a kill with this one.

His right foot barely hit the bottom step when he felt like his left arm had been torn off his body. Throbbing sensations ran through the arm and he lost feeling in that hand, allowing one of his guns to slip to the floor.

He grabbed at the spot that caused the most grief and felt the warm liquid spread into his right hand that still gripped the other weapon. It was a pain he had never felt before and the blood that continued to flow only made the dizziness that much greater. He turned, prepared to meet his fate.

"Put the gun down and I won't kill you," a feminine voice came from outside.

A girl. He was going to die because of a girl.

Ryan stepped from hiding, her gun raised and targeted directly to his center.

He didn't raise his gun to her, merely held it down at his side. Blood saturated his right hand after reaching up to find the wound on his left so much that the gun was too slippery to even attempt to fire a decent shot.

Ryan continued to move slowly toward him, now entering the house, the broken glass crunching under her boots with each step. Though he didn't drop the gun, Ryan felt him to be of little threat. The fear in his face said as much.

"Get it over with," he said in a shaky breath that left Ryan in shock.

"I'm not going to kill you. You just have to cooperate."

He pulled his gun up and just as Ryan was about to fire into his chest she stopped herself. Her eyes widened, realizing where he held the gun. His right temple.

"If you don't, I will," he screamed in agony.

He was crazy. Absolutely crazy.

"Whoa, whoa," Ryan began. It was a situation she had never dealt with before. "Just calm down, everything will be fine." Her words sounded stupid even to her.

"I'm dead either way."

"What's that supposed to mean?"

"If I don't complete my job, I'm dead," he cried out.

This was something she could work with. She had to cool him down, get as much information as possible.

"Look, you haven't killed anyone yet–"

"I don't care about jail," he interrupted her. "Jail would be better than pissing him off."

"Who," Ryan immediately asked, but the man only shook his head and pressed the gun harder to his skull. "Who," Ryan demanded. Her tone was cutting, causing the man to shake in fear. "Tell me," she begged.

Tears rolled down the man's face. He was screwed up. It was more than just fear.

"Damnit, who sent you? Sophia Delacruz?"

He jumped a bit when she said the name. Ryan knew that he knew her, but he only shook his head.

She had tried to rule Sophia out of the picture since the argument with Ethan, but there was something nagging her that wouldn't allow it.

"Did Sophia Delacruz have anything to do with this," Ryan asked, mentioning the full name once again.

"She would never!"

"You know her. How?" She fought to hold back her anger, but it spewed through with each word.

She continued to step closer, hoping the irrational person before her wouldn't notice. If she could get close enough and wrestle the gun from him, law enforcement would have someone in custody to interrogate.

"Her…" he began, his hands now shaking. "Her father," he concluded, causing Ryan to freeze in place only a couple yards from him.

Don't.

She didn't have the chance to stop him. Before she could say another word, try to convince him not to, the shot rang out and his body fell to the floor.

No!

She rushed to him, hoping that it was another screwed up shot like the many he and his accomplices had fired since all hell broke loose, but for once he had it perfect. It was instant.

The knees of her jeans had picked up some of his blood in her attempt to see if there was any life left in him. She rubbed her hands, now moist with his blood onto her white shirt, cursing herself that he managed to get one more pull of the trigger.

Then, she ripped her phone from her back pocket.

"We have a huge problem," she said once JD picked up.

"I'm on my way, but local law enforcement will probably beat us," he said coolly. "Is everything okay?"

"Fuck no, everything is not okay," Ryan screamed.

"Whoa, calm down. All I know is there was a break-in at the Lowell estate."

"A break-in? A break-in," she repeated. "Do you call three dead bodies a *break-in*?!"

Silence, and then, "Shit. Damn, Ryan, is everyone okay?"

"The family, I believe so."

"And you," he sighed.

She didn't know how to answer. It hadn't sunk in yet. Adrenaline still spiraled and surged in her veins, not allowing her to think, only allowing her to continue on.

CHAPTER 20

Ryan placed her gun on the entry table and sank into a nearby chair. There was a moment when she thought about checking on the Lowell family, telling them that it was safe again, but she decided to catch her breath first.

She didn't bother investigating any of the bodies. It would just be more names added to a growing list.

Light thumps told her that the people upstairs had come out of hiding. Upon lifting her head, the first person she saw at the top of the stairs looking straight into her soul, was Ethan. For a brief second, his eyes darted to the deceased at the base of the staircase, then back to her.

She wasn't sure what she expected, but when Danny tore past Ethan, bolting down the stairs and past the body like it didn't exist, Ryan's reflexes kicked in and, though lacking in energy, she quickly stood. His small body crashed into hers and dampness from his face soaked into her shirt. She wanted to push him away; the blood on her shirt had dried, but her jeans were still saturated at her knees.

"Thank you," he whispered. "You saved us."

Ryan forced herself to ignore the words; they were too full of emotion, and she wasn't good with emotion.

Eventually Danny slowly pulled away and turned with Ryan to face the rest of the family descending down the stairs.

The women cringed and clenched up as they stepped by the dead body. Oliver was packing Mia and tried to shield her eyes from the grotesque scene, but she had already seen it. It would be something that would bring nightmares in her future slumber.

Though Danny's reaction shocked her, he was a child, and had just gone through a traumatic experience. Ethan, on the other hand, should have known better.

He never took his eyes from her until she was in his arms. He tightened his grip and breathed her in. She was real, and alive.

Ryan was livid by his actions and immediately broke from the embrace. The confused look on Ethan's face told her that he hadn't thought of the consequences to his actions.

"What are you doing," she hissed. Her eyes were wide and enraged.

He glanced over her body, noting the blotches of blood on her clothing, but he could tell it wasn't hers. "I just wanted to make sure you were okay."

"I'm fine. Don't do that shit in front of your family."

If anyone had noticed, other than Danny, they gave little indication. They were still taking it all in, the busted glass, the dead body, the growing puddle of blood.

Ethan raked his fingers down Ryan's bare arm. It was a small gesture, but he needed to feel her. If his family had not been there, he'd have his lips all over her.

Everyone's thoughts were broken with the wailing of sirens growing louder by the second. While they all rushed to the front door, Ryan sank back in her chair. Ethan remained by her side. He tried once more, placing a hand on her shoulder, but her only reaction was to shake him away.

* * *

A slew of law enforcement tore through the home in all directions. Ryan kept to the side as the Lowell family allowed the hysteria to set in.

"Ryan Beckett."

The voice alone told her not to look up. This wouldn't be like the last time. She wasn't going to have a temper tantrum with Trevor Parker. She'd answer his questions and wait for JD, who would arrive soon. There were bigger things going on than a battle of words with Parker.

"Care to tell your side, since he's obviously not talking?" He motioned to the dead body behind him.

"There are two more out back."

She could tell that he wasn't expecting that, what with his bulging eyes and gaping mouth.

"Are they dead," he managed to ask.

"If they weren't, we wouldn't be here." Her words were dry and emotionless.

Instantly his attention flew from her and he began barking orders. Half a dozen people rushed through the crushed glass toward the edge of the lawn.

Every time she blinked she thought of each hit they had absorbed by her. Three to the chest. One in the neck. One in the head. One in the arm.

The last one troubled her. He didn't have to die. She didn't plan on killing him. Her thoughts drifted in a million different directions, but before she could process any further, the front door swung open and another group of men crashed through the chaotic mayhem.

Ethan continued to give a statement, but paused when he saw Ryan dart toward a man at the door. Delgado.

She grabbed his arm and pulled him out the door, out of sight. Ethan rushed through his words. Something was going on between them. He had been skeptical of their banter in his father's office that one day. There had definitely been a connection and he tried to ignore it, but he couldn't now.

* * *

"Where are we going," JD growled, disliking the idea that his men would know more than he did by the time they returned.

"I have to talk to you privately," Ryan whispered.

They moved quickly toward his car and didn't speak another word until they were in its confines.

"Care to tell me what's going on?"

"My head is a mess right now," Ryan admitted. She raked her fingers through her hair, and realized that somewhere along the way her clip had fallen out.

"That's obvious. You just killed three intruders."

"Two," she sighed.

"I thought you said–"

"The last one committed suicide."

JD was stunned. That was one of the last things he had expected.

"You might want to get out your notebook," Ryan told him. It was hard to smile, but she halfway attempted.

With hands slightly trembling, mostly from the two pots of coffee he consumed throughout the day, he did as she said.

"I'm going to skip to the end," she began, to which he nodded. "The man at the stairs, I tried to talk to him, to reason with him, but if he was going to fail his assignment, which he knew he was, he'd rather die. You should have seen him, completely terrified of not carrying out what his boss had instructed. I mentioned Sophia's name and–"

"Yeah, about that," JD sighed. Ryan had been a great deal of help over the years, generally she had a way of reading into things that he couldn't see. It hurt him to tell her that she wasn't even in the right ballpark with this one. "I think we need to look into something–"

She interrupted him, her words sucking the oxygen from the car. "It's her father."

"What?!"

"That's not all."

"Sophia Delacruz? Her dad wants Ethan Lowell

dead? How do you know?" His words were fast and racing.

"That man told me before he killed himself."

"Ryan this isn't making any sense..." His words trailed off.

"He had track marks, just like Cohen and Norman. I think Delacruz is part of a cartel and bringing in heroin." It was a blunt and speculating statement. "There. See what you can work with."

"Jesus, Ryan," JD gasped, still trying to process the fact that he had three dead bodies. Now his friend had just given him the tip of a lifetime. "I don't get it. I thought you said there was no way Ethan would be caught up in that sort of stuff."

"You're right," Ryan groaned. She rubbed her thumbnail across the bottom of her lip, the gears in her head turning at full capacity.

"And I'm guessing the idea that Ethan broke the heart of Delacruz's baby girl isn't an option to go on," JD ventured.

"There was something that struck me. I made note of it at the time. When you mentioned Sophia's name to them, did you–"

As though he could read her mind, JD interrupted Ryan. "Old man Lowell's reaction."

Their eyes met, and an imaginary lightbulb ignited.

"Okay," JD breathed heavily. "I'm going to look into Delacruz's business. If he's involved with a cartel and trafficking drugs into the country, chances are there's money laundering through his business."

"Great, so you take a drug dealer off the streets…"

"I just don't get how any of this ties back to Owen or Ethan Lowell. I'll do some digging, just try to be safe in the meantime."

Ryan huffed at the absurd comment, noting that they had just been targets at the family home. Not out in public. At the family home.

JD noticed Ethan watching them from the distance, while Ryan stared down at her feet, still deep in thought.

"Someone's looking for you," JD cooed.

Ryan jerked her head up, and made out the figure of Ethan, arms crossed, glaring from the mansion's entrance.

"Don't worry, I'm good with keeping secrets," JD laughed.

"What the hell is that supposed to mean." Her words were defensive, which only caused JD to laugh more.

"Hey, your personal business is just that."

"Oh my god," she squawked. "You have no idea how wrong you are."

"I've known you since you were a kid. I can tell when you're lying."

She knew he could. She also knew that this was now at least the third person to see some connection between them.

"You have a different energy since you've taken this job," he continued.

"It's not supposed to be like this."

"Ryan, the fact that we talk as much as we do, and

235

the things that I've told you, I could be fired tomorrow. Sometimes rules are broken, but shit works out."

Rules had been broken, but this was something that wouldn't work out. Ryan remembered the conversations before the shattered wine glass. She meant nothing to Ethan. He had a girlfriend that he claimed he was in love with. All she had been was a distraction for one night.

CHAPTER 21

"Can we talk," Ethan asked once again while Ryan bolted the door.

He had asked the question every few minutes during the drive back to his penthouse and she always had an excuse to dismiss any thought of a conversation.

"No offense, but look at me," she snapped.

That was part of the problem. He was looking at her.

"I'd like to put on clothes that aren't covered in blood and clean up a little."

Ethan nodded and stepped aside for her to go by. As she did, he grabbed her arm and pulled her in, allowing his body to melt into hers.

"I'm so thankful that you're safe," he breathed into her ear.

She wanted to give back everything that he put in the embrace, instead she pulled away.

This time Ethan saw something else in her face, in her eyes. At the mansion he knew they couldn't show any emotional connection in front of his family, and he had a momentary lapse in judgement when he finally saw her. Now they were alone, and she still held back.

Her face wasn't angry this time. She looked hurt, near tears. It tore him to pieces not knowing why. As if she could read his mind, Ryan shook her head for him not to continue and she went toward her bedroom. A minute later she came out with a change of clothes and disappeared into the guest bathroom.

Ethan couldn't have been more frustrated. He knew there was a storm of emotion rolling through her. He simply wished that if any of it was caused by him, she'd tell him as much.

He wanted everything on the table. She wasn't going to push anything away anymore. She wasn't going to run from him, not today.

"What the fuck, Ethan," Ryan screamed when she opened the bathroom door and found Ethan waiting outside.

"We need to talk, now." It wasn't a question. His demand was sharp and dominating. She'd be lying if she tried to convince herself that it wasn't a little attractive.

He clasped her hand in his and began to lead her toward the living room. It wasn't necessary and she was tempted to fight it, just as she had his embraces, but for just one more second she liked having his touch all to herself.

"Sit," he told her, motioning toward the couch.

Ryan glanced over at the accent chair that she had sat in that night she told him about her past, when she purposely distanced herself from him. He raised a brow and crossed his arms once she looked back at him. His thoughts were loud and clear. *No.*

She took a place on the fluffy couch and allowed herself to sink into its softness. It felt comfortable enough to fall asleep on, but the tension in the room wouldn't allow it.

Just as she had expected, Ethan sat right next to her, his left leg slightly crossed under his right, his body turned facing her.

"I figured it out," he remarked.

Ryan's eyes widened. That wasn't what she expected, and she wasn't sure how to respond. Rather than incriminate herself, she allowed him to continue on. His jitteriness told her he had a lot to get off his chest.

"Delgado. Jonah Delgado. JD."

Shit.

Ryan knew that JD could be heavily reprimanded for some of the stuff they discussed. They talked about a lot of private information on cases that she wasn't supposed to have any knowledge of.

"Ethan, you can't tell anyone, if you do he could lose–"

"His wife and his family? God, he's like fifteen years older than you, with a little kid. I never thought–"

She held her hand up, inches from Ethan's face. Her lips were tightly clenched together and her brows were furrowed enough to cause a headache.

"What the hell are you talking about?"

"You didn't know he was married," Ethan continued, shocked that Ryan could ignore the giant piece of gold on his left hand.

Ryan reached for the throw pillow behind her back and smashed it across Ethan's head.

"You're an idiot!"

"What the hell was that for," he screamed back, grabbing his head, although all the pillow had done was ruin his perfect intentionally messy hair.

"Yes, I know he's married! His kid thinks I'm one of her aunts," Ryan spat. Confusion spread over Ethan's face. "His father and my father were in the Navy together. Our families are friends. The only thing at risk is his job. I've been helping him with cases when I'm bored out of my fucking mind."

Ethan felt like shit. Clarity shot through his veins. Her research, her private calls, it all made sense, and he felt like an ass.

"You know what, Lowell, why the hell should you care anyway?" Furious at him for insinuating that she'd sleep with a married man, she decided to drag in his character. "You freaking cheated on your girl-friend!"

"Come again?"

"Oh, suddenly you're forgetting all the revelations from earlier?"

He skimmed over her face, redness from rage set in her cheeks and along her neck. It couldn't be more prominent how jealous she was. He tried not to allow it to affect him physically, but he couldn't control it. His attraction to her was going through the roof. There was only going to be one end to the conversation. He could only imagine one end.

"You remembered all that," he pressed on with a

teasing tone in each word.

"You want to flip out, thinking that I'm involved with a married man, but you used me. You claim that you love some woman, so then what was that night at the charity ball?"

He didn't want to use her own words against her, but a sick part of him got pleasure from watching her squirm. The longer he could keep the conversation going, the more she revealed about her true self. "According to you, it was a mistake."

She took a deep breath and exhaled loudly. "You're right."

"Are you contesting that?"

She forced herself to look into his eyes, searching. She saw nothing more than a raw hunger, a blazing desire. Maybe her vision was lying to her for once. What she was seeing couldn't be real. It was all made up in her head, what she had wanted to see.

She quickly stood, eager to get to her room and stay there for the rest of the day and evening. As if he were able to read her mind, before she could fully straighten herself, before one single step was taken, he had her back on the couch. His grip on her arm was firm, yet soft and delicate, like he was afraid of breaking her.

When she sank into the couch this time, their bodies were much closer than before. Their sides touched, and both felt the jolts of electricity radiating from every connecting spot.

He eased himself closer to her, so that she'd feel his breath on her skin with each word. "While I meant everything I said today, technically I don't have a girl-friend."

"Technically?"

A mischievous smile crept across his lips and a wave of glitter danced through his gaze on her, green sparkles like she had never seen. "I haven't exactly asked her yet."

Ryan's heart pounded. Breathing became difficult from the heat in the room. "I don't understand." She was both hoping and dreading that she did.

"All those words were said with only one woman in mind. You."

Relief washed over Ethan as he allowed the words to slip from his lips. He had finally put it out there. He was done with any games and ridiculous misunderstandings. All he wanted was for her walls to crumble for good. What he didn't expect was for her to shake her head profusely as her eyes welled up with tears.

"This isn't good." The statement was forced and lacking in what she intended.

He wasn't going to allow her rejection to be easy. "Why?"

"Emotions can't get in the way right now. The stakes are too high." She knew for the millionth time how robotic she sounded, but it was the truth. "Your actions today showed that."

"What? Because I didn't listen to you? Because I went after my niece and nephew unlike their coward of a father?" He didn't want to sound angry after basically pouring his heart out, but if this was her

242

reason for backing away, it was bullshit.

"No," she screamed. Ethan couldn't tell if she wanted to cry or punch him. "It's because whatever you feel for me, whatever that is, that caused you to disregard your own safety with concern to mine!"

"Do you even hear the crap coming out of your mouth?"

This time, rather than pull her back on the couch, he rose with her, asserting himself, towering over her.

"It's true." Her voice was so soft; Ethan could barely make out the words. "I don't want you putting yourself in jeopardy for me."

"Fine, I won't," he lied, knowing it's what she wanted to hear.

"You're saying all this now because you're thinking with something other than your head," she scoffed. Since they started their conversation she had seen the flashes of lust in his eyes, and it took everything in her to ignore it.

"Yeah, I am," he admitted. "My heart."

Holy shit. Unexpected.

Those words stopped her own.

His eyes tore into her, begging for a reaction, anything. Ryan was still having a difficult time processing everything he had said. While he never told her directly that he loved her, he had said it to his father. He insisted that those words from earlier were only about her.

Pain flickered across his face with each passing moment of silence. When he could no longer take another second, he silently excused himself to his bedroom.

He quietly closed the door and threw himself onto the bed. If he were to allow his insides to outwardly vocalize themselves, there was no doubt he'd be screaming in frustration. Instead he stared up at the ceiling, completely embarrassed by the outcome. He should have done more physically, but he couldn't, as much as he could only imagine one ending to the evening, he couldn't force himself on her.

Ryan stood on the other side of the door. There was no debate as to whether or not she needed to follow him. The pounding of her heart, and the tornado of butterflies in her stomach told her that. As much as she continued to think that it was only a physical attraction, that only her body was drawn to Ethan, she knew she was fighting with her heart on the issue as well.

Before she got the door halfway open, Ethan was already rising from the bed. He eyed her suspiciously with glassy eyes full of need.

"Why did you leave," Ryan found herself asking as soon as she swallowed the lump in her throat.

"I assumed the conversation was over," he answered coldly.

Ryan's eyes drifted from Ethan's, slowly making their way down his body. The t-shirt he wore was too tight, emphasizing ever muscle. His jeans hugged every curve perfectly, especially the growing length below his belt and down his left leg.

She couldn't help but bite her lip as she scanned back to his face. Her slow steps had gotten her to the point that there was only about a foot of empty space separating them. Ethan hadn't moved since he first bolted off the bed.

Her hand stretched to his chest, hard as cement, but it was unable to mask the rapid beating within. Her body absorbed every thump as it radiated through her, to her very own, until it matched his. It was in that moment that every reason, every reservation, every thought about why none of this should progress between them, ceased to exist. None of it made sense. The only thing that made sense to her was the fact that she had never felt what she was feeling right now, and it was something she could no longer ignore.

Ethan's breathing quickened into short and desperate gasps for air when Ryan began to trail her hand from his chest, along the top of his shoulder, until finally touching the skin on his neck. Her touch was soft and feminine, but the coolness of her hands did little to subside the fire spilling from his body.

He allowed his right hand to glide around her waist, and through the thin cotton shirt, he could feel the flames inside her bubbling to the surface.

She lifted herself onto her tiptoes and pulled the back of his neck down toward her. Their lips barely brushed and he could see the irritation in her narrowed eyes. He had felt the same, even worse, for far too long. It would be difficult to make her wait any longer, considering that his pants were about to split at the thought of what was to come. Even before that one night, all he could think about was making her his, in every way imaginable. He needed her to want the same.

He finally gave in and allowed their lips to meet.

It was a soft kiss at first, full of longing, both of them with the desire to savor every second. Ethan's hands skimmed up and down Ryan's back, and when they reached her hips, he couldn't fight the urge to pull her further into him, to show her how much he wanted this, how much he wanted her.

Her ass was so tight in her jeans, and he struggled to sink his hands into her, but when he did, the most adorable yelp pierced through her mouth and into his.

"You promise not to freak out this time," Ethan growled in her ear. He pushed her damp hair away and tenderly sank his mouth into her neck.

"I promise," she moaned, which only heightened his arousal.

"I mean it," he began, coming up for air. "I can't deal with you pushing me away again, calling this a mistake."

Fear quickly flashed across Ryan's eyes. "I don't want to push you away."

"But?"

"That's it," she smiled.

Just like that, like he had been given a green light, he pulled her to the bed with him. Their soft and slow touches becoming rougher and more frantic. Everything that had built up between them came rushing to the surface once again, but this time is was deeper. There were emotions swirling between them, more than attraction, more than lust, more than just sex.

As Ethan straddled her, careful not to put too much weight on her, the clothing began melting away.

The tips of Ryan's fingers sent shivers through Ethan as she slowly traced down his abs. She played with the top of his jeans, taking her time with the button and zipper.

Ethan lifted himself onto both hands, hovering over Ryan like he was in the middle of a pushup, and waited for her to continue working on his jeans. The confident grin on her face was more than he could take.

"You're driving me fucking crazy, but you already know that, don't you?" He breathed the words onto her cheek before going in for a deep kiss.

Her mouth parted to say something, but he didn't allow it, instead taking the opportunity to plunge his tongue in to meet hers. The noises she made at the simple action forced him to pull away until he was on his back beside her.

Ryan was confused for a minute, but once Ethan's remaining clothes hit the floor, excitement took over, and her body prepared itself for him, wanting to relive that one night over and over.

She reached for the buttons on her jeans but stopped when laughter poured from Ethan's lips.

"As slow as you are? No."

He ran his hands down her almost bare chest and momentarily kissed below her navel. The foreplay, if you could even call it that, didn't last long. Once her jeans fell onto the floor next to his, he was back on top of her, vehemently kissing every inch of skin other than her lips. Those he allowed to gasp and moan, to cause his undoing.

Ryan felt one hand slide under her back, and when the tightness from the underwire in her bra loosened, she knew he had the clasp unfastened.

Ethan pulled himself away for a second, scanning over her naked body, only covered by a pair of simple grey cotton panties, beneath him. The first time the darkness and the heat of the moment didn't give him the opportunity to fully admire her. He watched her cheeks redden at being put on display. While it was adorable, it was sad that someone so perfect had never been appreciated the way she deserved.

He couldn't, wouldn't, tell her now. It would ruin the moment, and she'd only ask questions. He had mentioned it before in a roundabout way, but maybe she didn't pick up on it. He tried not to let the nerves get to him as he thought about her being the first.

Ethan sank back into her, massaging her breasts while his mouth absorbed every confirmation of pleasure bursting from her lips. It wasn't until Ryan's nails dug out of his back and gripped around his cock, lightly stroking it just enough to tease him, that he broke from her mouth, suddenly unable to catch his breath from her touch.

"I need you," she whimpered.

He didn't know how badly until he began to slide her panties off and realized that they were drenched in her juices. He wasn't sure that he could get any harder, but as he gripped them in his hand, he could feel his cock react and pulse inside her palm.

Ethan was slow at first, teasing at her entrance, coating himself with her arousal, torturing the both of them before he thrust inside.

Desperately Ryan squirmed beneath him, bucking her hips up, begging for the smoldering sensations she yearned to feel. She couldn't stop the small cry when her body welcomed the inevitable. He filled her entirely, easing the longing ache to have him inside.

Ryan's hands balled up the sheets beneath her with each pleasurable thrust, their rhythm growing faster by the second. It was a combination of raw and rough, yet sweet and meaningful. She wrapped her legs around his waist, already slippery with sweat.

She propped herself onto her forearms, bringing her face closer to his, until they were buried in a savage kiss. She pushed back on his left shoulder and pulled at his right arm, causing him to lose balance and tumble onto the bed, their bodies still locked together.

"What the hell," he gasped. She was on top of him with a ravenous confidence flickering in her eyes. "Do you always have to be in control," Ethan laughed.

Ryan lowered herself, kissing through the stubble along his jawline, feeling his reaction inside her each time her lips came down on his skin. She sucked on his earlobe before whispering in his ear. "Trust me, you're in control."

When he met her eyes with his, he knew that he

was. She was giving him complete control over her body. She pulled herself up, her hands gripping his torso as her body sat perfectly impaled on his cock.

Ethan gripped both sides of her waist so tightly that he knew he'd leave marks once again, but her moans of ecstasy told him that she didn't care. Once Ryan began grinding into him, Ethan used his control over her body to make each thrust harder and deeper.

The feeling was new to Ryan; it felt different than before. Her eyes rolled back and she allowed herself to become totally lost in the sensations that Ethan sent through her body, as if he knew exactly what she craved.

When she bit down on her lip and all but stopped breathing, her walls clenching around him, Ethan pushed harder and faster, knowing that she was close. Her nails dug into his chest as screams erupted from her lips. There wasn't one thing Ethan could think of as being sexier than watching her ride out her orgasm, his name pouring from her mouth, begging him not to stop.

Knowing that he had caused such a rush of pleasure to radiate through her, was enough to bring him to his climax. He ferociously moved her against him as he continued to pound into her, needing his own gratification.

A rough groan tore from inside his throat, echoing throughout the room, as he released, filling her completely with his sperm.

Ryan felt Ethan convulse inside her; warming

sensations she had never felt before shot through her core.

Breathlessly they untangled, falling together in a naked and sweaty mess.

Once the calming and sleepy sensations drifted in, and after they both fell into the atmosphere that post-sex often brought, Ethan lovingly ran his fingers along the glowing skin of Ryan's arm. When he came to her wrist, he became hesitant, his heart pounding as he entangled their fingers together. Relief washed over him when a purr vibrated in her chest and she turned, locking their eyes.

Ryan scanned over Ethan's body, glistening from sweat. Red marks were painted across his pectoral muscles, his arms, and his lower torso. It wasn't until her eyes drifted farther down that Ethan noticed her face clench with concern.

"What's wrong," he immediately asked. She had promised she wouldn't freak out, but something now told him differently.

"What happened to the condom?"

Shit.

Ethan wasn't sure how to explain. It was another first for him.

"Ethan!"

"Things escalated," he began.

Ryan's breathing increased and though she tried not to show her panic in front of Ethan, he had already started to learn to read her impeccably.

"I'm sorry. That's never happened before," he announced sheepishly.

"What?!"

"I've never not used a condom. I...something about–"

Ryan's head was spinning. When she came to Ethan's room, she knew they'd ultimately end up having sex. Stupidly, she thought he had been prepared for that.

"If you're worried, don't be. I'm clean. I swear," he tried to reassure her.

"It's not that. Well, yes, there's that, but–"

"But what," he interrupted, pressing her on. She was now causing a panic within him.

"I'm not on anything."

The revelation hit him like a ton of bricks.

"I thought all women–"

She quickly cut him off. "I haven't had sex in the last ten years and I'm fairly regular, so there was never a need to put unnecessary medication into my body."

He couldn't tell her, but a part of him thought it was a little sexy. Given, he'd have to be more careful in the future.

"You know what, it should be fine. I think I'm around the time of the month where chances are pretty low."

Ethan could only laugh. When he first met the fiery woman in his father's office, he never imagined her being the first woman in his bed, let alone having this conversation with her.

"What's so funny?!"

"Ryan, it's not like you're sixteen and in Catholic

school. If anything were to happen, it wouldn't be the end of the world." Even he couldn't believe what he was saying.

"My line of work doesn't exactly allow me to think like that. Also, the fact that we're not..." She let her words drift away, not finishing the sentence once she saw Ethan clench up and drop his hand from hers.

He forced himself to ignore the latter part. "You plan on doing this job forever?"

"I'll retire when I have to."

Ethan hated hearing that. After the events that had taken place earlier, he wanted nothing more than for this to be Ryan's last assignment. "When is that? When there isn't a breath left in you to enjoy your life?"

"No!" She rose from the bed and began dressing. "You know, this whole thing tumbled downhill because you couldn't wear a condom."

Ethan slid his boxers on, followed by his jeans. The direction the conversation was going didn't correlate with his dick flopping around.

"Sorry that I wanted a different experience with you," he yelled back. He wasn't angry, but upset.

"What the hell does that even mean?" Ryan's arms flew up in frustration.

Ethan grabbed her shoulders and held her still. His eyes were stormy and conflicted.

"I wanted you to be the first woman, the only woman, that has ever been in my bed. I wanted to feel you. I wanted to feel what it was like to be with someone that I loved, with nothing between us."

253

Damn he was good.

His hands slid from her shoulders, down her arms, causing goosebumps to trickle over her skin. He finally reached her hands and clasped them in his. His thumbs massaged the backs of them while he pulled her impossibly close to him.

"There's so much that I want to say to you, but I'll wait. The look you're giving me right now is telling me as much," he laughed. It was an uncomfortable and nervous laugh.

Ryan took deep breaths. It was so much to take in. She had never expected such intensity from Ethan. The truth, the whole frightening and terrifying truth of it all, was that she was falling for him. Suddenly, keeping him safe was the only thing that mattered.

CHAPTER 22

Ryan: Good luck today!

Jeremy: You actually remembered.

Ryan: Sorry. It's been crazy around here.

Crazy was putting it mildly. Ryan was thankful that Ethan had no plans for Sunday. She needed a day where they didn't have to go anywhere or do anything.

Jeremy: Oh, I know. I saw a couple pictures from that charity thing this past week.

Ryan: And?

Jeremy: You haven't called to complain lately about this assignment.

Ryan: I haven't called period.

Jeremy: Haha. It's cool. Your love life is none of my business.

Ryan: Stop. There is no love life.

Jeremy: Those pictures look more like a couple and less like a "job assignment".

Ryan: Just go win your race!

Jeremy: I love you!

Ryan: Love you too.

Ryan didn't expect for there to be pictures, but of course. Rich people couldn't do anything for charity without it being plastered everywhere. She had to wonder, after the spat between Ethan and his father yesterday, if Owen Lowell would attempt to find out about the mystery person his son was supposedly dating. Too many people were sensing the attraction between them; it would only be a matter of time before Ethan's father would know, and something told her that he would be a little more than unhappy about it.

Ryan spent a great deal of time Sunday sorting out the mayhem of the day before. JD had insisted that he was on the verge of something huge and they'd be talking the following day.

To her surprise, shortly after lunch, Ethan had brought up her brother's race, but she had to decline watching it. Two years prior he had been in a little accident. It was nothing major, just a small crash that took out several cars. Those moments of uncertainty as she watched the television, hours away from him, caused her to never watch another race again. It might seem silly to some people, but she couldn't bear watching his races after that, knowing that she might be sitting in the comfort of her living room, chugging a beer and stuffing her face, and in an instant be an only child. The fact that she didn't own a television anymore also helped with that.

Jeremy came in second that day.

The evening was different. For the first time, Ryan didn't feel tense or uncomfortable around Ethan.

They ate dinner together, made by Ethan while Ryan was on a call, and though he put on a movie after, it was soon paused and they spent a great amount of time talking.

"Does that turn you off from the idea of marriage," Ethan asked after talking with her about the strained relationship with her parents since their divorce more than a decade ago.

"Not at all. I'm glad they realized it. I just hate that throughout the years they both put their careers before us." She was appreciative that, while they were on the topic of divorce, he didn't mention her own.

"When I asked you about your career–"

She quickly cut him off. "I've asked my brother the same. He's been in a couple accidents over the years. He always told me that if he's lucky enough to see his life flash before his eyes and make it back, then he'll quit."

"I take it the same goes for you," Ethan sighed. "If

you can make it back to the living after you see the *white light*, then you'll evaluate things?" He didn't mean for his words to come out as sharp as they did, but the idea of anything ever happening to Ryan tore at his insides.

"I don't know. I've never really been hurt," she admitted.

It only irritated him further. "Newsflash, you're mortal too. Maybe you've just been relying on luck for too long."

He gave her a kiss on the forehead. She knew he was upset, but only because he cared. Ethan then drifted off to his bedroom, closing the door behind him. They hadn't talked about arrangements between the two of them. Things first needed to play out with Delacruz. Ryan hadn't told Ethan that part, that she knew who was behind it all.

* * *

Then it was Monday morning.

As soon as Ethan and Ryan entered the offices, everything had to be turned off between the two of them. They fell into the typical work day they had done for a couple weeks now.

Through the walls Ryan could hear Owen yelling profusely at a contractor on the phone. Ethan pretended to ignore it but found himself flinching every time his father's voice broke past the solid barrier.

JD: We need to talk.

Ryan: Over text?

JD: Definitely not.

Whenever JD didn't want to communicate over text, it meant that he was scared of leaving a blatant trail of evidence as to what was being discussed.

While Ryan contemplated for a moment, another text came in.

JD: Make sure you're out of range from Lowell.

For once, she honestly didn't know which Lowell he meant. She looked up at Ethan, who actually seemed to be doing something productive on his computer.

"Just go," he said, not bothering to look away.

"Excuse me?"

He laughed, a genuine laugh. "I know you and your buddy have something to discuss that I don't need to be privy to. Just go." He gave her a playful wink and went back to work.

Due to the last text from JD, Ryan had a feeling that something colossal was about to follow as soon as she hit the dial button.

"Are you alone?"

"Dude, don't be all cryptic. You're scaring me."

She could hear the deep breath on the other end. No doubt JD was probably raking his hands along his receding hairline.

"JD? What's going on," she pressed.

"I've gone through a shitload of Emilio Delacruz's financial records and–"

"He's laundering drug money through his business, isn't he?"

"Damnit, Ryan," he hissed. "Do you want to hear what I've uncovered?"

His aggravation with her guess said it all. She was right. She said nothing and allowed him to continue.

"So, yes. He's definitely into some dealings with the cartels. I can't prove it yet, but I have no doubt in my mind that he's one of the major heroin suppliers in this area."

"I don't get it," she burst out, her voice piercing through the phone. "What the hell does any of that have to do with wanting Ethan Lowell dead?"

"Absolutely nothing."

Ryan felt her heart stop at the answer.

"Ryan?"

"Yeah," she barely answered.

"Delacruz shelled out five grand for an extensive and rushed DNA test."

JD's words didn't make sense. He went from drugs to *Maury* in a matter of seconds. Ryan tried to find a response but was unable.

"His accounts show that this was done within days of his son dying."

Ryan felt dizzy. Pieces began to interlock. She remembered how the little boy stood out on Sophia's Facebook page, but she hadn't seen it before.

"I'm going out on a limb here, but–"

Ryan swallowed hard. The words were so close to escaping from her mouth. *Ethan was the father.*

She stopped herself once she did the math. Ethan would have had to have been somewhere around sixteen or seventeen to father a twelve year old child. It didn't make any sense.

Then Ryan remembered the blood draining from Owen's face at the mentioning of Sophia.

She felt like an idiot.

One. Ethan didn't father a child with an older woman and then become great friends with her daughter years later. Ryan knew that.

Two. Owen reacted in a way that suggested that he was definitely hiding secrets.

Three. Emilio ran a DNA test, immediately after his son's death.

Four. Mrs. Delacruz committed *suicide* a short time later.

Ryan's head was a mess. A million different things were weaving back and forth but she hadn't yet put them all together.

"Mother fuck," Ryan gasped.

"Yeah. I thought as much."

"What do we do," Ryan immediately asked upon her realization.

"Look, Ryan," JD sighed. "I need to come in and talk with them. "I know that you and Ethan are...close," he said, trying to watch how his words came out. "This will be brought to light. I can give you about two hours, but you need to talk to him."

The fact that JD was thinking of her relationship

with Ethan, which she still had not figured out yet, meant a lot.

Ryan had never been as nervous around Ethan as she was when she returned to his office. Thankfully he was on a call when she walked in.

She took her seat in the same place she had left moments ago and stared at a blank computer screen. Her stomach became heavy, burdened from the news JD had just shared with her. Owen Lowell, rich business man, married to the same woman for more than thirty years, had fathered a child out of wedlock, a child that was now deceased, a child that never got to know his half-siblings.

"Travel arrangements are a little complicated at the time," Ethan admitted to the person on the phone. "I can try to be in Alberta next month."

Ethan was working on his own business venture. Ryan knew very little about it aside from the fact that he wanted to do it himself, apart from his father.

Ethan watched Ryan carefully, still focused on the man shooting him statistics on the other end of the phone. Something about her was off once she returned from her phone call, but he couldn't place it. He wanted to get off the call as quickly as possible.

"Alright, thanks. I'll be in touch," Ethan concluded.

He made his way in Ryan's direction, but she gave him little attention until he passed by her and she heard the click of the lock on the door. She closed her computer, set it on the table and rose.

"Sit down," Ethan insisted.

Ryan hesitated. There was no need for the door to be locked, at least that's what she thought, up until Ethan sat down with her.

He was impossibly close, and though she knew he didn't put on more cologne than usual, her senses latched to it right away, absorbing the effect.

He played with her hand in his. It was a sweet gesture, not at all sexual, but despite that, an ache grew inside Ryan, not just for sex. It was more than that for her now. She tried to only focus on Ethan and his soothing touch, but the nagging thoughts of Delacruz gnawed at her insides, waiting to spill out.

"Are you alright," Ethan asked. His voice was low and raspy, undeniably sexy.

The way he looked at her with so much care and concern made Ryan want to pounce on him. Something had changed in her since Ethan Lowell.

"I'm fine. There's just a lot on my mind," she admitted, knowing that he deserved to know what she knew, before JD bombarded Owen with a load of questions.

He leaned in closer to her. His other hand trailed up her arm, along the front of her neck, until his thumb stroked her jawline. "Am I part of what's on your mind?"

"Don't start," Ryan began, but she knew the words were useless.

The heat that Ethan's body emitted had caused her own to react in a feral way.

"This isn't the time or place," she continued. Her breathing had changed; the smirk Ethan was giving her right now meant that he felt it as well.

"For what," he teasingly pressed on. His hand made it to the back of her neck and he gently tugged her forward, their faces only inches apart.

"For whatever you're thinking."

Rather than pulling her the inch or two more, he leaned forward, but his lips didn't sink to hers. Instead, she felt the jolt of electricity running through her veins from a warm pinching on her neck.

"Don't leave marks," she softly moaned.

Vibrations from his laughter echoed into her body, and she could feel the need between her thighs growing. She tried to find the words. *We can't do this here. Your father is right next door.* They were in her thoughts, but she couldn't bring them out. She was losing herself in everything that was Ethan Lowell.

"I need you," he groaned into her ear while he slowly guided her down onto the couch and climbed on top of her.

"We need to talk." Finally. She was able to get something out. They did need to talk. There were so many things that needed to be discussed.

His eyes flared with desire when he slid his hand over her chest, concealed by too much fabric, much to his displeasure. "I have a condom this time," he chuckled.

Ryan had to focus. The lust couldn't get the best of her, although she was very much on the brink of ripping Ethan's clothes off.

He came down on top of her, his lips desperately after her own. He raked his tongue along her bottom lip, lightly pulling at it with his teeth, until she parted open for him to lay claim to her. His tongue ripped into her mouth just as she threw her arms around him, pulling him closer.

He loved that she tried to follow all her silly rules. It made his desire for her to break them that much stronger. Ethan palmed her breasts, which only caused her to fight back the inevitable moans. The kiss became hungry and deep, both wanting more.

Once Ryan lifted her knee and began massaging his bulging arousal, Ethan knew that he was done for. All the layers between them needed to go. Now.

The only thing that could have stopped them was a knock on the door. "Ethan?" The handle of the door wiggled, but didn't open due to being locked. A moment of uncertain silence followed, with a sigh from the person behind the door. "Come to my office when you get a break."

The tone in Owen's voice said it all.

"Shit," Ethan gasped. He scratched at the stubble on his face. "I never lock my door." His teeth tugged at his lower lip with a cocky grin.

"Jesus, Ethan," Ryan hissed, rising up. Her shirt had become untucked and rumpled and she desperately tried to compose herself, subduing the sexual need Ethan had moments before put inside her.

"Hey," Ethan began, wrapping himself around her from behind. "It's no big deal."

Ryan turned to face him, his arms still firmly around her. "We can't do this right now."

"Okay, tonight."

"No."

He gripped her tighter. "Stop, Ryan. I'm not letting you push me away anymore."

"I don't even know what that means. I don't even know what this is." She tore herself from his body.

"I don't know about you, but I was pretty clear. I want you." His voice was strong and demanding.

The playful glimmer in his boyish green eyes did nothing to quell her thoughts of something more. She didn't know what he meant when he said those words. She assumed it was all about sex, and though she tried to ignore it and not make a big deal about it, the word *love* had escaped his lips a few times lately. If they weren't careful, she knew that it wouldn't be long before she'd say something back.

"Let me get this shit over with my dad and maybe we can get out of here early today."

Then Ryan remembered. "Wait, I really need to talk to you about something."

"We'll talk tonight, all night if you want," he told her, quickly kissing her on the forehead.

As weird as it was to think it, Ryan started to have trouble telling herself that this was a job. The more time she spent around Ethan, the more it felt like a budding relationship.

Before she could protest, the door was half open and Ethan was beckoning her to follow. She glanced at her phone. It had been more than an hour since she spoke with JD. All she could hope was for Ethan's father to have a few quick words for him and for her and Ethan to have a few moments alone before JD arrived.

She could at least hope. Somehow, reality always had a way of knocking her on her ass.

CHAPTER 23

Ryan tried to stay out of the way in Owen Lowell's office, but the moment she followed Ethan in, she felt Owen's eyes heavily on her, watching her every move, even as he was deep into conversation with his son. He'd be stupid not to notice. Apparently everyone on the entire planet knew that she and Ethan had something between them. Even her brother knew from a single photograph.

If Owen knew, he said nothing, completely ignored it.

Just when Ryan thought the conversation had concluded, and she'd be allowed alone time to talk to Ethan in private, a knock on the door twisted her guts.

Allison poked her head into the room. "Mr. Lowell? Agent Delgado and two others are here to see you."

"Thank you, dear. Please send them in."

JD saw the look on Ryan's face instantly, and he hoped that his apologetic eyes got through to her. He knew that she hadn't had the chance to tell Ethan. Ethan would be the only one in the room unknowing of the information presented.

Pleasantries were made, and while Owen, Ethan, and Delgado took seats near the massive teak desk,

Ryan and the other two agents chose to stand. She didn't know their reasoning for doing so, but hers was simple. She didn't want to be anywhere around Ethan when JD began with the questions.

Ethan quickly sensed that Ryan was uncomfortable with the situation. Maybe it was because he knew about her friendship with Delgado; however, he couldn't be sure. He watched as she broke contact from him, refusing for their eyes to meet anymore, and stared out the windows into the city stretching beneath them.

"Mr. Lowell," Delgado began, directing his attention toward Owen. "I have a few questions for you."

"Me," Owen asked, appearing shocked.

"We're both busy men, so I'm not going to tiptoe around the situation."

"What are you talking about," Owen gasped.

"We're all but certain that we know who has targeted your son."

Wrong. Certain.

"Who?"

"Emilio Delacruz." Ryan loved how JD was able to keep his voice so monotone, but she knew inside his head he was dancing like a girl to her favorite boy band.

There it was. Ryan had to turn to see the reaction. Just as she expected, Owen clammed up and looked away from everyone.

"Now, I have a few theories as to why, but I'm hoping you can help me with that," Delgado went on.

"Dad, what's going on?"

The dagger twisted in Ryan's chest. Ethan would freak out if Owen confirmed what she and JD already expected. She hoped with everything that he didn't father a child with the mother to one of Ethan's old friends, but deep down, her expectations weren't too high.

"Can you give me insight on why Emilio Delacruz has sent people after your son," Delgado continued.

"Ethan," Owen began, ignoring Delgado's question. "You should go. I need to speak with Agent Delgado privately."

Ethan didn't say anything. He looked to Ryan for help, but her eyes said it all. She knew something. Everyone in the room knew something.

Delgado was relentless. "Here's what I discovered. Before the car bomb, right after Delacruz's son died, a DNA test was done."

Owen Lowell couldn't look anyone in the eye at that point. All the suspicions were correct.

"As if you didn't know, the results were that his son wasn't his. You can imagine what that would do to a father. His only son dead, and now to find out that it had all been a lie for the last twelve years. Is there something you would like to add or do you want me to continue based on theory?" Delgado's words were cutting. He clearly wasn't happy that Owen pretended to have no enemies this whole time.

"Dad?"

"I don't know what any of you want me to say," Owen began, defeat dripping from his face.

"Were you the fucking father," Ethan screamed,

bolting from his chair, even causing the other two agents in the room to step back. Their hands went to their holsters upon instinct.

"It was a long time ago, before you and Sophia were friends," Owen admitted.

"What the hell is wrong with you?! I had a brother? No. Sophia and I shared a brother, a brother I've met and never knew him as such, and now he's dead. Are you fucking serious right now?" Ethan's ranting boomed from the walls, causing Ryan to shudder in fear. She had seen him angry before, but those times were nothing compared to this.

The shock of the revelation caused Owen to be rendered speechless, but that wouldn't last forever.

"If Delacruz knew that you were the father," Delgado calmly began.

"I didn't kill his son," Owen shouted, slamming his fist down on the desk. "My son," he corrected.

Those words made Ethan dizzy. The admission sank in. He hated his father. Though their family could be a little dysfunctional at times, this was it. He couldn't imagine what his mother would think.

"I'm not saying you did. He died of a disease that wasn't caught in time."

"Then why would Delacruz care? It was my son that died, not his," Owen growled. His words were cold and harsh.

"For twelve years, he thought it was his son," Delgado concluded.

Ethan understood. Emilio Delacruz wanted to take the same thing away from Owen Lowell.

* * *

Ryan and Ethan didn't speak on the drive back to the penthouse. A million different beginnings for a conversation came to her mind, but all of them sucked. There was nothing she could say. The Lowell family lived a perfect and cushy lifestyle, at least that's how it appeared looking through those massive glass windows of their immaculate mansion, but glass could be so easily shattered.

"How are you," Ryan asked once she parked the SUV in the secure and private parking garage, amongst all of Ethan's toys.

His eyes ripped into her with such disdain. "I'm fucking peachy, Beckett." He jerked open the door and swiftly slammed it behind him.

Ryan had to quickly catch up to his pace toward the elevator that required a special key, which led them down a series of halls, only to another elevator to his penthouse. By the time the final elevator dinged, Ryan was nearly out of breath. She had been slipping on her exercise routine lately.

"You knew didn't you," Ethan screamed, throwing his keys and wallet onto the table near the door. His green eyes screamed even louder with the amount of pain oozing from inside. Ryan wasn't sure if his pain came from the revelation of his father's acts, or her not telling him immediately.

"I just found out," she admitted. "I told you I needed to talk to you, and–"

"So while I was basically dry humping you, you

knew all this?"

"Don't try to put it so eloquently." Ryan cringed, detesting how he made it sound vulgar and trashy.

"Screw how I'm saying it! You knew then, didn't you?" His words were so sharp, hatred lingering on his every breath.

"Calm down, will you," she begged.

He made his way to his bedroom, still in a frenzy. He was generally a tidy person, liking everything in a neat order. In his haste, and the turmoil of the day crashing through his mind, he flung his jacket on the floor halfway through the room. He didn't give a shit, the cleaners would take care of it no matter how it was presented to them.

He could feel Ryan hesitating at the doorway as he slipped his shirt from his shoulders.

She tried not to allow his broad and powerful back to divert her attention, but Ethan had become a walking distraction, with or without clothes.

"What," he snarled as he turned to face her.

He began undoing his belt and Ryan couldn't control her heartbeat once it hit the floor. The only thing left for him to remove was his pants, then he'd be in nothing more than boxers and she was already close to losing it after their session on the couch.

"I really don't have anything left to say to you, so I don't know why you're just standing there," he continued.

Ryan could feel her cheeks growing red from embarrassment. She fumbled for words. "I thought we could talk."

273

"If it wasn't clear to you out there, I'm not in the mood to talk." His pants fell to the floor and he kicked them aside.

Ryan wished he would have been in the mood for something else, but that wasn't happening.

"I'm wiped after today," he began, realizing that regardless of how frustrated he was with both the situation about his father as well as Ryan, he was coming off as harsh to someone he genuinely cared about. Maybe that was why he was so angry with her. He cared about her so much, and she kept him in the dark, like it was just part of her job. He was nothing more than a job, as she had pointed out on more than one occasion.

"Where are you going," Ryan found herself stupidly asking as he headed toward his bathroom.

He raised a brow. *Really?* "I'm going to go shower." He scanned her body up and down. He was aware that he had left her wanting from earlier, and her reaction to seeing him near naked proved that even more. "Alone," he added, before closing the door and locking it behind him.

It took every ounce of energy for him to not pull her in with him.

The long shower made him further realize that he had overreacted, at least with Ryan. When it came to his father, he still had words that he wanted to say, but he had to let his anger calm down so that every adjective didn't turn into a variant of *fuck*.

Ryan dropped her book and nearly twisted her ankle jumping from her bed to the knock on her door.

"Yeah," she breathlessly managed.

Ethan raised his brows with curiosity and glanced behind her, noticing the book on the bed, and only the book.

"You seem a little out of breath for just reading. Must be a good book?" He made his comment as lighthearted and fun as he could, still feeling awful for going off on her earlier.

"It's not that kind of book," she grumbled.

He had seen her bookshelf when she packed a few things before coming to his place. Nothing on it suggested raunchy romance. Knowing her, she was reading something that made college literature students cringe.

The words were so difficult for him to say, but for her, he had to. "I'm sorry. I took all my anger out on you–"

"It's fine, really," Ryan interrupted him.

The way he hovered, leaning into the door jamb, hesitant about making his way into her room, all while his eyes continued to drop from hers to her lips, made Ryan's insides scream.

"Do you want to come to the living room and talk," he finally asked, the lust in his eyes fading.

It was an obvious direction for the conversation; however, when Ryan first saw him at her door, she was hoping all that frustration from earlier had left him needing a release in a way other than with words.

They sat on the large couch; unlike the last time, they weren't even close to touching, the entire middle part of the couch separated them. If either minded, neither allowed the other to see it.

Both Ethan's eyes and voice were demanding. "Why don't you start from the beginning?"

CHAPTER 24

"I knew, or at least heavily suspected, it was Emilio Delacruz that day we visited your parents."

Ethan tried not to react, but when he tilted his neck from side to side, the crunching gave Ryan pause. "How?" The simple question came as more of an animalistic growl.

"The last gunman. I didn't tell you this," she began, hating to recount any of the deaths in her past.

Ethan shook his head. It was almost laughable that she felt compelled to lead in like that. There was a hell of a lot she didn't tell him. That much he knew.

Ryan sank into the couch and continued. "He was terrified of his boss. I tried to find a way to get closer to him, to get the gun away, but for him, death was easier than failing at his job."

"Wait, you didn't–"

"I wasn't close enough to stop him," Ryan sighed, though she didn't feel bad about him dying. She couldn't. He had threatened the lives of innocent people. "When I asked who sent him, he wouldn't say at first. Sophia had been on the top of the list and I mentioned her name, which seemed absurd to him, but he knew her. He knew her through her father. He wouldn't say his name, but I know now that it's

Emilio Delacruz."

"And the rest?" Ethan had made himself comfortable on the couch, but the part of Ryan that begged for his touch found him to still be too far away.

"I didn't want to mention Sophia's dad after your initial reaction to her. I also didn't have the faintest clue why he'd have you as a target."

"The call, earlier today?"

"That was JD, Agent Delgado." She felt the need to establish, though Ethan knew they were the same person.

"And he had everything figured out?"

"Yeah," Ryan sighed. "The only thing we don't know is how Delacruz found out it was your father, possibly a confrontation with his wife. I guess it really doesn't matter now."

Ethan appeared deep in thought. "Sophia's mom committed suicide." It was a statement that held an underlying question within it.

"Trust me, after all this, that will be investigated."

Ryan knew in her gut what the investigation would uncover. If Emilio Delacruz was going through this much trouble to torture the man who fathered what Delacruz thought was his child, then his wife caught the worst of it.

"Your father really pissed off the wrong man." Ryan had thought it to herself, but when the words came out, she realized that she'd have to tell Ethan everything.

Ethan watched her skeptically from his end of the couch. The twitch of her mouth and her inability to make eye contact said it all.

"Get it out. There's not much that's going to surprise me at this point."

Ryan laughed slightly. She could probably tell him that Delacruz was an alien from a distant planet and it wouldn't come as a surprise.

"Delacruz isn't in the parts business."

"I've seen his warehouse, yes he is," Ethan scoffed.

"He's using it as a means to hide where his money actually comes from." She didn't want to delay the truth by allowing Ethan to counter with her. "He's working with a Mexican cartel and he's one of the heroin suppliers in this area."

It took Ethan a minute to absorb what she was telling him, partly because she had said it so blunt and dry, as if it was something he should have known all this time.

"He's a really bad guy, Ethan. He knows a lot of people who would happily take you out for the right price."

"Basically I can't leave this place until he's caught," Ethan growled. He was angry, not with Ryan, with the mess that was his life right now.

"Even here isn't safe, but it's for the best at the moment." To her knowledge, Ethan had been very careful about keeping his home a secret and very few people had a means of getting to his door.

"They know where he lives. With all that knowledge of his crimes, can't they–"

Ryan cut him off. He was naïve to think it could be so simple. "It's believed he's in Mexico, but if he knows the FBI is looking for him, do you really think he's going to be at home waiting for the doorbell to ring?"

Of course she was right. He could only dream that it would be that easy.

"Now *we* need to talk." Ethan's tone was more somber than it had been during the entire discussion that took place.

Ryan looked at him with such confusion in her eyes. She thought the conversation had concluded. While it had been heavy and serious, he had another topic that was going to be addressed whether she liked it or not.

"What happens once this is all over," he asked.

"I guess you'll go back to whatever you did prior to a couple weeks ago." She pretended not to know what he was talking about.

"Cut the shit, Ryan. I mean us. What happens with us?"

She couldn't hide the erratic thumping in her chest when he said that. *Us*.

"We'll go about our lives just as we did before we met." Saying those words felt like acid, but the idea of a relationship was even more terrifying. Relationships ended, and she would rather have whatever it was that she and Ethan had right now, than to have him shatter her heart in a million pieces when he eventually got bored.

"I can't do that, and even though you're pretending you can, I know this is more than just sex for you." He slid closer to her. He couldn't stand having this conversation without being able to touch her.

"What makes you think that?"

He took her hand in his, which she willingly allowed, not even a hint of her trying to fight it. Ethan then cast her a teasingly sinister grin, which told her that the conversation wasn't stopping anytime soon.

"You're not the type of woman to sleep around with anyone. Why was it so easy for you to do that with me?"

"The first time was–"

"Choose your words carefully," Ethan interrupted. Holding her hand had only heightened his desire to have her back in his bed. If she said the word *mistake* again, he was fully prepared to show her differently.

"I just lost myself," she breathed heavily, diverting her eyes from his.

"I don't think you'd ever allow that," he laughed.

Ethan ran his free hand through his hair and all Ryan could think about was twirling her own fingers in it with him hovering over her. Great. Here she was trying to dismiss the idea of anything between them, and all she wanted was for him to be all over her.

"You know what I think, I think you feel something for me. I think you did that night, otherwise it never would have happened."

Her chest clenched as soon as he said the words. She would never admit how true his words were, but the gleaming eyes watching her every move told her that he already knew.

"And I think I've made it pretty clear how I feel about you," he continued.

That statement did nothing to calm the rapid fluttering inside her.

"I wish you wouldn't say those things," Ryan began, feeling the air around them growing heavy.

"What? That I'm in love with you?"

She couldn't take her eyes from his.

Ethan never thought the words would be so easy for him to say, but he had never felt what he felt for her with anyone else. If she was set on ending things, he had to let her know his feelings.

"You're just," she began. She didn't want to believe that he was being truthful, that would only make things that much harder. He had used the word love before, but there was an intense finality in the way he said it now.

"Let me stop whatever you're trying to tell yourself." He needed to make her see that she was different to him. "That's not something I tell women, and whether you believe me or not, that's not something I've ever told any woman."

Ryan felt increasingly dizzy and her insides were going nuts. Everything he was saying. The way he was looking at her. She wanted nothing more than to forget whatever the world had in store for them and to just be with him, to be with someone who made her feel like she was his whole universe.

Ethan pulled Ryan's hand up and placed it on his chest so that she could feel the beating of his heart. They stayed like that for a few moments. Though Ryan had lost all words, unable to form a coherent thought, Ethan still had a few.

"I know you can't and won't say anything back, and that's fine, for now." There was a playful and knowing glimmer in his eyes, and Ryan was torn between wanting to punch him or kiss him. "I just need you tell me if I'm wrong with one thing."

Ryan nodded, clamming up at what he might need her to say.

"Am I wrong in believing that you might feel the same?"

She held her breath at the question. *You're wrong. You're wrong. You're wrong.* She could repeat the words in her head over and over, regardless how false they were, but they wouldn't come from her lips. All she had to do was say two words and the romantic and passionate side of Ethan would slip away and they could leave everything between them in the past.

After a second more of watching the confliction in her face, "That's what I thought."

He pulled her forward as he fell backward into the couch. One hand tangled itself in her hair while the other held on to her waist. Ethan put everything he had into the kiss. If his words didn't tell her how much he wanted her, she would know now.

Her hair danced playfully over his face like soft strands of feathers tickling down his neck. If there had ever been a kiss that felt as good as sex, this could have been it. Without any words, both could feel all the emotions from the other pouring through. It wasn't a kiss that was rushed, in a haste to get to something more. It was a raw passion, a breaking point, each of them giving in.

Ryan felt the flames washing over her body with every movement of Ethan's hands. When they were together, he gave her all the feelings she never imagined. She tried to ignore them, hoping they'd go away, but the constant butterflies that swirled inside and the way her heart beat whenever he looked at her had become too much. If he wanted her, he had her.

Ethan momentarily broke the kiss to stare into Ryan's eyes. "Bedroom?"

She bit her lip and fought back a smile, not wanting to appear too eager, and nodded.

Ethan ripped her from the couch and she wrapped her legs around him. They fumbled to the bedroom in a tangled mess of desire.

Once Ethan had Ryan on the bed and she quickly began undressing, he almost forgot the outcome from last time. He rushed to the bathroom and strolled back in, waving a condom in his hands, which only caused an adorable laugh from Ryan's reddened and swollen lips.

"Third time's a charm?"

"What is that supposed to mean," she huffed, crawling to the edge of the bed and helping Ethan from his shirt and shorts.

"The first time, you freaked out, and called it a mistake," he teased.

"Stop reminding me," she squealed, pulling him onto the bed.

"The second time you said you wouldn't freak–"

"You didn't wear a condom!"

"Can I tell you something you'll probably hate," he

284

whispered in her ear. His voice was low and deep. It alone caused a penetrating arousal within Ryan. "That was the best sex I've ever had."

Ryan wasn't too sure about that. With her limited experience, hands down Ethan was the best, but she highly doubted she was the same for him.

"I mean it, Ryan," he continued, after noticing her uncertainty. "I've never gone bare, and it felt amazing. The fact that it was with you made it the best." He hovered over her, now completely sheathed. "I'd like to try it again, one day when we don't have to worry about the outcome."

Ryan's eyes widened and they both stopped breathing at the realization of his wording. Ethan placed his forehead on hers and began laughing.

"Too much, too soon?"

"You could say that," Ryan managed, the pitch of her voice rising.

His laughter faded throughout her once his lips fell on hers.

Everything Ethan had done to her body always felt new and different, but sex this time was above and beyond. Ryan couldn't even call it sex. It was so much more.

Ethan was gentle with Ryan; he had been the other times, but this time he made every touch lingering. He thrust into her not for the purpose of chasing a release. He wanted her to feel him, to feel all the missing pieces that couldn't be conveyed with words.

His eyes locked on hers with such adoration and

emotion. "Tell me you're mine."

If Ethan ever talked dirty to any of his lovers, he had never done so with Ryan. She had him pegged for the type that would, but he continued to surprise her.

She didn't know how easily the words could slip from her mouth, or what exactly he was asking for when he said that, but she meant them in every way. "I'm yours," she moaned in his ear.

He softly removed one of her hands from his back and brought it down near her head, entangling their fingers. It was a simple gesture, yet so intimate, and the way he looked at her when he did so told her that this was everything to him. She was everything.

Ryan pulled her other hand to his neck and sealed their lips together. Upon doing so, Ethan's movements became deeper and stronger, if that was even possible. Uncontrollable screams escaped Ryan as that pleasurable sensation shot through her, stealing every doubt and filling her with emotion that she had never known.

Ethan allowed himself to fall soon after into the euphoric bliss.

As if they had done it a thousand times before, they wrapped together beneath the covers and drifted away, leaving the rest of the world behind.

CHAPTER 25

Morning sunlight poured through the slits of the blinds, forcing Ryan to wake. With Ethan's arm wrapped around her bare waist, she allowed her thoughts to drift to the night before. A smile formed on her face when she twisted back to see him still peacefully asleep.

Past hesitation was replaced with a pure and undeniable clarity. She was absolutely in love with this man.

Ryan was able to slip from his grasp on her. He groaned slightly, but remained buried in sleep. She reached for Ethan's discarded t-shirt from the night prior and tossed it on. The smell alone caused sensations to tear through her core.

Groggily she sauntered from his room and through the kitchen, her mind set on a warm shower. The oven clock showed 10:27. She had never slept in that late. Generally, she had a difficult time with sleep, but last night changed that.

Thinking of Ethan, she filled the coffee maker and hit the start button. Regardless when he woke, she assumed that would be first on his list.

She finished her shower and wrapped herself in a towel before going back to her room to find something

287

to wear. It was established that they wouldn't be leaving until Delacruz was caught, so she could put the business side on hold for now. With that, she threw on a pair of cargo pants and a fitted t-shirt that accentuated both her slim figure as well as muscles.

She fought to suppress a laugh when she saw Ethan in his boxers pouring two cups of coffee. He definitely looked like he needed more sleep and his hair was a complete wreck.

"What," he playfully mumbled, although he was quickly becoming more awake by her presence.

"You look…"

"Devilishly handsome?"

Ryan bit her lip once he turned to face her. Even the way he sipped his coffee now turned her on.

Vibrations from the stand next to the door cut their moment short. Ethan grumpily went for his phone, but missed the call. His brows furrowed and his mouth twisted.

"Shit," he sighed, scrolling along the screen. For the last three hours he'd been getting calls and texts from his mother and sister, desperately pleading for him to get in touch.

"I need to make a call or two," he told Ryan, heading toward his room for privacy. He wasn't sure what they wanted, but he didn't want Ryan overhearing anymore of the madness that was his family.

At that, Ryan padded her pockets looking for her own phone. It was still on her nightstand from yesterday. After she and Ethan had *talked* she hadn't been back to her room.

Her face made the same expression as Ethan when she scrolled through more than twenty missed calls and messages.

Perkins.

Perkins.

Levi.

Perkins.

Levi.

Jeff.

It was a continuous cycle of those three names. She was surprised to see two more recent missed calls from Brett. Just as she was about to dial Perkins, the silent phone lit up with an incoming call. Brett again.

"Hello," Ryan hesitated after choosing to accept.

"Shit, Ryan. Everyone has been trying to get in touch with you."

"Is everything okay, what's wrong?" She tried to mask the panic in her voice, but something had to be seriously bad for all the calls.

"Where are you and Ethan," Brett asked.

"At his place. Why?"

"His family has been trying to get in touch with him for hours. They even called Perkins. I'm surprised he's not at Ethan's door by now. Jesus, are you just waking up?"

Ryan dismissed the question, immediately sensing the suspicion in Brett's voice. "What's going on?"

"Old man Lowell had a heart attack."

For a moment, Ryan's brain shut down.

Thankfully, Brett continued on. "He's in the hospital now."

Ryan let out a sigh of relief. "I'll get him there soon."

"Are you sure that's a good idea?"

Ryan was a little surprised that he would ask that, but concluded the conversation when she saw Ethan, now in jeans and a t-shirt, hovering in her doorway.

"Hey, I have to go," she said, quickly hanging up before Brett had the chance to close the conversation on his part.

"My sister told me not to come. They're just doing tests and–"

"I'm not going to tell you what you should or shouldn't do. If you want to go, we'll go."

He wanted to go. Despite knowing about his father's past, at the end of the day, Owen was still Ethan's father. Before Ethan outwardly expressed wanting to go to the hospital, Ryan was already grabbing her concealed holsters from the dresser.

"Seriously?"

"What?"

"We're going to a hospital."

"Are you forgetting what happened at your quiet little mansion?"

He knew she was right, and she wasn't taking any chances by not having at least one weapon on her.

* * *

Ryan had called ahead and had security at the

hospital reserve a parking spot in the small outdoor lot. She didn't like the idea of having to use the parking garage.

Ethan noticed that Ryan had become extremely antsy about leaving his sanctuary, and he'd be lying if he said he wasn't a little nervous as well. Things were escalating too fast and he only hoped that Emilio would be caught soon so that he wouldn't be in constant fear.

Ethan raised a brow and pointed to the sign on the sliding glass door. *Gun Free Zone.*

Ryan shook her head. "Don't start."

She turned briefly and examined the surroundings outside once they were in the glass doors. They didn't ensure any safety, and she didn't allow her thoughts to think for a minute that they'd be safe. Ethan anywhere in the public was one of the most dangerous things right now.

For a split second, Ryan felt at ease when Ethan grabbed her hand in the elevator. When she looked down and saw their entangled fingers, a whole new issue invaded her thoughts with the fuzzy lines that she and Ethan had created.

"Thank you for being here," he whispered in her ear. He didn't need to speak so softly; they were the only two in the small box.

"I'm a little obligated to be," Ryan admitted, trying to halt anything romantic, given the situation.

Ethan chuckled, sending happy echoes through Ryan. "In some ways, yes," he responded while tightly giving her hand a few squeezes.

He kept his hold on her down the hallway toward a large waiting room. His mother or sister had obviously told him where to go, because he seemed pretty confident in his sense of direction.

Ethan scowled at Ryan as she yanked her hand from his upon seeing his family, everyone minus his father and Oliver.

Gwen rushed up to Ethan, and Ryan quickly distanced herself from him. Though Gwen's eyes were now dried, her tears had infected them, leaving a puffy redness.

Seated in chairs, from the direction Gwen came, were Leighton with Mia cuddled on her lap, flipping through a colorful book with minimal words, and Danny next to her on a tablet. They all looked completely exhausted.

"Is everything okay," Ethan asked. "Why are all of you out here and not with dad?"

"Calm down, sweetie," Gwen began. "We just left his room. The doctors needed to do a few things."

"What the hell happened?"

"I don't know. He came home from work yesterday, visibly upset, and he woke early this morning with pains. Before I could do anything, he was on the floor." Gwen began to sob again.

Ethan didn't want to think that all the Delacruz stuff had gotten to his father, but he was pretty sure it played a large part. If Owen had talked to Gwen, he had obviously left that part out.

They sat in silence. Ryan firmly clasped her hands in her lap. Ethan had made a gesture with his eyes toward them, but Ryan shook her head. Too much had happened in the last few days. Openly bringing their relationship to light would have been the icing on a cake that was toppling to the floor.

"Mommy," Mia squealed, looking up to Leighton. "When is daddy coming back?"

Ethan made eye contact with his sister and she mouthed the word *London*. Apparently the divorce was really happening. Ethan was relieved for his sister. She kept most of her problems private from the family, but he knew that she hadn't been happy for years.

Oliver and Leighton had met through Owen. Ethan didn't intend to make the same mistake with Ella.

A doctor appeared and glanced around at the family. "Oh, there's more." He looked a little concerned before continuing. "Not all of you at once."

Leighton waved her hands for Ethan to go. "We've already seen him. I know he's as good as he can be for now. You should go."

Ethan rose, and looked down at Ryan. Her eyes widened and she shook her head. As much as she didn't want to be left alone with any of Ethan's prying family, she was certain that she didn't want to deal with Owen even more.

Ultimately, Ethan and his mother both left for Owen's room.

Ryan was left with the psychologist. The smirk on Leighton's face said it all.

"So," she began slowly, putting a squirmy Mia in the chair next to her, while giving her full attention to Ryan sitting across from her. "Until mother figures this out, or Ethan comes clean, I don't have anyone to talk to about it."

"What are you referring to?"

"Come on Ryan," she laughed. "What is the *deal* between you and my brother?"

Ryan didn't know how to answer that. It was still new and very unclear.

"He's changed since I was last in the states," Leighton continued, which quickly caught Ryan's attention. "And I've never seen him look at any woman the way he looks at you, but there's something about you that's a little troubling."

Ryan's jaw dropped. All this time she liked Ethan's sister, but now Leighton found her *troubling*.

Her laughter pierced the air. "Sorry. I don't mean it like that. I think you're good for my brother. I really do. What's troubling is the whole role reversal."

"I get that I have a masculine job, but I'm really not–"

"It has nothing to do with your job. More often than not, women tend to put their emotions out there first. Now, I don't know if my brother was just trying to piss my father off when he used that word the other day..." She paused when she saw Ryan's face clench, and it became obvious. "Wow, I never thought I'd see the day when my brother said that to a woman that wasn't related to him." Leighton sat back in her chair in disbelief. "Do you love him?"

It killed Ryan that Leighton had to ask that question. "I don't know." She knew, but she had so many other things to think about right now, and had to put the idea in the back of her mind. Besides, how could she admit that, say those words to his sister, when she hadn't said them to Ethan yet?

"I think you do."

Well, isn't she just a damn clairvoyant.

"You should tell him, it isn't–"

"I saw some vending machines back there, did anyone want anything, candy or soda maybe" Ryan asked, quickly interrupting Leighton before the conversation could get any heavier.

Leighton pursed her lips with happy satisfaction and shook her head, like she knew that she had won the battle and the war, that this was Ryan admitting defeat.

* * *

Ethan didn't know why he expected to see this frail old man in the hospital bed, but that most certainly wasn't the way he found his father.

Owen was angrily hitting the buttons on the television remote connected to his bed when Ethan and Gwen stepped in.

"You'd think for all the damn money they're going to charge insurance they could put in a fucking remote that works," he spat out.

"Honey." Gwen rushed to him and kissed him on the forehead. "You need to stay calm. The doctor doesn't want you stressing out about anything, especially something so trivial."

295

Owen paid little attention to his wife, instead focusing on Ethan. "I'm surprised you came," he huffed.

"Regardless how I feel about you, you're still my father."

"What is going on," Gwen asked, slowly enunciating every word.

Ethan wasn't going to bring it up. If his father ever wanted to reveal his secrets, that was on him. As far as Ethan was concerned, he wanted nothing more to do with any of it. He wasn't going to let his father's past get the best of his thoughts. If he allowed himself to care about it, then he was holding the burden as well.

"He knows about Rosa and the baby." The words were so careless and matter-of-fact.

"Oh," Gwen sighed.

Ethan's eyes bulged to the point that his eyeballs could very well have fallen from his face. *She knew. His mother knew.* It felt like his chest had just taken a full and direct hit from a wrecking ball.

"Ethan," Gwen began in her soothing, motherly voice.

"Stop, mom." He held his hand up. He had to pace, move around, something. If he stood in the same spot, he thought he might pass out. "You knew?" At first his voice was barely a whisper, but once the anger in him boiled out, "You fucking knew?!"

"Ethan..."

"Don't talk to your mother like that," Owen chimed in.

Like a madman, Ethan laughed at his father for correcting his language.

"Are you serious right now?! You want to lecture me?! You're the one who cheated on her! You fathered another child and–"

"Sweetheart," Gwen interrupted, grabbing Ethan's arm, trying to calm his temper. "We worked through this years ago."

"I don't know you, either of you. How could you stay with him? And what about the baby?" Millions of questions continued to pour through his mind. This was twice as horrible as yesterday.

"By the time we found out, it was too late, and Rosa wanted to keep the baby," Gwen responded. "We all agreed to cut our losses."

"What the fuck does that mean?!"

"It means she lived her life and we lived ours," Owen interrupted. "The affair ended before I even knew she was pregnant."

"Why does any of that matter? You know what, I don't care. You cheated on mom," Ethan growled. "And you," he began, trying to soften his words to his mother. "You stayed with him."

"It was for the best to repair things, especially for you and your sister," she admitted, but her face spoke differently.

"What you really mean is that you stayed for the money." He regretted his words the instant he saw their effect on his mother's face. It was the truth, though no one had ever said as much. By the time all this had happened, Leighton was already in college and Ethan was nearing that point. They weren't children that needed shielding from a divorce.

"Don't act all high and mighty. Look at you," Owen roared.

"Me? I didn't father a child with a married woman while I was married!"

To Ethan's surprise, his father laughed at him, but it was his next words that were cutting. "At least I wasn't fucking a prostitute."

"What the hell are you talking about?" Ethan's fists clenched in rage at whatever sick thing his father was insinuating.

Owen sat up straighter in his bed, attempting to look commanding and dominant. A heart attack had done nothing to cause him to change, not one bit.

"I thought hiring someone like Beckett would knock you down a few steps, keep you out of the spotlight," he laughed. Ethan only became more infuriated at Ryan's name coming from his father. "Hell, you even started coming to work, because you were too embarrassed to be out in public with someone who made you look like a pussy."

"Owen," Gwen whispered. "Please, stop this." Tears began to form in Gwen's eyes, and she was the only person Ethan felt even a little sorry for at that moment.

Owen ignored her, like her presence had faded from the room. "You do realize that I'm basically paying her to screw you."

Ethan had no words.

"Don't look so shocked. Everyone knows," Owen

scoffed.

"Ethan..." Obviously Gwen didn't know. "Is that the girlfriend," she hesitated. Her eyes tightened up, pleading for him to deny it.

"Yeah," Ethan acknowledged confidently; although technically he and Ryan hadn't clarified what their relationship was.

He had never seen either of his parents look so disappointed in him.

"So, all that, the other day at the house, the entire time it was *that* woman," Gwen gasped.

Ethan really hoped that her words weren't coming out as they sounded. Ryan was beautiful, confident, strong, determined, and smart as hell. She looked past the surface. She treated him like no other woman had. She was genuine and real. She made him feel things he never thought he'd feel for a woman. Falling in love with her had been too easy. She was anything but *that* woman.

"She's not good enough for either of you, right?"

His mother looked away, but his father only glared at him and shook his head.

"You come in here, after I've just recovered from something life-threatening," Owen angrily began. Ethan couldn't help but roll his eyes about it being so serious now, when earlier all his father cared about was a damn remote not working. "You want to get on me about my life, look at yours."

"I have," Ethan quickly responded. "I'm happy, and I couldn't be happier with my choices." With that, Ethan turned to leave.

Owen couldn't let him go without one more jab. "You can tell that whore that she's fired."

"Go to hell, *dad*."

CHAPTER 26

"Don't you want to stay a little longer," Ryan asked when Ethan practically pulled her like a ragdoll toward the elevator. "We just got here."

"I'm done." His voice was stern.

"You're fuming."

"I don't want to talk about it."

The doors closed and the silence on the way down was ominous and uncomfortable. Ethan didn't reach for her hand and for the most part appeared to be in a different world entirely. Ryan didn't press him to talk any further. Yesterday, after discovering his father's past, she had seen how he lashed out. Now that he had time to process it, she was sure that more words were exchanged, probably enough to give the old man another heart attack.

Ethan was a little confused when Ryan asked him to wait inside the doors of the hospital while she got the vehicle. She gave him some explanation about how someone could have known he was visiting and been waiting for them to return. It was a short walk to the parking spot, still safer than the garage next door, but she wasn't having it. Ethan couldn't wait until Delacruz was caught. As much as he cared about Ryan, he needed her assignment to end, for them to have a normal relationship, one where he felt like she actually *needed* him.

"Asshole," Ryan muttered under her breath as a black car tried to cut her off from exiting the lot. She swerved and went around, failing to even yield to the stop sign upon making a right turn from the lot.

Ethan ignored her and said nothing. He felt unsettled about various events from the past weeks, and yesterday and today was like someone dropped the whole damn Giza pyramid complex on him. Ryan sensed as much, but she wasn't good with any of the things girls were supposed to be good with. She tried to separate her feelings from daily life; obviously it wasn't healthy, but it had worked up until she met Ethan. Even now, she saw that he was troubled with family matters, but what could she say? Her parents were divorced. Hell, half the time she didn't even know which continent they were on. They barely spoke or saw each other, aside from holidays here and there. She was the last person to try to give Ethan advice on dealing with family.

"Are we going straight back home," Ethan asked, his voice breaking through the ancient rock music.

Ryan let out an exhausted breath. She knew Ethan was getting frustrated with his lack of freedom. "It's for the best. You'll be safest there."

Ryan glanced in both her side and rearview mirrors. Something felt off. The light she needed to take was red, but there was a green left turn signal. Trying not to look like a crazy person who didn't know their way around, she slipped through two lanes as

302

smoothly as possible and took it. From her peripheral vision, she saw that she was getting a look from Ethan.

"I know now isn't the time," he sheepishly began. "But there's something I want to ask you."

"Okay?" Ryan drew the small word out, forming it into a question.

A smile appeared on Ethan's face. Upon glancing over to him, her body heated up. She was definitely screwed when it came to Ethan Lowell.

"It's about us."

Ryan's hands tightened on the steering wheel and her mind began to race at what he could possibly have to say on the matter that couldn't wait. She tried to pay attention to him, but something in her gut wasn't allowing her to give him her full focus.

Ethan noticed with each passing minute since they had left the hospital that Ryan's behavior was changing. At first he thought it was due to his silence and moodiness that he projected after seeing his family. He had no intention of ever telling her what his father said. He also neglected to mention that she was *fired*. If she was, he was certain Perkins would inform her. Pushing all that aside, he knew that something else had caused Ryan to change. Her nervousness that she tried to conceal did little to help his own.

It was a simple question, and he wanted to make it more special so that it didn't sound like a little elementary school crush.

"Will you stop staring at me and say what you

need to say."

Her laugh was different; it wasn't real, which only created more doubt in Ethan's mind.

"Am I making you nervous?"

"No?"

"I know now isn't the time to ask, but I want this to be serious between us, and–" His words were quickly cut short as his right side was flung against the door when Ryan made a sharp and illegal left turn. "What the fuck, Ryan?" After looking around some more, he didn't even recognize the area. "Where the hell are we going?"

Ryan ignored his question, and hit a call button on the dashboard.

"Hey, I can't talk, I have some shit with a fu–"

"I'm in trouble," Ryan interrupted.

Ethan recognized the voice on the speaker in the SUV as the one belonging to Agent Delgado. A brief silence followed and voices in the background on the other end faded.

"What's going on?"

"We're being followed and I have a feeling it's going to get a little intense. I've shared GPS with you," she spat out.

Ethan looked in his mirror. The same black car that had cut them off at the hospital was still behind them. That wasn't a coincidence. Ryan had made some questionable turns that had gotten them nowhere near his penthouse, and now he realized why. For a good portion of the time, she knew they were being followed.

"Why didn't you tell me," Ethan yelled at her as soon as she got off the phone.

"I didn't want to worry you," she answered, far too calm for Ethan's liking.

Before he could reply, there was a piercing ding, followed by another.

"Fuck!"

Ryan made another sharp turn, this time to the right. The seatbelts did little for either of them at this point. She groaned at the street they had turned on. The last thing she wanted to do was put innocent people in harm's way, and the six lanes of traffic wasn't to her liking; however, the shots did cease momentarily.

She continued to weave in and out of traffic. The car that followed attempted to do the same, but they weren't nearly as fast and definitely clumsier about it.

"I really don't like this," Ethan groaned, clutching to whatever he could.

"It's bulletproof for the most part."

"I meant your driving at this point!"

Despite the tense situation, Ryan couldn't help but let out a genuine laugh; however, Ethan glared at her, finding there to be nothing humorous.

"You're forgetting who my brother is," she reminded him as she slipped from the far right lane through the center, to the left, in all of two seconds.

"I'm pretty sure driving doesn't count as a genetic similarity!"

Ryan hit another button and the screen in the

center of the dashboard extended into a grid of the streets. Taking her chances, she cut across three lanes of oncoming traffic and onto a two-way street.

"You're really going to have to trust me in a second." She looked back and though the car was farther behind, it wouldn't last for long. Personally, she didn't want it to. She just needed them far enough away from bystanders.

"I trust you."

"Yeah?" She glanced between the map and her mirrors. "You know all those fancy cars of yours?" There was a panicky gleam in her eye before she continued. "How well do you trust your driving?"

Ethan was about to ask her to repeat herself over the guitars and drums blaring throughout the car. Between her music and the bullets, it took him a minute to think clearly to process what she was saying.

"No! No way!"

"Ethan," Ryan growled, clenching her eyes for the briefest of seconds. "I have an idea, but I really need your help."

He knew he never really had a choice. He'd do whatever she asked.

"What's your plan?"

"How about I tell you as we go?"

Ethan closed his eyes and shook his head. "Jesus Christ, Ryan."

She glanced at the clock, it had been less than two minutes since she called JD. There was no way in hell that anyone, local or FBI, would make it in time to do anything. She veered onto a smaller street, now leading into the warehouse district. Technically the single lane was big enough for semi-trucks, though two cars in opposite directions could squeeze through.

Ethan didn't understand, as long as they were in the middle of the city, the firing was not as bad and only intermittent. Now it sounded like they were in the middle of a warzone.

Ryan hit the cruise control and quickly unbuckled both Ethan and herself.

"I need to get into the back. Grab the wheel and get over," she commanded.

The car jerked to the side as Ryan kicked the wheel before Ethan was able to have a firm grip. It threw her body between the seats, not giving her a clean entry.

"Ethan!"

"Next time, try giving me directions prior to executing," he yelled back.

Ryan popped the bottom of the seat up and its modification allowed it to swipe up and slide beneath just as a box rose. Ethan tried to look in the rearview mirror but couldn't tell what the hell Ryan had going on. Soon she had pipes that she began twisting together, and he heard a few clicks of the contraption locking in place.

"Is that a damn bazooka?!"

"No," Ryan only partially lied. It was an experimental weapon that an outside friend of The Agency was dabbling with. He was a mechanical engineer that began tinkering with weaponry, creation and improvement, all of course kept under the radar. He had given Perkins this as a gift. Ryan had fired it once for practice, but she never thought it would be something they'd have to use. When she was given the ST-5 as the mode of transportation, she was well aware of the secret hidden within.

"It's just something in case of emergencies, but I only have one use on it," she said as she began positioning herself.

Ryan glanced over her shoulder at the large GPS screen, judging from their speed, she only had about half a minute to give Ethan directions.

"I need you to listen carefully. You see that button on the dash, third from the left, eight pointed star?"

"Yeah?"

"When I tell you to, hit it. Also, scrunch up, keep yourself covered with the seat, the Kevlar will protect you." *Hopefully.* "Two streets ahead, I need you to make a sharp left. We good?"

Ethan didn't acknowledge her.

"Ethan!"

"I'm processing!"

They passed the first street.

"Okay, got it," he quickly confirmed.

He desperately wanted to ask her what the button was for, but he had a feeling he'd know soon enough, and surprisingly, not knowing made it a little more bearable than knowing what was to come.

Ryan didn't tell him the plan. So far he hadn't freaked out too much about the situation and she needed him to focus so that she could as well.

She felt the sharp turn of the vehicle but managed to hold on to her bearings and keep her position locked.

Halfway through the turn, "Now!"

The car behind them had barely made it around the corner when the back glass of the SUV whipped down upon Ethan pressing the ominous button. Two bullets made it in and then there was only the roaring sound of the explosion behind them.

The car burst into flames, glass and other particles from the vehicle shattering in every direction amongst the warehouses. The SUV drove approximately another three seconds before meeting its own fatal end.

The jolt from the collision upon passing a side street flung Ryan from the middle of the SUV to the driver's side. She felt her shoulder crunch against the door, and once the vehicle stilled, the pain that shot through her arm became excruciating. She assumed nothing was broken, but it would soon be a hell of a bruise.

Upon instinct she made her way out to open the driver's door and check on Ethan, knowing that he hadn't put on a seatbelt after switching with her.

"Hey," she breathed.

"What the fuck happened?"

They both looked over to the irate delivery truck driver. He was in the wrong, not expecting a speeding vehicle to be coming through the warehouse alleys.

"We have to get out of here," was all Ryan said as

she jumped back in the vehicle and began rummaging.

She pulled out several things; one was a gun that she tossed at Ethan. It was much larger than the ones he had seen her with, and he gave her a questionable look.

"That's my personal one, it's a Glock 20. Yes, I also realize how crazy I am putting it in your hands," she huffed.

He was fully expecting it to be over. She had taken out the car chasing them. "Why the hell do I need this?"

The look in her eyes said too much, and it sent Ethan's stomach churning to the point that he wanted to throw up. It wasn't about to be over.

"I'm really hoping I'm wrong," Ryan began, noting the time on the clock behind her; it had only been four minutes since she got off the phone with JD. The lack of sirens wailing made her heart pound that much faster. "Look, we have no transportation, and I can't have you out in the open. We have to find an empty warehouse and just wait."

"Just wait?! That's your solution?"

"I don't have a fucking drone up there telling me where anyone is. I don't know if there are more coming, but I'm not taking that chance," she screamed.

She found a spare magazine for her gun. She never hated herself more for being so unprepared. All they needed to do was make a quick visit to the hospital. Between the gun in Ethan's hand, and her agency issued one, they had exactly forty-five shots. It sounded like a lot, but she knew that every time she fired it needed to count desperately.

Ryan pulled something else from beneath the seat. "Put it on," she told Ethan as it flew through the air.

"What is this," he asked stupidly. Once the question came from his lips he realized it was a bulletproof vest and if the seriousness of the situation hadn't hit him yet, that did it.

Ryan helped him with it until he was completely strapped in. Their eyes finally met and he knew something was wrong. It was the unknown that frightened the both of them.

"Let's go," Ryan said, marching off before the delivery driver could make his way to them through the blockage.

"Wait," Ethan shouted, finding it difficult to keep up with her. "Where's your vest?"

She didn't answer, and he found her pace to be increasing. All the warehouses looked the same and he had to wonder if she knew where she was going or if she even had a plan prior to now. Come to think of it, nothing had been planned. Everything since leaving the hospital had just been luck with a little skill on her part.

"Ryan! Where the hell is your vest," he screamed. He yanked her, more forcefully than he wanted, so that she was facing him, and he wished he hadn't.

"I don't have one," she quietly admitted, a soft flicker of sadness in her eyes, confirming his worst fear.

In that moment, Ethan's heart sank.

CHAPTER 27

Ryan yanked the gun from Ethan's hands after examining the cheap handle to what appeared to be an abandoned warehouse. Two shots later it was busted enough for her to tinker with it and make it open.

"What the hell is this," he asked after she tossed the weapon back to him. Though she had complete control over it, he noted the way her arms jerked from the recoil.

"An awesome gun, but you're down to thirteen shots now," she calmly told him as they entered the darkened building.

The only light that poured in was from the windows at the top of the metal frame, and it took a moment for their eyes to adjust.

Ryan quickly studied the small building. It was extremely tiny compared to the rest of the warehouses, and completely empty now. An elevated platform about eight feet above them ran along the left side with a hall down the middle leading back. Ryan figured that it could have been used by an overseer or boss. Farther forward on the left, past where the platform cut off, there were gradual and wide metal stairs leading to the second level.

"There must be offices up there, hopefully access to windows," Ryan observed, quickly ushering Ethan up the stairs that made an abundant amount of noise.

The stairs cut to the left and there was only one room. There were no doors, no nothing. The stairs simply ended in a large room. When Ryan examined further, she encountered the hallway that led to the platform.

"It seems this is the only place in here. Everything else is just the one story warehouse floor."

At the far wall, the one that ran even with the front of the building, there was a vertical sliding window from floor-to-ceiling, with the exception of about a foot, allowing the room to receive more light than the downstairs. It was a crappy angle, but she would be able to keep an eye on the entry door. After all, they'd be easy to find with the handle broken.

She was shaken awake when her phone buzzed.

Perkins.

Before she could finish a two syllable answer, his voice was booming through the speaker.

"I got an alert that the ST-5 was involved in a collision!"

Of course he did. The damn vehicle was so secure that if a grocery cart tapped it, he'd be alerted.

"We're fine, as fine as we can be. Everything is fine."

"You just said fine three times. You're up shit creek aren't you?"

Ryan turned down the volume on her speaker,

realizing that Ethan was eyeing her. "Pretty much," she responded. After briefly pulling her phone away, she realized how fast everything had happened. It had barely been six minutes since she talked to JD. "Just so you know, I'm in building 39 in the warehouse district. I had to get him out of the open. I'm not sure if there are any–" her voice stopped immediately as three figures began approaching the outside of the building.

She had two options. She could fire now and completely give away their hiding spot, and possibly end up wasting ammunition in the process. The other option was to allow them to enter the building and either use the platform or the stairs to her advantage.

Every part of her screamed the latter, but three against one *again*, was pushing it. It all boiled down to what would keep Ethan the safest.

"I have to go," Ryan whispered, ignoring Perkins protesting on the other end.

Ethan rushed to Ryan, transfixed on something outside the window. "What's going on?"

"Get back from the window," she insisted, much to his displeasure, not answering his question.

He did as he was told while she slid the window for just enough of an opening.

The angle definitely wasn't ideal for her, but with the men so close to one another, she was quite certain that if she caught them off-guard, she could immobilize all of them within four seconds of the first shot.

Just from what she could see, they each had a

pistol, but only one actually had it in his hand. He was her first target. Judging from the looks of it, they were nothing more than common gangsters, simple drug dealers. She didn't anticipate for them to have incredible drawing abilities nor to be expert marksmen.

Ethan flinched as soon as the shots rang out. He hadn't seen what was beneath the window, but he fully expected glass to shatter at any moment. To his surprise, nothing.

Silence ensued and Ryan attempted to relax, even if only for a brief second, as she leaned against the wall.

Thirty-four. That was how many shots were left between the two guns.

"How many," Ethan eventually asked.

Ryan tried to get her breathing under control, but this was hands down the most nervous and insecure that she had ever been in a situation. "Three, and I used more shots than I intended."

Ethan held out the gun she had given him but she only shook her head. He had no idea why she gave it to him. If push came to shove, he knew how to use it, though what he'd end up hitting would be an entirely different story.

Just like an atomic bomb, a massive burst of the world crashing down, it happened. The shattering of the glass, though quick and instant could have easily been in slow motion. Ethan stepped to the far wall and Ryan dropped to the ground, only covered by the foot of ledge beneath where the window once was.

There was one person darting about down below. She hesitantly peaked over the ledge and fired twice, but missed.

Thirty-two.

Focused on the crunching glass beneath her and the echoes of the shots ringing in her ears, she missed something critical that Ethan did not. In the seconds since the disintegration of the glass and the missed shots, Ryan allowed frustration to consume her, knowing that she had very little ammunition to waste. It wasn't until she attempted to rise that Ethan threw her against the wall, covering her with his body as shots came from the stairs on the other side of the room.

Blindly she fired around Ethan as another shot rang out. When his body jolted against hers, she knew that he had taken one of the hits. As if she were a machine, she quickly changed out magazines, the numbers ticking in her head.

She managed to push around Ethan and fire at the second shooter, sending him backwards, careening down the stairs from which he came.

Twenty-six.

Ryan rushed back toward Ethan. "What the fuck were you thinking?!" She tried to hide her emotions; she couldn't let them get the best of her right now.

"I heard the stairs," he began, wincing in pain.

Ryan began examining him but saw no blood, not even a drop. The vest had protected him.

"Shit. I thought that would feel more like paint-ball," he laughed, but it was insincere and did nothing to mask his fear. He only wanted to try to alleviate the seriousness of their situation.

Ryan didn't want to cry and tried her best to stifle away the tears.

Fuck being a girl.

Once she was able to look into his eyes, "You saved me."

Ethan simply pulled her in tightly, praying that it wasn't the last time he'd be able to hold her, and kissed her on the forehead.

Mere seconds felt like minutes, and a minute fell into what seemed like an hour. Both knew it hadn't been that long. Both knew that help was on the way. Unfortunately, help wasn't as fast as the evil pouring in.

"Ethan, I need you to get down the hall between here and the platform," Ryan urgently insisted.

Anger flashed across Ethan's face. "You've got to be kidding! You'd be dead if I weren't here."

He towered over her, not budging for a second.

They heard it. With the sounds of the pounding footsteps and lack of sirens, they knew that this could be it.

Ryan fought back tears, but she felt one or two escape.

"Then you'll have to help me."

Ethan's heart raced. This wasn't a video game. There was no do-over.

"Stay away from the window," she began, motioning him to the side. It was the side of the room more hidden upon reaching the top of the stairs from below. Ryan took the opposite side. The shooters would encounter her as soon as they rounded the last corner of the staircase.

Ethan didn't like the setup one bit. He was the one who had some type of protection when Ryan had nothing. With the steps growing louder, he wasn't able to argue with her. At least he was doing something other than hiding in a corner, relying on her to save him.

Ryan's voice grew quiet. "You take whoever is on the farthest right, I'll take care of the rest," she instructed, avoiding eye contact. "Aim for the torso. Trust me, that gun will do the rest."

She then raised her gun and held it toward the large entry, prepared to fire at the slightest movement.

Her sense of hearing was still in the distance, searching for the sounds of help with each passing second, yet still fully aware of the footsteps rushing toward them. One second, then another, passed. Sweat dripped down her back and her heart worked at an unrecognizable speed.

She glanced toward Ethan, fully expecting him to be a wreck, but if he was, he was damn good at hiding it. She had been hesitant putting that gun in his hands at first. As much as she hated to admit it, she really needed him right now.

Ryan easily took the novices by surprise. She was quicker and more accurate with her shots. They continued to round the stairs which was insanely stupid after the first man was taken down. They should have hid around the corner, waited, perhaps even shot blindly, not continue to walk right into her line of fire.

Fourteen?

Two more rounded the corner and Ryan took the first, the one on the left. The one on the right nearly exploded, thrown backward into the wall, blood staining the stone as his body keeled over and rolled down the stairs from which he came.

It was Ethan's shot. Ryan couldn't believe it. She had hoped he wouldn't choke, and he didn't. She wanted to give him a high-five or a hug, but quickly thought more logical thoughts. This was far from over and they were too low on ammunition.

Nine? She was gradually losing count between the two guns.

There was an ominous silence. Not a single step was heard. Not a click of a gun. Not even a breath. Ryan lost count of the bodies.

Like the speed of an enraged black mamba, two bodies darted from around the stairwell, and they were prepared.

The pain was instant, but the adrenaline kept her standing long enough to unload the rest of her gun. Thankfully Ethan stepped in once Ryan stopped firing.

Letting his guard down, forgetting what may have still lurked below them, he rushed to Ryan to steady her, leaning her against the wall as she slid to the floor.

"What the hell happened?"

"I'm out," she breathed. She looked down at her leg and clenched her teeth so tightly that they were on the verge of cracking. "Fuck," she hissed.

Ethan couldn't see the wound, but the hole in her cargo pants said enough. Blood flowed through and down her leg, turning the khaki fabric below her left knee a deep crimson.

"How many do you have left," Ryan asked, attempting to draw Ethan's attention away from her leg. Her last count had been nine between their two guns, most of those shots belonging to Ethan.

"I...I don't know," he stammered. "I know I wasted some."

He put the gun in Ryan's lap for her to take out the magazine and check. She tried her hardest to hide her disappointment.

Two.

"What can we do about your leg," Ethan quickly asked, watching the tiniest puddle of blood form on the floor.

"Nothing. It's fine."

Everything was fucking fine.

"FBI," a voice familiar to the both of them shouted from below.

"Oh, thank god," Ethan gasped and pulled Ryan in for a hug.

She winced and tried to hide her pain from the movement.

"I don't want you trying to get down those stairs. Wait right here," Ethan insisted, and before Ryan could contest, began his descent down.

He tried to avoid the bloodbath of dead bodies draped along the stairs, but found that his shoes were soon sloshing through the mess. He had a pretty strong stomach for the most part, but seeing what his gun had done to one of the men brought his insides to the verge of expelling everything he had in him.

Ryan breathed a sigh of relief and allowed the breeze from the shattered window to wash over her. It was all over.

Her stomach tightened at the quietness from the faint wind. Where were the sirens? Sounds of vehicles? Shouting officers?

She looked toward the stairs and knew something was wrong. She had allowed Ethan to leave, completely unprotected. If her heart ever completely stopped beating, it was in that moment.

CHAPTER 28

Ethan stood frozen in the middle of the stairs once the warehouse floor came into view. Before him were four satisfied faces, two that he knew. Emilio Delacruz was one of the men, along with two of his lackeys. The other face took Ethan further by surprise. It was the voice that had called out.

Brett.

Ethan had only met the bodyguard once, on the night of the charity party. He was flabbergasted that one of Ryan's own coworkers was playing for a different team.

"Is she dead," Brett asked. The way his words came out, not even bothering to say her name, caused Ethan's blood to boil, but seeing the four guns in his presence meant he couldn't do anything about how he felt.

Brett scoffed and rolled his eyes when Ethan didn't respond, and instead directed his attention to Emilio. "He's all yours now. We'll check upstairs while you have your fun."

"About how long until we've got problems," Emilio asked.

"I think it's been roughly ten minutes since the alert on the crash, so not long. Make your seconds count."

Emilio Delacruz motioned toward Ethan with his gun, and Ethan moved in the direction he was told. Soon he was off the stairs and on level ground with the man. He hated where he was standing. Behind Delacruz, he could see the platform, but he couldn't see Ryan down the hall. All he could do was wait helplessly for the ringing of the shots that would soon come.

* * *

Ryan knew something was terrifyingly wrong, but what? FBI wasn't in the building, she was certain about that much, although she had been positive that she recognized the voice that called out.

With only two bullets left and the guns of her enemies down the stairwell or below the window with their dead bodies, she had no chance.

Her mind started racing into overdrive; she tucked the large gun into the back of her cargo pants, put aside the pain spewing through her leg, and limped down the hall, knowing her only chance of surviving would be getting her hands onto another weapon. She didn't have time to dwell on her mistakes, but that didn't stop her from taking a second to curse herself for not having her body armed from top to bottom.

There was a little cubbyhole with a locked door. It was enough to conceal her from blatantly standing in the open, and for once she had to hope like hell that both luck and skill would be on her side.

Footsteps carried up the staircase, growing louder with every beat of her heart.

Gunshots rang out like a hailstorm, but they were all located in the room she had just been in. Knowing that the shots were there and not below where Ethan had gone was the only thing that gave her a glimmer of hope.

"Did she climb out of the window," one of the men asked.

"These ceiling tiles are pretty fucked up," another mentioned. "Maybe she's up in the rafters."

"No," the familiar voice sighed.

Ryan couldn't place it, but she knew that person, and it most definitely wasn't anyone from the FBI.

"She couldn't have gotten up there," he hesitated. "Unless she's injured and pretty boy helped stow her away."

There was a silence as the three men contemplated.

"Check down the hall," the familiar voice whispered, though it was loud enough to cause Ryan's intestines to clench.

As the footsteps began to approach she knew every movement had to be precise and accurate, injured or not.

* * *

After the string of gunfire died and he could still hear the men's muffled voices, especially the one that he knew to be Brett, Ethan's heart broke. Ryan was good, ridiculously good, but even the best heroes and heroines had their limits. There was no possible way for Ryan to have survived. It sounded like the Fourth of July up there. The smell from above floated down and filled his nostrils. He couldn't even focus on the man pacing back and forth spilling some awful speech.

"Did you really think she was that invincible," he laughed, watching Ethan as he stared over and above his head to the platform. "I'll give it to her," Emilio began, motioning behind him to the emptiness. "She was good. Kept you alive a lot longer than I would have thought."

"Why are you doing this," Ethan asked, an almost whisper. He had to block out thoughts of Ryan or else he'd crumble. It would have been one thing for him to mess up the only relationship he ever wanted to have, but this outcome was too unfair.

"I intend to take away from your father everything that he took away from me," Emilio growled.

* * *

He was right there. Ryan could smell the scent of cheap cologne as the floor creaked beneath him so subtly. The shine of his shoe was the first glimpse of him that she encountered, and after one more step, she went for it.

She put all the force and energy that she could muster into her right arm as she attempted to choke the life from him. It was difficult, and apparently the car crash had left her with more hurt limbs than she anticipated. He was much taller, so much so that she dangled from his neck while she pulled him backwards and he gasped for air. For a second he tried to fight back, but she had taken him by surprise and he took too long in calculating his next move. Slowly he sank beneath her, his gun still dangling in his left hand. She quickly grabbed it as soon as her feet hit the floor.

Ryan knew that he wasn't dead, and though it was unnecessary and it would be just another memory to add to her growing list of haunting nightmares, she took two shots, making sure that he'd never wake again.

* * *

The two gunshots startled both Emilio and Ethan.
Hope.
If Ryan was dead, those shots would have been unnecessary.
Maybe they were putting her out of her misery.
No.
With as many shots as he heard earlier, something drastically different had to be taking place. Ryan had to still be alive. She had a thought process unlike anyone he had ever met. She had to have come up with some plan.

* * *

Another man placed himself in the hallway, and full of frustration, Ryan unleashed fire from the gun she had just confiscated, sending him flying backwards across the room.

That final click made her sick once again.

All she had was the Glock 20 with two shots. She knew that she still had at least one more asshole to take care of, and there was a big uncertainty as to what waited below.

* * *

Ethan saw Emilio Delacruz begin to get panicky and nervous and had to wonder if he was aware that his men were gradually being taken down by an injured *girl*. At least that's what he hoped. He tried not to let his satisfaction pierce through him, only to be short-lived.

* * *

"Come out," a lone voice rang out. When Ryan hesitated, "I know you're empty Ryan. Get the fuck out here."

She could be defiant, stand in her hall of safety and wait for him to show himself, that is if he truly believed that she was empty. Then she had about a millisecond to nail him with two shots.

Two damn shots.

"I'm not coming in a darkened hallway sweet-heart," the voice huffed, quickly growing impatient.

Ryan knew help was coming, she only had to wait a little longer.

Ethan.

She needed to get to Ethan as soon as possible. Hiding in the hall wasn't doing him any favors.

"Who are you," she asked, finding her voice.

"Just get out here. I have no intention of firing right away," he laughed.

Ryan had to trust more than her gut. Her gut was telling her that he was scared of her, and as long as she had the mountaintop, the cover of darkness, she'd have the upper hand.

Then her heart got in the way.

Waiting added to the security of her life, but what about Ethan?

It wasn't until that thought crossed her mind that she was certain. She loved him with everything she had, and as cliché as it seemed, she couldn't imagine life without him.

She felt like shit at the realization that he had already told her everything he needed to. Him. Ethan Lowell. The same guy who never brought women to his bed. Never had actual relationships. Cringed at the thought of his best friend getting married. He had told his whole damn family that he was in love with someone. He had told her that he loved her, and she never said it back. He never even asked her to.

She had to stop thinking. She had to do what she

had been trained to do.

Take out all threats.

Torn, but knowing what needed to be done, Ryan hesitantly made her way down the hall toward the office. She kept her gun concealed in the back of her pants. Coming out with a drawn weapon would only lead to another storm of gunfire. If he thought she was unarmed, maybe that bit would work to her advantage.

She had no idea where in the room this man was located. Based on how his voice bounced, she assumed near the window, but the last thing she was about to do now was rely on assumptions; however, she was also relying on his word to not fire immediately, even though he was certain where she would step from.

That final step knocked her off her feet. She had heard that voice before, but she never expected to find the traitor that stood before her.

His sinister smirk told her that he reveled at knowing that he had taken her by surprise.

"I guess now is a good time to admit that I'm glad you turned me down for that coffee, otherwise this could have been more awkward than it already is," Brett laughed, twirling his gun around with no respect for the weapon.

Ryan swallowed heavily and masked her shock. "It makes a lot of sense now."

"Excuse me," he gasped.

"You never call or text me. This morning I made one mistake, answering your call. I thought it was strange that you asked about going to the hospital."

"Oh, save it," he snorted. "Everyone knows the two of you couldn't be reached because you were probably going at it like rabbits."

"That's what this is about then," Ryan asked through gritted teeth. "Why would you turn your back on your career to help a criminal?!"

There was a sparkle in his eyes with his answer. "Why do people like me do anything? No, it had nothing to do with you and *Prince Charming*. Honestly, you're not that much of a catch," he laughed. "When was the last time you looked at your paycheck?"

Ryan sighed in disbelief. "Money."

"Before I took this job, I knew a lot of shady people." Brett began his speech proudly, which only further sickened Ryan. "I kept in touch with them, and when I heard about Delacruz's offers, I decided to get in on it."

"For how long?"

Brett laughed nervously at the question. "After the gala."

"You knew where he lived," Ryan began.

"I also knew how difficult it would be to target the office or his penthouse, although plans were in the process of execution. Then this fell into our laps. It really could not have been more perfect. I do have to admit," he exhaled with a hint of amusement. "I didn't expect this sort of ending. I must say, I see why you're one of the favorites, why Perkins thinks your shit doesn't stink."

The anger and jealousy that flooded Brett's face

was bordering on deranged. Ryan had always been a pretty good judge of character; this was something completely out of left field for her.

She had to do it. Regardless of the evil she saw Brett exuding, it would still be one of the hardest things she'd ever have to do, to kill someone she knew.

Thankfully, Brett had underestimated her.

The moment, the briefest second, his gaze tore from her, she took her chance.

She closed her eyes after the first shot and fired the second. She couldn't look him in the eyes, to see his face. Selfishly, she didn't want to live with that image.

Zero.

The hits were so powerful and instant. The impact sent Brett flying backwards to the window that was no longer there. Then he was gone.

Four seconds. That was all the time that Ryan allowed herself to process what had just happened, who she had just killed.

She still didn't know what awaited down the stairs.

Upon hearing muffled voices down the hallway echoing into the silence of the room, Ryan chose a different means.

* * *

"My father didn't kill your son." Ethan knew the comment was bold, but so was Emilio's accusation.

He laughed, the sort of laugh all the villains in cartoons possess. "You have no idea, do you," he spat.

When Ethan could only reply with a look of confusion, Delacruz continued on.

"My son had a life threatening disease. He was happy and full of energy, though he was always the first to take ill, common colds and such. Apparently, that wasn't the case this time, and when we found out that something was wrong, treatment was too late."

"I don't understand what–"

"It was a genetic disease," Emilio roared. "One that doesn't run in my family or the family of my *late* wife."

With the amount of fury that was erupting from Emilio, Ethan knew that Sophia's mother had never committed suicide. Her death was at the hands of the man standing in front of him.

What he was hearing sounded incredulous. Emilio Delacruz had to be insane. None of what he said made any sense.

Ethan shuddered when two shots rang out from above. These were different than all the other blasts he had been hearing in the passing seconds, yet there was an eerie familiarity to them. They were from the gun Ryan had given him. There had only been two left. His heart raced. He didn't know what was taking place, but he knew that she was most positively still alive.

He had to prolong his situation for as long as he could, but the crazed man before him, flailing his gun as he spoke, made it difficult for Ethan to begin to form words, let alone coherent sentences.

"Do you want to know the funny thing," Emilio laughed, though it was a laugh full of hurt and rage. "You and your sister were lucky. The percentage of this shit passing from parent to offspring is only about ten percent, but my son inherited it."

"Your issues are with my father," Ethan managed, finding words once again. "I can't bring back your son, but–"

"No!" The word alone was enough to cause the building to rattle. "Your father deserves to feel what I felt when I lost what I *thought* was my son."

Ethan allowed his gaze to flicker upward for a second after seeing movement within the darkness beyond the platform.

Ryan.

He quickly brought his attention back to Emilio. The last thing he wanted was for the lunatic to see Ryan and turn his gun on her first.

Despite it being the faintest of glances, Ethan was acutely aware of one thing. Ryan was unarmed, and he couldn't imagine what the hell she must be thinking right now.

Silence fell after Emilio's last words and the only thing heard was his pacing back and forth as he tapped on the gun. He suddenly stopped as he and Ethan heard the sounds at the exact same time. Though the wailing sirens were distant, it wouldn't be long now. Everything would soon be over.

The next sound Ethan heard made his breath

stop, and then he watched as the gun rose. Everything beyond the barrel of the gun became an isolated blur.

* * *

Ryan told herself that it wouldn't be so bad. She had done more dangerous things in her lifetime. It would be no different than the time Jeremy dared her to jump from the roof into the pool; however, landing in water was a lot different than splattering on concrete.

* * *

The sirens grew louder, but there was no way they'd make it in time. Emilio Delacruz wasn't about to go through everything he had endured and not end up killing the son of the man he hated most in the world.

A series of fast and heavy footsteps echoed through the building, breaking the tension between Ethan and Emilio.

Emilio turned in the direction of the clanging metal above, but it stopped once Ryan hurled herself from the platform through the air like a wingless angel. Emilio tilted his gun from Ethan toward her, but before he could pull the trigger, his body was slammed to the concrete.

He kept a firm grip on the gun, accidentally pulling

the trigger in the process. The ringing of metal screamed throughout the building.

"Ethan get out," Ryan shouted as she wrestled with the man. She had noticed Ethan attempting to approach from her peripheral vision.

"You're fucking crazy if you think I'm leaving you!"

Another shot burst from the gun, but this time Ethan could feel the breeze from it cut near his face before it pierced the wall behind him.

The sirens were so close now, just not close enough.

"Ethan! Get out! I'm begging you," Ryan cried.

The next shot sent pieces of concrete flying from near Ethan's foot.

He knew if he didn't leave, Ryan's sole focus would be on keeping him safe, disregarding that of her own life, so he did exactly what she asked.

✳ ✳ ✳

For being in his fifties, Delacruz was not an easy fight for Ryan. It didn't help that her body was near exhaustion from the crash and the gunshot wound. Throwing punches and wrestling for control of the gun, all while she felt her leg continuing to lose blood, became one of her more difficult fights. Her body was running on nothing more than adrenaline and the relief of knowing that Ethan was finally safe from this demonic monster.

Ryan made a choice, going all in for the gun.

When she did, Delacruz's other hand closed in

335

around her neck; however, she was able to bring the gun down, though it was his finger still on the trigger. He still had several rounds left and that only made her need for the gun that much more vital.

Just as Ryan was able to almost pry the gun from Delacruz, his finger pulled the trigger one more time, and she collapsed to the side.

It was unnatural, unlike any pain she had ever felt in her life. She gripped her stomach with her left hand; she didn't need to look down to know that her hand was already drenched in warm blood.

Delacruz began to stumble up, and Ryan put an end to his existence. With every ounce of fight she had in her, through vision that was blurring, she rolled on her back and pointed the gun in his direction. The shots were slow. She let him suffer. First a leg, then a shoulder. He collapsed to his knees once one tore through his chest. That was when Ryan put him out of his misery. One in the head.

She remained on her back. A part of her told her to try to get up, but her body was no longer responding. The pain was fading fast, to the point that she felt nothing. All she wanted was sleep, and that's when she knew that she was dying.

Somewhere between the agonizing ending of her life, and the finality of death, Ryan was jolted back by the voice of an old friend.

"Jesus. Fuck. Ryan..."

The look in JD's eyes told her that she probably looked a lot worse than how she felt.

"It's fine," he reassured her as soon as he saw the sadness creep upon her face.

"We all know what fine in this line of work means," she managed to breathe.

He couldn't help but laugh through the pain he felt at seeing her like that. "You have to be *fine*," he began, emphasizing the word. "There's no way in hell I'm giving your parents any bad news, and can you even imagine what my parents will do to me if they find out–"

Ryan interrupted him, still trying to lessen the severity of her demise. "So, I have to live so you don't get your ass kicked by a couple retired SEALs?" Before JD could answer, Ryan could hear the medics breaking through. She grabbed JD's hand for one request. "I need to see Ethan. Immediately."

"He's safe. He's with–"

"It's not like that," she managed through the tears that began to wet the side of her face.

One look at her and JD didn't bother asking any questions. He stepped aside from the medics beginning to prep her for transport and radioed to a fellow agent outside.

Seconds later, a panicked Ethan was bursting in.

There was blood. So much blood. Seeing Ryan on the ground like that, he knew that it was hers. Half of her clothing was drenched in the liquid.

One of the medics eyed him suspiciously, but moved just enough to give him room to talk to Ryan.

"Ryan..." He couldn't even begin to search for words. He felt as though his own life was slipping away in that moment.

Ryan mustered up all the energy she had in her and pretended she wasn't as bad as she knew she was. "I need to tell you something before they take me away," she began. *Before I die.*

"Don't," Ethan managed, not wanting her to continue. He didn't want to cry, but the tears were right there. "Tell me when you're out of surgery or whatever." He knew exactly what she was going to say and a part of him, the part that wasn't falling to pieces like a damn baby, was so angry at her for doing this.

"Ethan, I have to," she breathlessly insisted. Her body was shutting down; she didn't have much time.

"Don't you dare say it. Not now. Not like this. Not because you feel bad for never saying it. Not because you think you won't have another chance to–"

"I love you."

He couldn't blink away the tears anymore. They were words he wanted to hear from her ever since he had first said them, perhaps even before that. Hearing them now made him feel like his world had just exploded. If anything happened to her, a part of him would always wonder if it was really her talking or just the moment.

CHAPTER 29

Agent Delgado, or JD as Ethan had now come to know him as, put all his duties aside and drove Ethan to the hospital. Both of them had argued that Ethan ride in the ambulance with Ryan, but her condition had taken a turn for the worse and the medics wouldn't allow it.

Along the way JD insisted that Ethan should get looked at. Ethan didn't care. There was only one place he needed to be. With Ryan.

He had sustained a small cut above his left eye during the collision with the delivery truck driver, and he most definitely could feel the bruising on his back from the bullets. It was all minor, nothing a small bandage and some ice wouldn't solve.

He tried not to think about Ryan, at least not how he last saw her, but red continued to flood his tear-stained eyes. All he could see was her fighting for life, and blood. There was so much blood.

"I'm not really sure what to say about all this," JD started after getting past all the nonsense about Ethan looking after himself.

"I'm not a fragile toddler that just lost my goldfish." Ethan didn't mean for that to come out as rudely as it did. Hell, he didn't even know if it was rude. With the emotions running through him, he felt drunk, in a daze, to the point he couldn't remember the words after saying them.

"Just know that Ryan is a fighter."

Too damn cliché.

"She's not bulletproof, and she's where she is because of me."

JD could see it. He had seen shifts like that before. Now that everything was hitting Ethan, the anger at himself was surfacing above the sadness. He should tread lightly, perhaps to the point of disengaging conversation altogether. There was no doubt in his mind that there was absolutely nothing he could say that would help Ethan.

* * *

Before JD could put the car in park, Ethan was already headed inside to the emergency room.

By the time JD caught up with Ethan, he was going ballistic on some poor nurse that clearly looked to be nearing the end of her shift as well as nearing retirement.

"Like I said, you're going to have to wait."

"Do you even know who I am?" Ethan felt gross once he said those words. It was the exact shit his father would say.

"Oh, honey. I know you did not go there," she sang, snapping her fingers. "You could be Denzel and I'm still not moving any faster. So you can see about where you rank right now."

Ethan was fuming. "Look, *Madea*–"

"Have you lost your mind? You can take your en-titled ass–"

JD approached the counter and announced his presence with an awkward cough. Ethan had already attracted a good amount of attention and was only further embarrassing himself.

"He belong to you," the barely five foot woman asked, her voice so piercing that it garnered more attention.

"No," JD abruptly answered, then quickly changed his mind. "Well, that all depends."

Nina. Her name was Nina. It was clear as day on the giant freaking nametag and Ethan had the nerve to insult her with that bullshit comment.

While Ethan tried the most ridiculous approach ever to getting his request through faster, JD decided to be more reasonable with the situation.

"FBI," he announced as he flashed his badge. He had to admit, it gave him satisfaction in doing that at times; however, what he wouldn't admit was that he wasn't above Ethan's tactics.

"And?"

JD had expected a different response. Ethan must have really gotten to the woman.

"This is an investigative matter. I'm going to need your full cooperation."

Technically, he wasn't entirely wrong; however, he realized he was laying it on pretty thick.

Like it was no big deal, "Gunshot victim?"

"Yes. Ryan Beckett. Can I get a status on her? Can

341

she be seen? Is she–"

"Hold your horses." Her voice was lower, calmer, not screeching. "She's already in a room. They're going into surgery immediately. It doesn't look–" She stopped herself.

Even though he was a belligerent ass a few seconds prior, the white look on Ethan's face caused her to stop talking.

"Do you know anything else," JD pressed on, but she only shook her head.

* * *

Later, JD insisted that Ethan go to his family in another wing of the hospital and inform them of everything that had happened, although he was certain they already knew. Hell, it was probably all over the news.

It took a lot of convincing, but finally, the lifeless body that had once been Ethan Lowell, left the waiting room to go to his family. JD had to promise him that at even the slightest bit of knowledge, he'd call.

Ethan walked down the same hall he had earlier in the day with a lump in his throat. He had needed Ryan on the elevator like before. He needed her now. He needed to feel her hand in his again.

"Uncle Ethan," Danny exclaimed. Something about seeing his family again felt like a weird sense of déjà vu.

Before any of them said another word, a shocked silence took over. They began to evaluate him, eyeing him from head to toe.

"What the hell is going on," Gwen asked, forgetting that grandmotherly tone and language for a second.

"Ethan," Leighton exhaled, tears forming in her eyes after looking at the broken man that was her brother.

"What are you wearing," Danny asked, not yet realizing the impact of what was going on.

Ethan then remembered he was still wearing the vest. The vest that Ryan had given him. The vest that she needed more than him.

All he could do was slump in a nearby chair with exhaustion. He thought they would have known by now, obviously they didn't.

"Ethan," Gwen screamed.

"Oh, god," Leighton gasped. "Oh god, no. Where's Ryan?"

Ethan only shook his head. His mother covered her mouth, but Leighton rushed to him, embracing him. He couldn't cry anymore. He was drained.

"She's in emergency," he managed. "It's over. Everything is over."

"What are you talking about? What happened," his sister pleaded, although she was now on the verge of tears.

"She saved my life," was all he could say. Anything after that was a blur.

Silence followed. Ethan continuously checked his phone, but nothing. What did he expect? He didn't know a thing about gunshot wounds. He didn't know what organs might have been damaged, or even if they could be repaired.

He ran his fingers through his hair, focusing his attention on trying to push away the tears that crept through the darkness inside of him. He couldn't think like that. He couldn't think for a moment that anything bad would happen to Ryan, but damn if life didn't have a shitty way of dealing cards.

Before he met Ryan, he was content. Then, of all people, he had to finally fall in love, in love with the most difficult woman he'd ever met. Now for the first time, he couldn't imagine his future, he couldn't imagine tomorrow, not without her.

Danny sauntered toward Ethan just as he was about to go back to Ryan's waiting room in another wing. "Hey." He plopped down in the chair next to Ethan.

"Hey, kiddo." Ethan's voice was graveled and strained.

"I said a prayer," Danny began with a bit of uncertainty. "Mom said you're supposed to do that kind of shit."

"You're ten," Ethan growled. "Where did you learn to talk like that?" He desperately didn't want to think about prayers or talk about Ryan.

"Have you heard mom? Besides, with this divorce and everything, I'll probably need therapy anyway."

"Again, you're *ten*. Think about whatever fucking cartoons you kids watch, or video games, or bikes,"

344

Ethan scoffed. He rolled his eyes at his own language. He was a horrible role model.

"She's going to be okay," Danny assured him, bringing the conversation back to Ryan.

Ethan closed his eyes and groaned. Danny was just a kid. He couldn't tell him to piss off.

From his peripheral vision, he saw Danny dig something with a glimmer of red from his pocket. He turned to see a small metal car. Danny pensively twirled it in his hands before sighing and handing it to Ethan.

"Here. I think you need this now."

Ethan didn't have words, and Danny continued on after seeing the confusion.

"I was really scared the other day. I mean, I saw Aunt Edna in a casket, but I'd never seen a dead body like that."

Ethan cringed. He was sick of the dead bodies piling around him.

"Anyway, I guess she figured as much."

"Ryan," Ethan asked, his stomach clenching with her name falling from his lips.

"Yeah. Before you left, she gave me that."

Ethan looked at the little red car. It was fairly old. The paint was faded in several places and the shiny silver metal came through.

"She said she flipped out before her brother's first big race and he gave her that. She said it wasn't the ideal shape for a worry stone, but she always treated it as such. It got her through difficult times and maybe I could use it. Does that sound like bullshit?"

"No," Ethan managed, choking down the lump in his throat.

"I thought you might need it now, or maybe she needs it back."

"Since when did you get to be so–"

"Mature," Danny added, but with a sparkle in his eyes. "Does that mean I can cuss?"

"Absolutely not," Ethan laughed. It was a pathetic laugh, but it kept him from falling apart again.

From a far off room, the one where Owen Lowell temporarily resided, Leighton waved for Ethan to come. He needed to get back to Ryan. Being around his family was doing nothing for him. He especially didn't want to see his father after the conversation earlier that day.

Ethan wanted to throw Danny from the room as soon as they walked in and saw what was on the television. What the hell were they thinking? Danny didn't need to see that, and Ethan didn't want to relive it.

"We don't have a definitive body count, and crews are still examining exactly what happened here. The last we've been informed has been nine; however, we are expecting a much larger count based on what we're hearing from those on the scene behind us," the perky and upbeat newscaster informed. "If you can see," she began pointing. "We believe this all began with a car chase that left the vehicle behind me exploding. It will take time for crews to determine just how many were killed and the identities of the victims."

Victims.

Ethan wanted to put a fist through the television.

Someone with a headset, no doubt from the news staff, pulled the anchor away and turned off her microphone to hand her a piece of paper and whisper something. Her eyes widened in surprise like she had the scoop of a lifetime.

"This is that," she gasped. Her voice in the distance was still very much heard.

She quickly composed herself and glanced over the paper before returning to her spot. Behind her Ethan could see the covered bodies of the men that Ryan had shot from the window.

"I have just been informed that this is what we can hope will be the end of the attempts on Ethan Lowell's life. Earlier this month, we reported on a car bombing, as well as an attempted stabbing, and not to mention the Lowell residence being targeted. We know now that these were all efforts made by Emilio Delacruz, who is suspected to be involved in drug trafficking."

Ethan was just about to grab the remote attached to his father's bed and shut the stupid blonde up, when she said words that gave him the smallest bit of relief.

"I have also been notified that one of the deceased bodies is in fact that of Delacruz."

It should have been a happier moment, but while Delacruz was dead, it was at Ryan's expense. She was clinging to life because of him.

"Ethan Lowell was removed from the scene prior

347

to our arrival, and it has come to our attention that his bodyguard was transported to a hospital after sustaining life-threatening injuries from what took place here."

Quickly, Ethan shut the television off at the mentioning of Ryan. Four sets of eyes sank into him. Mia continued playing with a doll on the far side of the room near the window.

Danny spoke first with a simple, "Whoa."

"He didn't need to see that. Fuck," Ethan growled, waving his hands between the three adults. "I didn't need to see that."

"I've seen worse," Danny admitted. "She's like some freaky action hero."

Ethan needed to get away from his family. It was all a damn movie to them. Meanwhile, he could still feel the buzzing in his arms from the gun. It was all too real. He'd never be able to get those images out of his head.

"I need to go," he whispered, suddenly feeling lightheaded.

✳ ✳ ✳

"You should feel like shit," Gwen scolded Owen once Ethan had left.

"For what," he shrieked.

"Everything you said to him about that woman. That woman might die because she protected him!"

"That was her job," he snorted.

Leighton was unaware of precisely what had taken

place earlier. She knew that her father and Ethan must have had some words, as Ethan had left more furious than ever.

"Danny," Leighton called to her son. "Here's some money. Take your sister to the vending machines."

"You're just trying to get me to leave so I don't hear the grown-up conversation," he scoffed.

Leighton knew she was going to have her hands full with him once he entered his teen years. Thankfully, he realized the intensity of the day and did as his mother requested, dragging his sister from the room with her doll in one hand and his in the other.

"What's going on here," Leighton asked, not directing her question to one specific parent.

Owen huffed and turned to the blank television.

"So many things," Gwen sighed. "Apparently your brother and Ryan have formed some romantic relationship."

Leighton wasn't following. "Yeah. So?"

Gwen looked at her shocked. "You knew?"

"Are you kidding? I knew before anything even happened," Leighton laughed. Her father now turned to look at her. "I could tell it from the first night I met her that Ethan was falling for her. What's the big deal?"

"The big deal," Owen hissed, enunciating every word carefully. "Is that she is *not* the type of woman that Ethan should be with."

Up until that comment, Leighton's attitude had been light and she found humor in the fact that Ethan had gotten attached to someone so different than any girl she had ever seen him with. Now, her father struck something else inside of her. Rage. Scalding rage.

"What the hell is that supposed to mean," Leighton spat. She tried to keep her voice down, but the realization hit too close to home.

"We just always pictured him with a lady," Gwen began with uncertainty. She tried to find a nicer way to say it than her husband.

"A *lady*? You mean someone with a fucking tiara on her head? Someone who doesn't work because she comes from money and doesn't need to? Someone like a congressman's daughter? Is that what you're saying?"

"Watch your language," Owen roared.

"No," Leighton told him. She calmed the fumes flowing from deep within so that she could finally say what she needed to. "Both of you are ridiculous. Worst of all, I'm just as ridiculous because I let you have a say in the same thing you're trying to do with Ethan. I married the asshole that you approved of, that *you* were happy with. I know you're going to protest, but believe it or not, Oliver and I are getting a divorce. I'm miserable, and if I stay in this marriage a second longer, I'm going to lose it." She gave a manic laugh at the thought. "Do you know how envious I am of what those two might have? Ethan fucking adores Ryan. You'd have to be blind, deaf, and stupid not to see it. You can say it was her job, but she might die now because his life meant more to her than her own."

Leighton saw that she was getting to her mother. Gwen had started to tear up and could no longer look at her, but she continued on.

"You know what, dad? I don't want my children around such antiquated beliefs." She tried to find a way of putting it nicely.

Owen now gave his daughter his full attention. "What are you insinuating."

"I'm saying, if either of you want a healthy relationship with your grandchildren, you better damn well hope that you can make things right with your son first."

Leighton heard her mother gasp, but she couldn't take anything else from them. She had said her piece. At that, she slammed the door behind her, much to the dissatisfaction of the judgmental eyes coming from both the nurses' station as well as a few residents of the waiting room.

Gwen remained in the room with Owen, the only thing filling the space between them being that of silence.

Leighton reminded her so much of herself many years ago. Both of their children possessed a fire that she once had, one that over the years had dwindled down to nothing more than a flicker.

"I'm not going to object," she admitted after a great amount of thinking.

"What are you talking about?"

Gwen turned, now facing her husband. They had loved each other at some point. Despite the affair, she still loved him. They just never had that passion. It was a convenient marriage and they got along for the most part. They both knew that. There was a love, one of care and understanding, but not the sort that should have been between a husband and wife.

"About anything."

"Anything?" Owen was still confused by his wife's short phrases.

"The kids. Ethan and Leighton. They're adults. They can do what they want," she announced.

"Oh, really," Owen began, sitting up straight, anticipating an argument with his wife now. "What happens when they continue to screw up?"

"Ethan is nearly thirty, he's calmed down a bit in recent years, and Leighton did exactly what you wanted up until now. Owen, she's never talked to us like that before."

"You didn't answer my question." His voice was teetering on the verge of yelling.

Her eyes turned to small slits as they bore into him. "I'll love them and accept them like any parent should do."

He knew that those words were meant to be a jab at him. He cared about his children in his own way. He wanted what was best for them and their image.

"All this shit started hitting the fan because of that–"

"Don't bring her into this," Gwen interrupted. She paced the room and avoided eye contact with her husband. He made it difficult to stay calm at times. "This would have happened one day. One day both Ethan and Leighton would have gotten tired of the pressure. Leighton and Oliver didn't just suddenly decide to separate upon meeting Ryan."

Owen growled and looked away. The last part was true; he knew that. He wouldn't admit it, but Ryan coming into their lives had nothing to do with his daughter's impending divorce. What he hated most about Ryan was the effect she had on Ethan and the fact that he couldn't have found that with someone like Ella Daniels.

Gwen eventually left, leaving Owen to his own thoughts.

The grandchildren.

Leighton couldn't have meant what she said. It had to have been an empty threat in the heat of the moment; however, Owen didn't want to take that chance. He didn't think that he was a bad influence on the children, but obviously his daughter thought differently.

Frustration. All he felt was frustration at the realization that Gwen was right. He could control a billion dollar empire, but he had no control over his children's lives. They were making sure that he knew that.

CHAPTER 30

The day could not have gone by any slower. Ethan was surprised that after agonizing hours, he was still in a waiting room, now not only with JD, but Perkins, Levi, and Jeff. After overhearing a call JD made, Ethan became aware that Ryan's brother was dropping everything and getting on the first flight he could in hopes that he'd arrive shortly after midnight.

He couldn't help but ask why Ryan's parents weren't being called. The relationship between parents and children was strained in Ryan's family, but he would have assumed they would be informed. He was surprised when JD told him that Ryan definitely wouldn't want that. Both her parents were in different countries and there was really nothing they could do anyway.

Ethan's thoughts turned to a dark place buried within. Maybe there was nothing anyone could do.

* * *

Ethan was stunned when later in the evening he saw a familiar face rushing towards him, followed by several more.

Zach.

"Dude! God, I'm so sorry." He stumbled for words as he embraced Ethan.

It wasn't their typical bro hug but Ethan refrained from pointing that out.

"What are you doing here?"

"I saw on the news and...I tried texting...Then Leighton," he began, but wasn't able to express a coherent sentence or thought.

Ethan looked behind his friend to see Leighton coming down the hall, with both his niece and nephew in tow.

"Danny insisted," she told him before he could ask. If she was being honest, her reasoning for being there was only partially true.

Ethan eyed his sister suspiciously while she and the kids took seats across from where he was standing.

"Fine," she admitted with the faintest of laughs. "I couldn't be around the two of them any longer."

"What happened?"

Leighton twirled her hair for a moment, hesitating. Then she brushed it away like it wasn't a nervous habit of hers. "I got tired and just exploded, okay?"

Ethan had to stifle a laugh. Suddenly, he didn't want to know what happened once he left. With his sister, anything was imaginable.

"You do know you're going to give him another heart attack."

"As stubborn as he is? It would take more than an atomic bomb landing on that thick skull of his to hurt him," Leighton scoffed at her brother.

Zach sat down next to an exhausted Leighton and as soon as he did, Mia, sugar pulsing through her veins, leapt onto his lap, suddenly intrigued by the gold cuffs on his earlobes. Zach didn't seem to mind and allowed her to entertain herself. Ethan smiled at the thought. His best friend was better and more affectionate to his niece and nephew than their own father. Hell, Oliver left them as soon as the divorce was brought up.

Ethan had planned on staying at the hospital, all day, all night, however long it took until he knew that Ryan was okay. He just never expected the rest of the people around him to stay for so long.

* * *

"You know," Ethan quietly began, treading into dangerous territory, as soon as Leighton excused herself to go to the restroom. "She's pretty much single now."

"What the hell does that mean." Zach attempted to angrily whisper back, trying not to wake the ball cuddled against his chest.

Ethan shrugged. "Just thought you'd like to know." For a long while the waiting room had been so tense, this was the first time that he could let out a breath. The change of subject doing only the slightest in easing his nerves.

"You do know I'm getting married," Zach spat back.

Ethan found it odd how riled up Zach got at the mentioning of Leighton. He had a crush on her in another lifetime, a lifetime before she married a British cunt while still in college.

"I'm revoking my request for you to be the best man after that comment," he grumbled.

Ethan, however, couldn't help but notice the illuminating redness that crept to Zach's face.

"Holy shit," Leighton shrieked, rushing back.

"You look like you've seen a ghost," Zach chuckled as soon as she took her seat next to him.

Her eyes, filled with worry, flashed toward Ethan. "Worse."

"Why are you looking at me like that? What's worse?"

Leighton motioned behind her with a small movement of her head.

Shit. Gwen and Owen Lowell. Mom and dad.

"He must have gotten the approval to leave," Leighton groaned. "Whatever he says, we just need to ignore it and remain calm."

One could never have guessed that less than twenty-four hours ago, the man calmly walking toward them had a heart attack. He looked far better than he did when Ethan first saw him in his hospital bed that morning.

Ethan, nor Leighton, acknowledged either of their parents when, to their surprise, the two of them sat down. Leighton shot Ethan a horrified look. *What the hell are they doing?*

Owen Lowell cleared his throat, commanding the

attention of even those outside of their family. "How is she," he asked.

"Seriously," Ethan scoffed, slumping back in his chair.

"I genuinely care, damn it!"

"Owen, you promised," Gwen growled.

Owen sighed and calmed his increasing temper. "I'll make this quick so we can all move on," he began, gesturing between Ethan and Leighton. "You kids are adults. You can make your own decisions. I might give my *opinion*; however, I won't disown you based on your choices."

Ethan met the eyes of his sister. The speech was ridiculous. Their father had never been good with apologizing; hell, they didn't know if he ever apologized in his life.

Before either could respond to Owen, he pushed aside what he had just said, acting as though he had been dunked in the water and cleansed of any past wrongdoing.

"Now, how is Miss Beckett?" This time the question didn't come through gritted teeth.

"We don't know. We haven't been told anything," Ethan replied.

Ethan and JD shared a sinister glance when Owen huffed and made his way to the information desk.

"Excuse me, Miss," he began, trying to get a good look at her nametag. "Nina."

"What can I do for you," she asked dryly.

"My family and I need to get an update on Ryan

Beckett. She came in hours ago and we haven't received any information on her."

"Surgery," she replied, not bothering to look at the man as she skimmed through some papers.

"I'd hope that's obvious, considering. Surely you must have something less vague to report." Owen tried to remain composed, but her demeanor was off-putting and annoying.

"Nope."

"Do you know who I am? I could have–"

Nina threw her papers down and interrupted Owen. "Are you the daddy to that one?" She motioned with her eyes in Ethan's direction.

"Yes, that is my son. Look, I'm not leaving until I get something more than 'surgery' as an update."

Nina rubbed her temples, suddenly feeling a migraine coming on, as she reached for the phone that was buried under a pile of papers. She turned from Owen and tapped out a few numbers.

"Yes, can I get someone to come update Ryan Beckett's family," she said in a low tone through gritted teeth. "Thank you."

Before Nina could hang up the phone, Owen was back in her face. "Well?"

"Someone will be here shortly," Nina growled. "Now, if you could please sit down," she insisted, louder than intended, but it got her point across and Owen happily left her station.

Another twenty minutes passed before a doctor walked through the double doors, a clipboard in hand. He didn't need the clipboard; it was either good news or bad news.

"Ryan Beckett's family," he called out.

Everyone in that small space of chairs stood. The doctor, Dr. Harrison, eyed them all suspiciously. There were several men of various ages, an older woman, and another woman with two young children before him.

"Parents or siblings?"

The group looked from one to another, knowing that none of them were actually of any relation to Ryan.

"We're her family," Perkins stated.

Dr. Harrison let it be. It had been a chaotic start to his shift and it was only getting worse. He didn't have the time or effort for something so tedious.

"I apologize no one came sooner. We're short and," Dr. Harrison began before letting his words trail off. The people before him only cared about one thing and he was doing nothing more than delaying. "Alright, so, Ryan's surgeries went well, and she's been placed in a room. Her condition is still–"

"Where's her room," Ethan asked immediately. "Can we see her?"

Dr. Harrison's eyes clenched and Ethan knew that something was wrong. Something didn't go right.

Dr. Harrison tried to explain that while the surgeries went as well as they could have hoped, Ryan still wasn't in the clear. The gunshot to her torso had missed all vital organs, much to the surprise of everyone. The trauma, however, had left her in a comatose state. The doctors were certain that she'd come out of it, but when they couldn't say. All they could do at this point was monitor her.

CHAPTER 31

Two days later.

Eventually everyone dispersed. They had to. They all had lives to get back to. Everyone came at various times over those days to check in, but nothing had changed.

Ethan couldn't be convinced to leave, which only brought up another slew of problems between his family and the hospital staff. He did get a room at the hotel directly across the street for the purpose of a shower; however, he didn't sleep there. Once Jeremy had gotten in from his flight, Ethan insisted that Jeremy keep the room for however long he'd be around.

The days were draining. Seeing Ryan so helpless, talking to her only for her to not respond with sass and sarcasm, killed a part of Ethan.

"Dude, you need to get up and move around. You look like shit," Jeremy told Ethan. He fished in his wallet and took out a few bills. "Here, stretch your legs and get us some coffee."

Ethan glared at Jeremy. There was no way he was taking his money for some lousy hospital coffee. On the other hand, he knew Ryan's brother was right. He hadn't complained one bit about his arrangements, but the chair was destroying his back.

"I just want someone to be here when she wakes up," Ethan stressed, not allowing himself to think that she wouldn't.

"I will stay here the five minutes it takes you to get some damn coffee," Jeremy laughed. "You won't be missing much."

Ethan reluctantly agreed. As soon as he rose from the chair he felt like collapsing. His back screamed in anguish and his legs felt like pudding from sitting for days.

* * *

Jeremy towered over his sister. When he got the call from JD, he allowed himself a few moments to fall apart and break down. As much as he wanted to throw himself on his sister and beg her to wake up, to be okay, he had to be strong, both for her and for Ethan. Despite the last couple days, Ethan was resilient. Jeremy had seen that the moment the hospital tried to tell him that visiting hours were over. He could be dominant and aggressive, but he had one weakness, and Jeremy was looking at her.

Jeremy rubbed Ryan's hand. It wasn't warm, but it wasn't a deathly cold either. Wrapped in her lightly closed fist was that ridiculous trinket he gave her many years ago. He fought back something between laughing and crying.

"I can't take seeing you like this again," he admitted, thinking back to the time he last saw her in the hospital. She looked a lot worse then. This time she didn't have the bloody bruises covering her from face down. This time she looked pristine, like she was peacefully sleeping. "I can't lose you Ryan. You're my baby sister. I don't know what I'll fucking do if you don't make it through this." He couldn't stop the tears from falling now. Once he got to the airport, he managed to put them away. For days he kept them bottled inside, but not anymore.

"I wish I had a video of that shit to show your racing buddies," a soft voice croaked, nearly sending Jeremy against the wall in shock.

"Ryan? Oh my god! Oh my god! Holy shit! Am I fucking hallucinating right now?!"

"Shut up," Ryan groaned. "My head is killing me."

Ryan slowly began to open her eyes. Thankfully, someone had dimmed the room, but the little light that was there still bothered her and caused her to wince.

"I can't believe it. You're awake!" Jeremy rushed back to her and embraced her, which only elicited a painful scream.

"What the hell, man?!"

"Sorry," he told her, softly pulling away.

Ryan felt like she had been hit by a truck. She was able to clearly recall every moment up until when she was placed in the ambulance. She could feel that her torso was heavily bandaged. She had to wonder what all she lost. Maybe a kidney? She was still alive, at least for the time being, so it's not like they had to pull out all her intestines. With the way she remembered feeling when the shot hit her, she couldn't imagine that she'd still be here.

Jeremy continued rambling. His excitement did nothing for the pounding in her head. He laughed maniacally and talked about someone being pissed, which caught Ryan's attention.

"What are you talking about?"

"Your boyfriend. He's going to freak out when he finds out that he missed you waking up." Jeremy then acted like he was thinking for a moment. "Maybe you can pretend to be out of it and do all this again?"

"Are you high right now," Ryan spat. She clenched her fists and in doing so made note of the cold piece of metal. She brought it to her face and couldn't help but feel a warming sensation. "Where did this come from?"

"Your boyfriend. I can't believe you kept that all these years," Jeremy shyly admitted.

"Please stop saying that word," Ryan groaned, although that one word did send her mind to one person. "Shit. Ethan. Is he okay? Was he hurt?"

"Yeah, yeah. He's fine. He's been with you the entire time." Jeremy ran a hand through his wavy blonde hair and continued to pace. He always had a problem slowing down and sitting still, but this was beyond that. His hands were shaking. His sister was going to be fine.

Jeremy watched Ryan look around the room, void of anyone but the two of them.

"Oh, I practically had to tell him that if he didn't leave that chair his ass was going to rot off. Seriously, he's been here the entire time." Jeremy then chuckled, remembering something he made a mental note to tell Ryan. "When I first got here, it was really late. Most of your people, or whatever you call those guys, had to leave. The hospital tried explaining to Ethan that he couldn't stay in your room with you."

"I'm guessing that didn't go well," Ryan asked. Jeremy's smirk had been enough to answer.

"Are you kidding me? He and that old man of his told them if they tried to throw him out they'd buy the whole fucking hospital and have all of their jobs. It was crazy. I think the staff finally just didn't want to deal with the Lowell family anymore."

Ryan was speechless. The old man Jeremy referred to couldn't have been Owen, although it was definitely a fiasco that she could imagine coming from both of the men.

Eventually Jeremy's excitement calmed down and he fell into the chair near Ryan's bed. His facial features suddenly turned serious. Ryan watched as he grabbed a folder from the small table near her bed.

His face was grim when he brought up the next topic. "Perkins dropped this off for you." He was reading whatever was in the folder. It couldn't have been much as thin as it was, no more than a piece or two of paper.

"Are you going to tell me what it is or do you enjoy being all ominous and shit," Ryan huffed once Jeremy became silent.

His voice was soft, almost like he felt a little bit of pain for her when he finally told her. "It's your resignation papers."

Ryan's eyes doubled in size.

"It's not what you think," Jeremy quickly began. "They don't want to lose you, but he was pretty sure that you'd want these."

"You suck, you know that." It was an insult, but the look on her face told Jeremy that she wasn't entirely upset. "I wake up from a coma and you throw my resignation papers at me."

"Okay, stop. You're being a drama queen right now," he teased, putting the papers back on her table. "Tell me you're going to sign."

Ryan grumbled a bit, but if there was anyone she could talk to about this, it was Jeremy.

"I came back." Her words were barely audible, but Jeremy heard them loud and clear and knew from past conversations what she meant.

That hadn't happened to him yet. His life hadn't flashed before him, threatening to take everything away. Hers had. She was one of the lucky ones that found a way back.

Jeremy knew that it would be something new for her, but she was still so young. There were many other things she could pursue. Without a doubt in his mind, he knew continuing that line of work wasn't going to be it.

Jeremy rubbed his hands together and gave a clap. "Now, on to the good stuff."

"Jesus, Jer. I've been awake for like three minutes. Can you just let me rest?"

"Not even a little. You've basically been sleeping

for two days while the rest of us were losing our minds." He rose now and began pacing again.

"Get on with it." Ryan gave in with an eye-roll.

"You and Ethan Lowell?"

"Oh hell, what did he tell you?"

"Plenty."

Ryan's eyes nearly popped out of their sockets.

Jeremy noticed and tried to dismiss what she must be thinking. "Oh, god, no! He didn't tell me anything about the sex."

"There is no sex," Ryan screamed.

Jeremy shook his head playfully. "I really don't want to know about that, but trust me, I know there was sex."

"Get out. Just get out."

"Are you in love with him?"

The question, a simple question, took Ryan's breath away. She was just coming to terms with her feelings when everything fell apart.

The answer was obvious to Jeremy.

"Maybe you should tell him, you know, when you're not dying and all."

Ryan had to admit, it was a crappy thing to do. Ethan probably didn't know if she really meant it. People say a lot of stupid stuff on the verge of death, or so she heard.

"Speak of the devil," Jeremy whispered at the first creak of the door.

"Sorry it took so long," Ethan began. "Some idiot teenager couldn't comprehend that this is a hospital and not freaking Starbucks."

The look Jeremy gave him wasn't what he was expecting. Jeremy's smile couldn't get any wider. Ethan could practically see all of his teeth. His lips were stretched so much that most of his gums were showing.

"What's wrong with you?"

Ethan followed Jeremy's gaze toward the bed. One of the coffees fell from his hand as every good emotion known to man flooded through him once he looked into those insanely perfect blue eyes.

Jeremy grabbed the other coffee. "That one was yours," he announced, stepping over the dark puddle on the floor. He gave Ryan a quick wink and closed the door behind him, leaving her alone with Ethan.

Ethan slowly walked around the room toward her, the shock on his face more than a little evident. He looked like the same person she had left days ago, but his eyes were different. They were strained, puffy, and aged from either crying or the lack of sleep. Ryan had to go with lack of sleep. She couldn't picture someone like Ethan crying over anything. He'd never tell her how wrong that thought could be.

His eyes never left hers, which only made the pain in her body now mingle with a bubbly uncertainty. She couldn't read his face, couldn't tell what he was thinking. It only made her heart beat that much harder and faster. At least it was still beating.

"Please say something." Her words were rapid and breathless.

His hand softly trailed along her face and she had nothing in her to fight against leaning into his touch.

It was welcomed and warm. It made her feel alive.

"Can I kiss you," he whispered, already leaning toward her.

Ryan smiled and shook her head. "I'm not glass. I'm not going to break."

Ethan knew just how wrong she was. She was human, which meant that she most definitely was breakable. He had already seen that.

Before another second could pass he leaned in and pressed his lips to hers. What passed between them was electric, full of desire, need, and love. Ryan tried to rise, not wanting the kiss to end. If it was up to her she'd never break away from another. Her body didn't cooperate and she fell back to the bed with a yelp.

"Are you okay," Ethan gasped.

"Yeah, I'm just a little sore. Sorry."

He pressed his forehead to hers and let out the biggest sigh of relief.

"I'm so glad you came back to me. I don't know what I would have done if something had happened to you," he admitted. There was a rawness in his voice as he fought back all the horrible thoughts that had flitted through his mind over the last couple days.

Ryan allowed everything to sink in. "I can't believe it's finally over."

"Over?"

"Unless you have someone else trying to kill you," Ryan joked.

Ethan's eyes were narrowed, appearing to be deep in thought as they ran up and down Ryan's body.

When he didn't say anything to her comment, "If so, I guess you'll have to get a new bodyguard."

"You're really resigning," he asked. He was shocked. Jeremy had told him that she more than likely would, but all he could think about was her waking up. He never gave much thought to anything beyond that.

"I love this job. It was something I was good at, but I can be good at something that involves less gunfire," she laughed.

It wasn't a happy laugh. It said a lot of things, but pure blissful happiness wasn't one of them.

"I know you'll miss it."

She shrugged. "I can do other things that make me feel like I'm helping people."

In typical Ryan behavior, the conversation took a turn, with her becoming frustrated with leaving the hospital. Ethan tried to explain that it would be a while before she could even think of leaving, but she only insisted that she could take care of herself. Somehow he knew that she probably could.

After the conversation dwindled, other thoughts flooded Ethan's mind. An overdue conversation crept to the forefront. He knew it wasn't the time for something so serious, but he also knew that for once, Ryan couldn't run away from it.

Ryan sensed it immediately. Just based on the way Ethan was now looking at her, she knew exactly what he was going to bring up. Her stomach turned to knots and for a moment she wished she could fall back asleep.

"What's going to happen with us?"

Ryan expected Ethan to ease into it, but there it was. It could not have been more forward or blunt.

She hesitated. "We go on with our lives like we did before all this–"

"That's bullshit and you know it." He couldn't hide his annoyance.

Ethan paced the room. He expected this to go differently, but with Ryan, he should have known better. They were probably two of the worst people when it came to a relationship.

"You told me you loved me. I need to know if you meant it or if you were just–"

This time Ryan cut him off, surprised at how easy that one word was able to slip from her lips. "Yes."

Ethan felt like his heart might explode. Once Ryan continued her confession, he knew he had to do everything in his power to keep her.

"I should have told you sooner," she admitted, finding it difficult to keep eye contact with the way Ethan was gazing at her. "You were right about everything."

Ethan slowly began moving back toward her bed. "What are you talking about?"

"I never would have let things physically progress if I hadn't felt something for you."

His heart nearly stopped when he realized what she was saying.

"I was scared," she confessed.

Ethan grabbed her hands in his. "I'd never hurt you, in any way."

"I know that." She tried not to cry, but Ethan's face was already starting to blur.

"I know relationships haven't been the best for us, but now that the whole Delacruz thing is all over, I'd like to keep you around."

Ryan raised her eyebrows at the odd wording. "Keep me around?"

"Not as a close protection officer," he lightly chuckled.

"Good, because I'm *retired*." The words felt strange to say. It felt even stranger to feel so relieved in saying them.

"There's been something I've wanted to ask you for a while," Ethan began. His words were a little shaky and Ryan could feel the temperature of his hands increasing. "Ryan Beckett..."

Ryan felt oddly dizzy and the room started to spin. "Oh, god," she inhaled before he could go any further. "Please tell me you're not seriously proposing to me like this!"

The laughter that roared through him eased the tension and she had an answer to that notion.

"No. When I propose to you–" Ethan quickly stopped his flow of words upon realizing what he was saying. "Shit. I didn't mean...I just meant that if–"

"*If*," Ryan now teased. She was thankful it wasn't happening now, but she'd be lying if she said something permanent wasn't a possibility.

"You're making me nervous," he groaned.

"Are you trying to ask me to be your girlfriend?"

Redness faded into Ethan's face. "Well, now you

just ruined it."

Ryan couldn't help but laugh. She had never seen him so uncomfortable and yet so adorable. This was not the same man she met when she first walked into Owen Lowell's office. "Wow. Are you sure I'm really awake? I'm not dreaming this?"

"Not the reaction I was hoping for," he huffed. He knew she was enjoying this, but he didn't care. He'd give anything to hear her laugh.

"You do realize how you reacted to that word a couple weeks ago. You practically vomited."

He remembered his reaction in the restaurant that day with Zach. Even then he was severely aware as to how attracted he was to Ryan.

"Do you plan on giving me an answer?"

Ryan couldn't stop smiling. Sure, she was in a hospital bed with a screwed up leg and torso, but the man before her made all of that bearable. "Somehow, I think you always knew the answer would be yes."

Before she could change her mind, or heaven forbid say she made a *mistake*, Ethan pressed his lips to hers, more gently than he had wanted. He'd have plenty of days to ravish her and leave her breathless, but right now he needed to simply feel her, to have just a taste of what could be his forever. *Yes*. It was all he needed to hear. Almost all he needed to hear.

He pulled away slowly, but not so far that he couldn't feel her rushed breathing on his skin.

Ryan noted the mischievous sparkle dancing through the green eyes fixated on hers.

"As much as I enjoyed hearing that," he began,

swallowing the lump in his throat.

Ryan knew where he was going and she wasn't about to make him wait a second longer to hear it. "I'm in love with you, Ethan Lowell." The words that she found to be so difficult to say in another lifetime fell out with such ease. They felt so right.

The sensations that pulsed through Ethan were unlike anything he could have imagined. Despite the happiness he felt with Ryan's confirmation of a relationship, hearing those words made him the happiest he had ever been.

"And I am crazy in love with you, Ryan Beckett."

He entangled their fingers together, never wanting to let go. Hopefully, he'd never have to.

THE END

www.ingramcontent.com/pod-product-compliance
Lightning Source LLC
Chambersburg PA
CBHW051320250626
47155CB00007B/2394